I0725899

FORKS IN THE ROAD
A Western

by
Tamera Lynn Kraft

M Zion Ridge Press LLC

Mt Zion Ridge Press LLC
http://www.mtzionridgepress.com

Copyright © 2019 by Mt Zion Ridge Press
ISBN 13: 978-1-949564-70-9

Published in the United States of America
Publication Date: October 15, 2019

Managing Editors: Tamera Lynn Kraft and Michelle L. Levigne
Editor: Michelle L. Levigne
Cover Artist: Tamera Lynn Kraft

Cover Art Copyright by Mt Zion Ridge Press LLC ©2019

All rights reserved. No portion of this book may be reproduced or transmitted in any form or by any electronic or mechanical means, including photocopying, recording or by any information retrieval and storage system without permission of the publisher.

Ebooks are *not* transferrable, either in whole or in part. As the purchaser or otherwise *lawful* recipient of this ebook, you have the right to enjoy the novel on your own computer or other device. Further distribution, copying, sharing, gifting or uploading is illegal and violates United States Copyright laws. Pirating of ebooks is illegal. Criminal Copyright Infringement, *including* infringement without monetary gain, may be investigated by the Federal Bureau of Investigation and is punishable by up to five years in federal prison and a fine of up to $250,000.

Names, characters and incidents depicted in this book are products of the author's imagination, or are used in a fictitious situation. Any resemblances to actual events, locations, organizations, incidents or persons – living or dead – are coincidental and beyond the intent of the author.

Novels by Tamera Lynn Kraft

Lost in the Storm
Red Sky Over America
Resurrection of Hope
Alice's Notions
Soldier's Heart, From the Lake to the River Anthology
A Christmas Promise

The Story Continues

Fork in the Road tells the story of Jed Jackson and his orphaned brothers. Jed was a character created in the novel, **Lost in the Storm, *Ladies of Oberlin Book* 2**. Here is a list of novels in this story universe.

Red Sky Over America, ***Ladies of Oberlin Book 1*** tells the story of Lavena's friend and college roommate, America Leighton.

Lost in the Storm, *Ladies of Oberlin Book* 2 is the story of Lavena, a war correspondent who tries to get a story out of her hero, Captain Cage Jones, but he won't cooperate because he has a secret he doesn't want exposed. If Lavena doesn't get the story, she'll lose her job.

Soldier's Heart (free as an ebook only on the Mt Zion Ridge Press website) is the story of Noah Andrews, a sergeant from the Ohio 7th, after he returns home. It is also included in the **From the Lake to the River, Buckeye Christian Fiction Authors 2018 Anthology**.

The Aftermath, due to release in 2020, continues the story of Nate and Betsy Teagan, and Cage and Lavena.

I hope you enjoy all of them.

Dedication and Acknowledgment

I dedicate this novel to my son, Jonathan Kraft, for whom one of my main characters is named. He is a great husband, father, and son. I love him very much and am proud of the man he has become.

I would like to acknowledge the Wyoming Territorial Prison Museum for helping me with my research.

Author's Notes

This novel is a spin-off of LOST IN THE STORM: Ladies of Oberlin Book 2, and is about the lives of Jed's brothers.

You may notice during the novel, Joshua and Jonathan are referred to as JJ and Kid sometimes. Although they call each other JJ and Kid, they aren't referred to by those names until they start going down the wrong path. The name changes by the narrator are intentional.

I hope you enjoy FORKS IN THE ROAD.

Chapter One

Friday, August 21, 1863, Lawrence, Kansas

Twelve-year-old Joshua Jackson strolled home, secure in the belief nothing could go wrong after a day of fishing unless you were a fish. Rod propped on his shoulder and carrying the day's catch, he meandered barefoot beside his kid brother.

Jonathan, two years younger and two inches shorter, swiped his blond curls out of his eyes. The sun blazed red in the western sky. It'd been a hot day and showed no sign of cooling even though it was almost suppertime.

Joshua paused and sniffed the air. Smoke. Stretching his neck, he searched past the mound to the other side of the grasslands. Billows of black fog blocked his view.

"Fire!" Joshua dropped the rod and fish and charged up the knoll. "Run, Kid."

Jonathan tore alongside through the tall grass.

As they drew to the top of the hill, Joshua grabbed his side and gasped for air. Smoke blocked his view of the house. Flames shot up from the barn. Jonathan drew his hand to his mouth.

Joshua pushed through the thick black cloud. His eyes watered. Where was his family? Two men on the ground. He cut his stride short, approaching them slowly. One's dark green shirt was blotted with reddish brown stains. Blood.

Joshua choked back the moan coming from his throat. "Pa."

Jonathan bolted toward them, but Joshua grabbed him and dragged him to the cornfields where the old oak tree stood.

"Stay here," he ordered.

"No! Let me go." Jonathan kicked and screamed as he fought to get past his brother.

Joshua wrestled him into a bear hug. "Stop it."

Jonathan collapsed against the tree and let out a whimper. "But they're hurt."

"It's not going to help if we rush in and get ourselves killed. You stay put. I'll check it out."

Joshua staggered to where his father and Jeremy, his sixteen-year-old brother, lay slain. He squelched the urge to vomit as he closed Pa's dull brown eyes. Heat flushed his face as he strained to see through the smoke. He had to find Ma and his brother, Jacob. The barn had been destroyed, a few beams still burning. The house nothing but smoldering embers.

Maybe they ran from whoever did this and got away. He still couldn't see them.

He tripped on the shovels he'd tossed on the ground earlier and fell with a thud. Pa had told him to put them away, but he'd forgotten in his rush to go fishing. The lump in his throat threatened to choke him, but he swallowed it back.

Pulling himself to his feet, he wiped his scraped hands on his pants. A hacking noise came from behind. He spun around.

Ma crouched beside Jacob. So much blood. It soiled her blue calico dress and dark blue apron and smeared her hands and face. Had she been shot too?

Joshua's knees weakened. He scrambled to kneel beside her and tried to check the wound on her swollen, bleeding arm. She yanked it away. He rubbed his stinging eyes and waited for her to tell him what to do.

She hugged him, coughing though her tears. "Thank God, you're alive. Where's Jonathan?"

"He's at the oak tree. Wha... what happened?"

"Raiders." Her eyes glazed over. "I told your pa and brothers to run, but they stayed to protect the farm. He told me not to worry. They weren't after civilians, only soldiers." Her words caught. "The devils gunned them down and kept shooting."

"Ma, you're hurt. What did they do to you?"

"I tried to stop them. The no-account that killed your pa pushed me onto the woodpile is all. I'll be fine." She swiped away her blond curls matted with sweat and blood. "It was Mr. Hart."

"No." Joshua drew his fist to his mouth, remembering the tall schoolmaster who had given him the worst whipping of his life, probably the only one he didn't deserve. "What you're saying doesn't make sense."

"You listen." Ma grabbed hold of his arm and sputtered out a cough. "Mr. Hart didn't just quit teaching here. He's wanted for murder." Her bottom lip quivered. "He's Quantrill."

"Mr. Hart... Quantrill?" Joshua blinked. "What do I do?"

"Take Jonathan to the river and hide."

The idea of hiding didn't set right with Joshua. Pa stayed. "I can't leave you like this. You're hurt."

"They're killing any men and boys old enough to bear arms. If they come back, I'll keep them here as long as I can. You go now."

"No." His lungs hurt when he took a breath. "Come with us."

"Do you want me to have to bury two more sons?" Ma gazed at her bloody hands and wiped them on her apron. "They're not after me, they're after you. You can come back in the morning. I expect they'll be gone by then. Now, git!"

Joshua tottered like he'd been kicked in the stomach. He opened his mouth, but before words came out, she flashed him a steel blue glare he dared not defy. He turned and ran to the oak tree where Jonathan sat rocking with his knees drawn to his chest.

"Come on, Kid. We have to hide."

"But what about Ma and Pa? They all right?"

"I need you to act grown right now. Raiders attacked the farm. Ma's hurt, but not bad. Everyone else… They're all dead."

Jonathan's glassy blue eyes gazed though the tangled curls falling over his face. He stopped rocking.

"We've got to get out of here. Ma will be all right." He tried to sound confident for Jonathan's sake, but the words come out in a rasp. "They're only after us."

The ground rumbled, and a dust cloud encircled horses and the men who rode toward them. Jonathan drew his knees in tighter and stared toward the farmhouse. Joshua yanked on his sleeve, but he didn't look like he planned to go anywhere.

"Kid, we have to hide. We have to go now."

Jonathan blinked, then shot up and ran. Joshua chased after him, dashing over the knoll, through the high grass. He caught up when they were halfway to the river. The thunder of horses' hooves filled his ears.

He considered stopping, maybe finding a place here to hide, but the rumble shook the ground and drew closer. He grabbed his brother's arm and picked up the pace.

Soon, they reached the banks of the Kansas River. They collapsed under some bushes by the riverbed. Joshua panted, still trying to catch his breath and hold back the panic in his gut. Jonathan wailed.

"You got to quiet down, or they'll find us," he whispered.

Jonathan put his hand over his own mouth and muffled the sound of his crying.

The thump of horses' hooves grew louder. Three men rode in their direction. Jonathan started to get up, but Joshua grabbed his arm.

"That's Mr. Hart," Jonathan whispered. "He'll help us."

"No, He's Quantrill. Kid, he killed Pa."

Jonathan's eyes widened, but he kept quiet.

Quantrill and his men stopped a few feet from them. Joshua lay on his belly in the dirt beside his brother and waited, his heart pounding like Indian war drums. He willed the raiders to ride away, but they didn't.

More horse hooves rumbled, more men riding to the clearing. They were close enough that Joshua had to hold his hand over his mouth and nose to shield it from the dust the horses stirred.

"So, how'd it go?" Quantrill said.

"Lawrence won't soon forget the lesson we taught them today," a thin man with a bushy beard said. "We shot every man and boy we could find."

Jonathan let out a whimper, and Joshua poked him. He clamped his lips together.

"Good job, Bill," Quantrill said. "Did you get Lane?"

"Na, he got away, but we got most of those jayhawkers."

"That's a shame. I would have liked to have shown him the wrath of the Missouri raiders. Guess it can't be helped. We did what we could. He won't soon forget this day."

Joshua tried to grasp what he heard. His pa and brothers murdered because they wanted to kill Senator Lane?

"Anyone see the James boys?" Quantrill said.

"They were right behind us," Bill said.

Two young men rode into the clearing. One looked more like a boy. He had to be close to Jacob's age, maybe fourteen. The other wasn't much older than Jackson.

"What took you so long?" Quantrill said.

"Jesse and I thought we'd take a large withdrawal out of the bank to help the cause." The older one spat onto the ground. "We couldn't make the bank manager see it our way, so we shot him."

"Good." Quantrill chuckled. "Dirty Yankee banker. Let's get out of here, men. We did what we set out to do."

The riders galloped away.

Jonathan doubled over and sobbed, locks of hair hiding his face.

Joshua's heart raced. "We can't go back. Ma said to hide out 'til morning."

"We lost the fish. What'll we eat?"

"Don't reckon we'll be eating tonight. We'll fret about that in the morning."

Jonathan wailed until he gasped for breath.

Joshua put his arms around his brother and held him until he fell asleep, but he didn't dare doze. He sat against a rock and let the kid use his lap for a pillow and watched in case the raiders came back.

The night air caused a shiver to run through him. He wouldn't be able to sleep anyway. The lump in his stomach made him half-sick.

He wrapped his arms around himself and listened for the clamor of horses. Other than the crickets chirping and an owl hooting, the night was quiet except for Jonathan's sobbing gasps. *Please, Lord, don't let them come back.*

Chapter Two

The sun rose on the horizon. An orange hue lit up the sky but did nothing to lighten Joshua's despair.

A monarch butterfly with orange wings, black lines, and white dots perched on his foot. He watched it for a minute before nudging his brother to wake him. The butterfly flew away.

Jonathan peered at him with a dazed expression.

"Time to go home, Kid."

When they returned to the farm, the fires had burnt themselves out. Where the barn and house once stood, smoldering embers and ashes remained. The smell of charred cornhusks made his stomach churn.

Joshua found his ma a few feet away digging in the dirt and took the shovel from her. "You go rest. I'll do this."

Ma collapsed onto a tree stump near where the house lay in cinders. He pressed his lips together. She was ailing, he could see, but he didn't know what to do about that. It was already a hot day. At least, he could bury the dead before the flies got to them.

He dug the shovel into the hard ground. Jonathan grabbed another shovel and scooped some dirt. Joshua was grateful for it. A man shouldn't bury his family alone. The heat from the sun poured down on them, and sweat drenched their shirts, but they kept digging all morning.

When the sun was high in the sky, Jonathan threw down the shovel. "I'm hungry."

"I know." Joshua removed his straw hat and wiped his face with his bandana. "After we get this done, we'll go to town and try to find some food."

"My arms hurt, and I'm hot."

"We're almost done. Please, I need your help."

Jonathan wiped his eyes with his sleeve and grabbed the shovel.

When they finished, Joshua stood over Jacob's lifeless body. Flies had already started to gather where holes splattered the middle of his brother's chest. He smelled the blood, could almost taste it.

Jacob had wanted to fight in the war, but Pa wouldn't allow it. He didn't want him ending up like this. They'd already lost one son at Bull Run, and another was fighting somewhere in Virginia.

Maybe Jacob had attacked the raiders before they shot him. Joshua liked to think so.

His voice quivered. "Kid, grab the arms." He grabbed both feet, and Jonathan grasped the arms. They struggled to lift Jacob's body, but it wouldn't budge.

"We're going to have to pull him to the grave. Come on."

They worked together to drag each of the bodies and shove them into the holes they'd dug. Jonathan collapsed on the ground.

Joshua knelt beside him and gulped for air until his breathing slowed. "Come on." He stood and reached a hand out to his brother.

They filled the graves until a mound of dirt covered the last one, Pa's grave.

A man rode in from the path that led to Lawrence. Joshua ran to his ma's side, shovel in hand, and squared his shoulders, determined to stand his ground and protect her.

Ma stared past him, trembling. He felt her forehead. She was burning up.

The man riding toward their farm was still too far away to recognize. His mount was brown like Quantrill's. Joshua clenched the shovel with both hands. If only he had a gun.

The rider drew nearer. Unruly gray hair, hazel eyes, a black sack suit, and a derby hat. Joshua's grip relaxed. It was the preacher. His shovel hit the ground with a thud.

Rev. Fisher ambled to Ma's side. "I've been making the rounds to my congregation to see the damage caused by the raiders. Rose, how did you fare?"

Ma stared at him but didn't answer.

"They killed Pa, and Jeremy, and Jacob," Joshua said. "Jonathan and me hid. Ma's arm is hurt, and she's burning with fever. She's shivering, and there's no blanket to cover her. They burned everything. We don't even have a place to sleep. Nothing's left."

"I'm sorry, boys." Rev. Fisher placed his hand on Ma's shoulder. "Rose, you're hurt. Let me see."

Ma held her arm out.

The preacher turned her swollen arm over, rubbed his finger over a dark purple spot before letting go, and brushed his hand across her cheek.

"I need to take you into town, but I don't have a wagon. You'll have to ride my horse." Rev. Fisher turned to Joshua and Jonathan. "Boys, help your ma."

Jonathan hurried to where Ma sat, and they each took one arm and helped her to the horse. She mounted without saying a word.

Rev. Fisher led the horse with Ma as they strode behind to the Methodist Church where they'd marched to the front last Sunday during a revival service and vowed to serve God through any adversity. If this was the hardship the evangelist was talking about, Joshua wanted none of it.

He and Jonathan supported their ma as they walked between rows of wounded men lying on blankets covering the floor. Moans and cries choked out murmurs of conversation. The stench of blood and sweat made his stomach churn.

"I'm sorry there's no doctor to treat your ma." Rev. Fisher set his hand on Joshua's shoulder and squeezed. "Some of the ladies are helping, but Doc Griswold... well he..." The preacher's voice trailed off, and he sauntered away without another word.

Joshua found an empty space and helped Ma lie down. Groans came from the others, but he ignored them. He only cared about his ma. She grasped his arm hard enough that he winced, but he didn't pull away. He leaned closer to hear what she had to say.

"Give me your word you'll do whatever it takes to watch out for your brother. Don't you leave him."

He wiped his hand over his face. "I give my word."

Ma turned to Jonathan. "Mind what Joshua tells you."

"I promise." Tears flowed down his brother's face.

Ma closed her eyes -- still breathing. He listened to each labored gasp for air and took air in and out as his ma's chest rose and fell.

Mrs. Miller leaned over their ma and placed a cool cloth on her forehead. Her hair formed a bun on the back of her head, but wisps fell loose on her round face. She knelt on the floor and examined Ma's arm. Joshua relaxed a little. Mrs. Miller was Ma's best friend and often treated neighbors when Doc Griswold was busy. She'd know what to do.

She turned toward them, face ashen and bottom lip trembling.

A heaviness swept over him. He could tell this was bad.

Jonathan let out a gasp. "Is Ma going to die?"

"I'm not going to lie to you, boys." Mrs. Miller blinked twice. "That's a rattler bite."

"It'll be all right, Kid." Joshua tried to sound confident, but his mouth felt like it was full of cotton. "Ma's going to be fine."

"Do you give your word?"

He flustered at the question and, try as he might, could not hold back the tears. "No, I'm just praying she will."

"It's not fair. James died in Bull Run only a year ago. Now Pa, Jeremy, Jacob. The only brother we have left is off fighting in Virginia. It's not fair."

"I know, Kid. It's this war. I wish it were over." He wiped the tears off his face and set his hand on his brother's shoulder. "I'll give my word on one thing. I won't leave you. I'll take care of you like Ma said."

Chapter Three

It had only been yesterday since Joshua leaned by his ma's cot and held her hand as she took her last breath. He helped Rev. Fisher, Mr. Miller, and Jonathan bury her beside his pa and brothers.

Jonathan stood at his elbow where he'd been since Ma died. Rev. and Mrs. Fisher and Mr. and Mrs. Miller completed the circle around the graveside. If there hadn't been so many funerals the last two days, more people would be there. Folks loved Ma and Pa.

The sun beat down, and Joshua had a hard time latching hold of the words Rev. Fisher said over the graves. Something about seeing them again, but it all blurred as if a fog resided in his head.

Rays beamed with not a cloud in the sky to shield them. It wasn't right the sun should shine so brightly on a day like today. Shouldn't it be raining? Shouldn't the gloom clouding his thoughts cover the landscape so heavily he wouldn't be able to see the graves in front of him?

"Amen."

The sound of Rev. Fisher's amen broke through the haze. The funeral had ended. Joshua wiped the back of his neck with his bandana. When would there be relief from this heat?

"Reverend, you know our situation." Mr. Miller, a thin man with calloused hands, said. "There's barely enough for the fourteen children we already have. We can't take these boys in permanent like. If you like, we can have them stay with us a couple of days, maybe a week, until you make other arrangements."

"That would be a kindness," Rev. Fisher said. "The town's sending word all over Kansas. Folks will be coming in Saturday to give the orphaned children good homes. If you could keep these two until then, I'd be much obliged."

Joshua stared at Rev. Fisher, exhausted from the emotions he tried to hold in. "Jedidiah's in Virginia." His voice echoed hollow in his ears. "He doesn't know yet."

"Don't worry, Son. We'll send word to your brother. As soon as he can get back, we'll let him know where we send you boys, but we need to find you a good home to live in for a spell."

Jonathan looked straight ahead. He hadn't spoken since Ma died, hadn't even cried. Maybe he'd never speak again.

He took his brother by the hand. "We need to go to Mr. and Mrs. Miller's house now."

Jonathan didn't respond but followed where he led.

After they hiked a half hour, Joshua surveyed the Miller property. The raiders hadn't touched the cabin, barn, or crops. Mrs. Miller said when they came by, she'd hidden Mr. Miller in the well until they left.

Why did the raiders destroy some people's lives and leave others unscathed? He didn't begrudge the Millers their good fortune. They were decent people, but where was the fairness of it?

"Joshua," Mr. Miller said. "You and Jonathan can sleep in the barn loft. There's plenty of hay. I'm sorry we don't have room for you in the house."

"That's all right, Sir. We'll be fine. Thank you for your kindness."

After supper, he led his brother up the ladder to the barn loft. "You still hungry?"

Jonathan stared past him.

"I'm still hungry. I bet you are too. Remember how Ma used to say you ate as much as ten grown men?" He squelched the desire to cry.

Jonathan didn't answer.

He raked the hay out so they could have a comfortable bed. Soon the patter of raindrops hit the roof. Maybe it would cool things off. "Kid, how long are you going to keep this up?"

Jonathan turned to him and blinked.

"Answer me."

Nothing.

"Please." He swallowed the lump in his throat. "I need you to talk to me. I can't do this alone. Ma told me to look after you, and I will, but you promised Ma you'd mind me. You going to break your word?"

Tears filled Jonathan's eyes. "I'm sorry, JJ. It hurts sooo bad."

JJ, the name Jonathan had called him when he was little and couldn't pronounce Joshua.

His chin quivered. "I know, Kid, but we're all we've got."

"I'll try," Jonathan said through a sob.

"Let's get some sleep."

"JJ."

"Yeah."

"Are..." He wiped the tears off his face with his sleeve. "Are Ma and Pa," another sob, "in Heaven?"

Joshua's voice grew thick. "Yep, I reckon they are."

"Can they see us?"

"I guess so."

Joshua lay back and listened to his brother's stifled sobs until the kid fell asleep. Rain started beating against the roof. He was soothed by the sound, as if all of nature grieved with him.

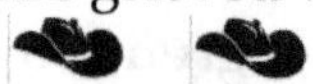

Joshua grabbed his brother's sleeve and followed Mr. Miller to the church. He had tried to convince Rev. Fisher to let him and Jonathan work the farm and live at home, but the preacher wouldn't budge, saying they were too young to stay on their own. If only Jedidiah were here.

When they arrived at the church, Rev. Fisher stepped over to them. "Mr. Miller, thank you for taking care of these two."

"Not at all." Mr. Miller gazed down at the boys. "You boys be good for whoever is blessed enough to have you."

"We will," Joshua said.

They wrapped their arms around Mr. Miller and hugged him. Mr. Miller paused before pulling them in tight.

Rev. Fisher pointed to the stage. "Boys, go stand with the other orphans. Some folks will be coming in to get a look at you."

Joshua pulled his brother with him as he squeezed in among the children. His heart ached for them. He and Jonathan weren't the only ones who lost everything.

Couples wandered into the church. Many came on the platform and pored over the children. Some of the couples felt their muscles. They better not feel his.

One man nudged him. "Open your mouth, boy. I want to get a gander at your teeth."

He wanted to refuse, but he needed to make sure Jonathan got a good home, so he didn't cause a fuss.

Maybe this was how the slaves felt. That must be why Pa had hidden them on the farm before the war started and why Ma would get so stirred up when she heard how they were mistreated.

Now he was the one on the auction block. After the man examined his teeth and squeezed his arms, he moved on.

One couple closed in on Jonathan. The young woman said to her husband, "Oh, Emmett, look at those blue eyes. Let's take him."

Jonathan's glance darted around, and he bit his bottom lip so hard it started to bleed.

Joshua stepped in front of him. "Ma'am, if you take my brother, you have to take me too."

"We're only looking for one child." Emmett pointed to a younger boy with blue eyes and said to his wife, "Will he do?"

She nodded, and they took the boy to the clerk recording the adoptions.

Rev. Fisher tromped over to him with a scowl on his face. "You're keeping your brother from having a good home. Is that what you want?"

"I'm not going to break my word to my ma or to Kid."

"You might not have a choice," Rev. Fisher said.

Joshua clenched his jaw.

Rev. Fisher put his hand on his shoulder. "I know you want to stay with your brother, but you need to put him in God's hands."

"Where was God when my folks were killed?"

"It wasn't the Almighty who did that."

Heat rose to the back of his neck. "I won't leave my brother alone."

"If you don't let him go with a good family, you might both end up in an orphanage back east. Is that what you want?"

Joshua widened his stance and folded his arms.

"You mind what I say." Rev. Fisher marched off the stage.

Many couples came through the church. Some wanted to adopt one or the other of the brothers, never both. Each time, Joshua refused, and they chose another child.

As the day wore on, the number of children dwindled as they left with their new families until the Jackson boys were the only two standing on the platform.

Joshua's feet hurt, and his stomach rumbled. He hadn't had any breakfast, and he knew Jonathan would be hungry too. The kid was always hungry. Maybe it would be better to go to an orphanage. They'd feed them, and he'd be able to take care of his brother like Ma wanted.

He started toward Rev. Fisher to tell him that when a man and woman entered the church. The man's face looked thin and stern, his shoulders broad, and the muscles in his arms bulging. His clothes were dirty, and he smelled of sweat and tobacco. The woman, also thin, wore a plain, tattered, black dress and bonnet. She kept her dull eyes down and her shoulders slumped as she followed her husband's lead.

The man trooped on stage, grabbed Joshua's hands, and gaped at them. "You've done hard work. You'll do."

"I'm not leaving without my brother."

"That him?" The man pointed at Jonathan.

He nodded.

The man grunted and looked Jonathan over. "I'll take them both. Where do I sign?"

Joshua let out a sigh of relief. It'd be all right now. They'd be together.

Rev. Fisher escorted the man to the clerk. After he gave his information, the man motioned for the boys.

"You call me Mr. Greer or Sir," the man said.

Joshua and his brother nodded.

"Come on." They followed him to his wagon.

"Get in," Mr. Greer said.

The boys climbed into the back of the wagon and sat with their legs dangling over the edge.

"Sir, I want to thank you for taking us both," Joshua said.

Mr. Greer's hand swooped down and clipped him across the face. "Boy, don't you ever sass me like you did in there again. I took you both 'cause I'm needing farm hands. You do as you're told, and I'll give you a place to sleep and food to eat. You cross me, and I'll whip you good. You get what I'm telling you?"

Joshua rubbed his stinging cheek. "Yes, Sir." He threw a glance toward his brother. How would he protect him now?

Chapter Four

Joshua rubbed his lower back where he ached from riding so long. They rode through grooves in the hard ground and jerked about, holding onto the sides for support. The wheel hit another bump, and he landed on top of his brother as the wagon veered away from the path.

The journey ended at dusk on a hillside surrounded by black oak and cedar trees. Enough land had been cleared for a barn, a log cabin, and a farm barely large enough to scratch out a living.

Mr. Greer stopped the wagon in front of the barn and climbed down. He shot back at the boys. "Get over here."

They jumped off and followed Mr. Greer to an old rundown shed standing twenty feet from the cabin. An oak tree shaded it with its massive branches. Mr. Greer opened the roughhewn door made of slats of pine and pointed inside.

As the boys entered, Joshua stepped over to a small potbelly stove and nudged his foot against the straw mattress and pile of horse blankets in the corner of the dirt floor. The shed was small, only about six-by-six feet. Light shone through some of the worn planks.

"Here's where you'll be staying," Mr. Greer said. "You eat at seven in the morning and seven at night. You work between meals. The rest of the time, you stay put. Don't come near the house bothering me or the missus."

"What about lunch?" Jonathan said.

Mr. Greer took a step toward him.

Joshua darted in front of his brother. "Mr. Greer, Sir, we're not sassing you. Just asking."

"No lunch. No time for that. This be a working farm. Any more questions?"

"Sir," he said, careful to keep his tone respectful. "After we bring in the crops for the year, will we be going to school?"

"I didn't bring you here for schooling," Mr. Greer said. "You'll be chopping wood and earning your keep in other ways."

Joshua slumped as if his arms and legs were weighted down with anvils. Ma and Pa both wanted them to finish their schooling, and Kid was so smart, they all knew he'd make something of himself, but it was better to stay on Mr. Greer's good side for the moment. He forced a tight-lipped smile. "We'll do a good job for you, Sir, and I thank you for giving us a place to stay until our brother comes home."

"I thought you were orphans." Mr. Greer placed a wad of chewing tobacco in his mouth.

"We are, but our brother Jedediah is fighting in the war. Rev. Fisher said he'd let him know where we are."

Mr. Greer raised an eyebrow. "He on the side for Southern independence or is he a Yankee?"

"He's with the Union Army," Jonathan said, "the Ohio Seventh."

Mr. Greer spat. "Fisher's not letting him know nothing 'cause he don't know where you be."

Joshua's chest tightened. "What do you mean?"

"I had me a couple of slaves, but they run off. I heard about Quantrill giving Lawrence a good whipping, so I got an idea to replace my workers with a couple of Yankee orphans." He leaned against the door frame and chuckled. "All I had to do was give them the wrong name and such. They were glad to get rid of you. You work hard, and I'll treat you fine. You go against me or try to run, and you'll wish you weren't never born. We cotton one another?"

A knot formed in his stomach. "We understand everything, Mr. Greer."

"Good. Supper's in an hour. If you be late, you don't eat." Mr. Greer left the shed and closed the door.

"What're we going to do?" Jonathan said.

"I don't know." Joshua rubbed the back of his neck. "How do I know?" Jonathan sniffled. "Stop it," he said a little harsher than he meant to. "We're not going to let Mr. Greer know he's getting to us. I know it's hard, Kid, but no more crying."

Jonathan wiped his face with his sleeve. "I'll mind whatever you say, JJ. I promised Ma."

Joshua almost told his brother to stop calling him JJ like he was four years old, but he didn't. If it made Kid feel better to call him that, it was worth it.

Besides, it was more important to figure out how to get out of this horrible place. He paced six steps to the edge of the shed. "We can't leave yet. You heard him. If we get caught trying to run off, I don't even want to think on what'll happen to us."

Six steps back. "We work hard and do everything he says while

I work it all out."

"JJ, I'm afeared."

He stopped pacing and placed his hand on his brother's shoulder. "Me too, but I need you to back me up. Can you do that?"

Jonathan nodded. "Why do you reckon God's letting this happen to us?"

"I can't rightly say God has anything to do with this." He swiped his hand over his mouth. Better to believe God didn't exist than to think He'd let this happen. "We're on our own here. We need to get washed up."

They found the old pump in front of the house and washed up the best they could without any soap or towels.

A monarch butterfly landed on the pump.

They entered the one-room cabin about half the size of their home in Lawrence but more than twice the length of the shed. It had a dirt floor, but unlike the shed, there were no slits in the boards, and a small window let in a sliver of sunlight.

Supper cooked over a small hearth on the back wall. A rifle hung on hooks above the mantel. A wood-frame rope bed with a tick mattress and quilt and a wooden chest sat against the wall to the right.

Mrs. Greer grabbed some plates from the shelves and set them on the roughhewn wood table in the middle of the room. She kept her eyes lowered and never uttered a word. The boys found seats on the bench as she placed the food on the table. Mr. Greer grabbed a piece of squirrel meat and bit into it.

Jonathan stared at his plate. "Mr. Greer, shouldn't we say grace?"

"I put this food on the table, not God."

Joshua threw his brother a look to warn him not to say any more.

Jonathan closed his eyes for a moment then dished out his food.

For the first time in as long as he could remember, Joshua didn't pray over his meal. Why bother praying to the God who allowed Quantrill to kill his family? They ate in silence.

When supper was finished, Mr. Greer nodded to them. "Make sure you're up bright and early in the morning, boys. Got a full day's work ahead of us."

Joshua raised an eyebrow. "Mr. Greer, tomorrow's Sunday."

"Yeah," Mr. Greer said. "Just another day 'round here. Ain't got time for no religious foolishness keeping me from working my farm."

That night, Joshua tried to sleep. He knew tomorrow would be a hard day, but he was wide awake. A coyote howled. It sounded close. An owl hooted. Even the noise of the crickets seemed louder than ever before.

Jonathan hurled off his covers and turned toward the wall. Looked like he wasn't getting much sleep either.

When Joshua finally did doze, that day invaded his dreams.

He and Jonathan rambled through the tall Kansas grass in their bare feet until they came to the edge of the Kansas River. They plopped on a limestone rock, baited their hooks with the night crawlers they'd caught the night before, and cast their lines into the water. They dangled their feet in the cool river before either of them said a word or caught a fish.

Jonathan sprang up when a catfish latched onto his line. He pulled it out of the water and unhooked it. "Do you think Jedidiah will be all right?"

Joshua peered sideways at him. "Of course, he'll be all right. Ma and Pa's praying for him, every day."

"They prayed for James too before he was killed."

As the day wore down, the boys picked up their catch and started home.

"Ma's going to be pleased," Jonathan said. "Ten catfish and a white bass ought to be plenty to feed the whole family."

He chuckled. "I reckon there might even be enough to feed you."

"Maybe, if you don't eat too much."

They strolled through the grassland toward home. Joshua smelled smoke and stretched his neck to see where it was coming from. Billows of dark clouds circled the knoll.

"Fire!" He charged through the fields. His chest heaved from running, but he couldn't get any closer as if he were running in place. Every time he reached the top of the hill, he found himself at the bottom.

He made it to the top again, grabbed a shovel lying on the ground, and pulled himself to the other side. Flames shot out of the ground, blocking him from getting to his family. He ran through the fire, scorching the hair on his head and arms. His green shirt caught on fire, and the flames engulfed him, burning his flesh. The fire died away. He froze in his steps.

Bodies in pools of blood.

He woke with a start and heard something. Jonathan was sobbing in his sleep again.

Chapter Five

Even at ten years old, Jonathan knew what it was like to work hard on a farm, but as he harvested crops, he couldn't keep the pace Mr. Greer set for him. He stopped picking beans for a moment to catch his breath.

Mr. Greer took a swig from his jug. "Get on with it. I ain't got time for you to be beating the devil around the stump." He parked himself under a cedar tree and watched them work.

The sun rose in the sky without a cloud to shield its beams or a breeze to relieve the heat it yielded.

At midday, Joshua turned to Mr. Greer, who hadn't moved from the shade the tree provided. "All right if we get a drink from the pump?"

"No breaks." Mr. Greer's speech slurred, and he drank another swig. "Get busy."

Jonathan worked as fast as he could in the sweltering heat, but as the day wore on, his stomach churned. Sweat poured into his eyes, and he felt woozy. He didn't know if he could stay on his feet much longer without at least a sip of water.

"That's it for today," Mr. Greer said.

Jonathan let out a sigh of relief, staggered to the pump, and lapped his fill of water. It felt good going down his parched throat. He poured some water over his head before falling to the ground.

Joshua took a few gulps and plopped next to him.

"You didn't get enough done today." Mr. Greer's breath smelled like whiskey. "I reckon you'll do better tomorrow. Get cleaned up. It's almost time for supper."

He hurried to wash up like he'd been told and followed Joshua into the house.

"What's this slop? I told you no more stew." Mr. Greer lunged toward his wife and punched her in the face. A reddish-purple mark appeared on her cheek. "You make this again, and I'll shove it down your throat."

Jonathan bristled and took a step toward Mrs. Greer, but Joshua shook his head and held a hand out to let him know there was nothing they could do. He ran his tongue across his teeth, everything in him wanting to stop this, and sat at the table.

Joshua glowered at Mr. Greer with those dark eyes of his, and Jonathan bristled. He knew that glare, the look of Joshua heading straight into trouble.

"I'm hungry." Joshua sat at the table and flaunted a defiant grin at Mr. Greer. "Stew sounds mighty tasty, Mrs. Greer. Thank you for making it for us."

Greer's thin lips tightened. Tension hung in the air like morning dew on grass.

Jonathan held his breath, wanting to protect his brother, but he couldn't think of how.

"Well, woman, I don't got all day." Mr. Greet sat on the other bench. "Get that slop on the table."

Mrs. Greer dished up the stew. When Mr. Greer looked the other way, she glanced up and nodded before lowering her eyes again.

When Jonathan turned to toss some beans into his basket. Joshua pitched some in his basket too instead of his own. He seethed. "JJ, stop that."

"Stop what."

"Trying to protect me."

"You're smaller than me. It's not fair to be expecting you to do a grown man's work."

Mr. Greer came toward them. "Get a wiggle on." He spat out a wad of tobacco and plopped down under the cedar tree as the boys stepped up the pace, but Joshua wouldn't stop throwing beans in his basket.

At least there was a breeze.

At the end of the day, Mr. Greer called out, "Quitting time, boys. Jonathan, you done good. Get washed up for supper."

He strode to the pump and grabbed the handle.

"Joshua, come with me," Mr. Greer said.

His brother tucked his hands in his pockets and followed Mr. Greer into the barn.

Jonathan began to wash up. He heard a swishing noise and a howl and stopped cold. He knew that sound. Someone was being whipped. He ran toward the sounds, determined to stop Mr. Greer from beating his brother, then halted. What could he do? It would only make things worse.

He fell to the ground and doubled over. The lashing and groans coming from the barn made him sick to his stomach. He wiped the tears off his face and covered his ears, but he could still hear.

Joshua would be mad at him for crying again, but he couldn't help it. A hand rested on his shoulder, and he startled and turned around.

Mrs. Greer pulled him into the house. "You won't help your brother none by getting in trouble too. You stay put here 'til it's over."

If only Pa were here, he would stop this. He sat on the bench almost afraid to breathe. It seemed like hours.

Mr. Greer sauntered into the house, sat, and dug into his food as if nothing had happened.

Jonathan sniffled. "Where's Joshua?"

"He didn't do enough work today," Mr. Greer said. "Don't work, and you don't eat. Now dig in. We're not going to waste food."

The knot in his stomach killed his appetite, but he forced down food, afraid not to eat. He tried to figure out a way to hide a biscuit or a piece of meat in his shirt so he could take it to Joshua later, but Mr. Greer kept too close of an eye on him.

Supper ended, and he was dismissed from the table. He raced to the shed... empty. He bolted to the barn and flung the doors open.

His brother lay face down on the dirt floor. Whip marks lined his back. Blood oozed from some of the lashes. All of them appeared red and painful. The welts dug into his wrists where ropes had tied him to the post.

"JJ." He ran to his side.

Joshua attempted to pull himself up by grabbing onto a milk stool, and winced.

Jonathan helped him to the shed and laid him on the straw mattress. "That was a fool thing to do, I might've picked enough beans on my own to keep us both from being horsewhipped. I can hold my own."

"I didn't get beat 'cause I helped you."

"Then why'd he do it?"

"Mr. Greer shot his mouth off about Pa being a dirty Yankee and not teaching us right. He called him a few words we've been taught not to say..." Joshua murmured. "I hit him."

Jonathan gasped.

"I know. I tell you not to get his back up, then I haul off and clout him."

"JJ, you're the one who said we're in this together. From now on, we share what we harvest. Then neither one of us gets in trouble."

"Or we both do." Joshua tried to rise, grimaced, and lay back down.

"Either way, we're together. Agreed?"

Joshua nodded.

"I'm going to get a rag and wet it."

"It'll be all right."

"I'm going to help you whether you like it or not. I not a baby. You aren't in this alone."

Joshua grinned through gritted teeth. "Kid, when did you grow up?"

Chapter Six

Fourteen-year-old Joshua and twelve-year-old Jonathan rushed into the cabin for supper.

"You're late," Mr. Greer said. "When you're late, you don't eat."

Joshua pressed his lips together. "You said not to come to supper 'til we finished cleaning the barn."

"Don't care. If you'd get a wiggle on instead of being a lazy, no-account Yankee, like your pa, you might get done in time."

Jonathan's hands balled into fists. "You take that back. I won't stand for you talking about our pa like that. He's more of a man than you'll ever be."

Mr. Greer stood and pushed the stool back. "You getting some sand in you, boy?" He lunged toward him. "I'll learn you."

Joshua's stomach knotted, and he moved in front of his brother. "Don't touch him."

Mr. Greer sneered. "You going to take the thrashing for him again?"

His heart pounded in his ears. It took everything in him not to lunge at Greer. "Yeah, if that's what it takes for you to leave him be."

"Stop it!" Mrs. Greer dropped the tin plate she was holding. It made a ding as it hit the dirt floor. Her voice lowered. "I won't let you beat those boys again, Amos."

Mr. Greer's hands fisted. "Get out to the shed."

Joshua bit his bottom lip.

"Go." Mrs. Greer wiped her palms on her apron. "I'll be fine."

He rubbed a hand over the heaviness in his chest. Maybe he should stay. That might make it worse. He didn't know what to do.

Mrs. Greer turned to him. "Just go."

He tugged Jonathan by the sleeve and headed outside. When they reached the shed and huddled in front of the potbelly stove, he tried to light it, but his hand shook so much, he couldn't get the flint to catch.

Jonathan's voice quivered. "I'm afeared he's going to hurt her."

"He is." He gave up on the fire and started pacing the length of the shed. They should have done something, but he didn't know what to do that would have helped her. "If we'd stayed, we might have made it worse."

"Why'd she do it? She knew he'd beat her."

"Don't fret." He dug into the dirt at the corner of the shed and pulled out a volcanic repeating pistol. "We'll get bullets soon, and when we leave, we'll take her with us. This, most likely, will be the last time he lays a hand on her."

"It doesn't set right, us sitting here doing nothing while a fine lady like Mrs. Greer gets hurt. Maybe we should pray for her or something."

Joshua's jaw twitched. "Do what you want."

The shed door slammed open, and Mr. Greer stood there, his gray hair disheveled and his eyes ablaze. "Boys, get out here. Mrs. Greer had an accident. She fell on a knife. Always was clumsy."

"Is she hurt bad?" Jonathan said.

"She's dead."

Joshua's heart dropped to his stomach.

They pushed past him and ran to the house. Mrs. Greer lay sprawled on the floor in a pool of blood, just like... like the day they went fishing. He knelt beside her and swallowed back the bile in his throat.

Mr. Greer stood in the doorway fidgeting with his hands.

"Did she fall on a knife five times?" Joshua grabbed the bloody knife still in her chest and stood, holding it at his side. If Greer wanted to kill them too, he wouldn't make it easy for him. Jonathan stepped to his side.

Sweat beaded on Mr. Greer's forehead. His gaze darted from the boys to his dead wife and back to the boys. He wiped his face with his bandana. "Get some shovels and bury her. And get that blood washed up."

Joshua's hand closed tighter around the handle.

"Nothing you can do for her." Mr. Greer features hardened showing none of the fear from a moment earlier. He grabbed the shotgun hanging on the wall above the fireplace, swung around, and pointed it at Jonathan. "But you can keep your brother alive."

Joshua's knees weakened. He dropped the knife and nodded to Jonathan. They picked up Mrs. Greer's body and carried it outside.

"What are we going to do?" Jonathan said.

He furrowed his brow. They were witnesses now. They couldn't wait until Greer conjured up the nerve to get rid of them. One way or another, they needed to get away soon.

Joshua stuck his head out the shed door and peered around, a calmness sweeping over him he hadn't expected. "The coast is clear."

Jonathan loaded the pistol and crept to the door of the house. He nodded to him and stood with gun drawn.

Joshua skulked to the barn, saddled the horses, and loaded supplies as quickly as he could. He led the saddled colts out of the barn, then slipped to the other side of the door beside his brother.

He nodded to Jonathan, and they crashed into the cabin. Jonathan pointed the pistol in Mr. Greer's face.

Joshua grabbed the loaded Henry rifle hanging on the wall. Without taking his eyes off Greer, he opened the sugar bowl and dumped out the silver dollars he'd seen Greer stash there.

He stuffed the change into his pockets. "Between this..." he jiggled the change, "and the horses and supplies we're taking, it should make us square for the work we've done over the last couple of years. Don't you think, Kid?"

"Yep."

"You run off with my money," Mr. Greer said in a screechy tone, "and I'll hunt you down."

"Now I wouldn't do that if I were you." He kept his voice calm and even. "We just want to get away. We don't want to shoot you."

"I'll... I'll get the law after you."

"Now, Mr. Greer." He moved closer and aimed the rifle barrel inches from the man's face. "If you do that, we'll just have to tell them how you murdered your wife not more than two days ago."

"You didn't see what happened."

"The sheriff wouldn't have a hard time proving it if we tell them about the stab wounds we saw when she was lying in her own blood." Joshua cocked the lever of the Henry rifle. It would be so easy to pull the trigger. He wanted to. His finger pressed slightly on the trigger.

Memories of about a month before the raid flittered through his mind.

Three men in Confederate uniforms had knocked on the door asking for food. His shoulders had tightened and his fists had balled, but he'd held back from attacking them. Pa had warned him of the dangers of letting his anger take hold. Ma had fed the soldiers, and Pa had sent them on their way.

The yearning to shoot Mr. Greer overwhelmed him just as it had when those rebel soldiers came to their house in Lawrence, but he could feel Pa squeezing his shoulder the way he did that day as if he were standing behind him. He removed his finger from the trigger and released the lever.

They backed out of the house and mounted the horses.

An owl hooted. A coyote howled. Joshua's heart pounded.

Every sound magnified as they rode into the night. "Which way you think we should head?"

"West," Jonathan said. "We were riding east when we came to this farm, and there are mountains all around. I think we're near the Ozarks. Lawrence has got to be west of here."

Joshua leaned back in his saddle. His brother always did have a good sense of direction, but knowing where they were and which direction to head after two years? He couldn't help being amazed. "West it is."

By daybreak, they came to the Kansas River running near their farm and nudged their horses on until they approached the road to Lawrence.

Jonathan patted his horse's mane. "Should we ride into town first or go to the farm?"

He stared at the road leading to town. "Lawrence. Rev. Fisher probably knows where we could find Jedidiah now that the war is over."

As they rode through town, he couldn't help gawking at all the new buildings on Massachusetts Street. It was as if he'd never grown up in this town. Everything had changed.

The new Round Drugstore, the new courthouse, general store, and houses lined the streets. Eldridge Hotel was erected at the same place the old hotel had been. The House Building where Pa had bought farm equipment and guns was the only store still standing from before the raid.

All of the debris removed, the evidence of that day gone.

A chill traveled up Joshua's spine.

As if it had never happened.

They rode on to the Methodist Church where they dismounted and stepped inside. Rev. Fisher sat on a pew near the front.

Joshua cleared his throat.

The preacher turned toward them, and relief washed over his face. "Thank God, you're safe. When we found out the man who took you gave us false information, we feared the worst. The sheriff had men scour the area for you, but by the time we realized what had happened, they couldn't find a trail."

Heat rose up Joshua's back. If Fisher had let them work the farm like they wanted instead of delivering them into the clutches of a mad man... He tried to keep his voice calm. "We're looking for our brother. Do you know where he is?"

The preacher looked at his hands. "I'm sorry, boys. We haven't heard anything, and he's not back from the war yet."

Joshua's heart dropped to his stomach.

"He might still be alive," Jonathan said.

Rev. Fisher set his hand on Jonathan's shoulder. "I wish that were true more than you know, but if he's not home by now, he didn't survive."

Everything inside Joshua wanted to grab the preacher by his collar and punch him in the jaw. He tried to remind himself it wasn't Rev. Fisher's fault that Quantrill killed his ma and pa and two of his brothers. It wasn't even the reverend's fault that the war claimed James and Jedediah, but he *was* to blame for sending him and his brother off to live with a monster the way he did. He stuffed the anger down.

"Boys, I know you've been through a lot, but I can find you another home, a good home where you'll be together, or you could stay on the farm. You're old enough now."

Joshua's jaw twitched. "We best be on our way." Before Rev. Fisher could answer, he marched out with Jonathan at his side.

Rev. Fisher called out, "Boys, wait."

He pretended he hadn't heard him call out because if he had stopped and turned back, he wasn't sure what he would do. He was done with Lawrence and with Rev. Fisher.

They mounted their horses and galloped north toward the river.

Once they reached the farm, Joshua dismounted and surveyed the ground lying unplanted, empty, still scorched from the fire. All the work Pa and his brothers put into the land, for it to end like this.

They strode over to the graves and removed their straw hats. The farm reminded him too much of that day... blood, death.

"Nothing left for us here," Jonathan said. "What do we do now?"

"Let's keep riding west. See where the road takes us."

Jonathan nodded, and they mounted their horses and rode the

path leading past the Miller farm. Mr. Miller stood in the fields planting, and Joshua almost stopped to say good-bye, but the yearning to get away was stronger. Mr. Miller glanced up, and he waved as they passed. He waved back.

As evening approached, he searched the horizon for a place to stop. Up ahead, the tall grass of the prairie gave way to a clump of trees near a stream.

"Good place to make camp," Joshua said. "Maybe we could stay a couple of days and catch some fish."

"Sounds good to me. All this riding gets a body wore out."

They stopped to set up camp next to the river. The water was bluer than the Kansas River. A flock of geese swam downriver, oblivious to any predators that might lie ahead.

A monarch butterfly flittered past them and landed on a branch lying on the ground near the riverbank.

Cottonwood, hickory, and elm trees all surrounded the campsite creating a serene refuge. The aroma of foliage and water was thick in the air. Joshua took a deep breath through his nose to take in the smells.

To the west, the sun setting behind mountains lit the sky with orange, yellow, and red. It struck him with awe. Such beauty and horror shouldn't share the same world.

While Jonathan gathered sticks and started a fire, Joshua unsaddled the horses and grabbed a couple of mason jars, one with beans and one with peaches, out of the saddlebags, along with an old copper pot.

"I expect we're going to get sick of beans and beef jerky before long," Joshua said, "but I got us peaches."

"We can fish and hunt some game along the way. Be good to have meat, even if it's just rabbit or squirrel."

"Be mindful with the bullets. They're all we got."

"I will." Jonathan opened the beans, poured them in the pot, and set it over the fire. The last sliver of sunlight disappeared behind the mountains. "JJ, how far you reckon we ought to go?"

"It's been two years since it happened. Why do you keep calling me JJ?"

"I don't know. You call me Kid."

"I've always called you Kid because you're my kid brother, but you stopped calling me JJ when you were around four."

"Do you mind?"

"No, I guess not. Call me whatever you want."

"So, JJ, where are we headed?"

"All I know is I want to get as far from Kansas as I can, and this road leads to Colorado. Let's stay on it as long as we can and see where it leads us."

Jonathan poked the fire with a stick and bit into a slab of beef jerky.

Joshua gazed at stars and trembled at how close he came to killing a man. "Kid, you ever get mad?"

"Nope. I'm too busy being afeared to get mad. I reckon I've been scared so long now I don't pay it no mind anymore. Why, you mad at somebody?"

"Yeah."

"Who you mad at? Mr. Greer? 'Cause I don't blame you none."

"Him more than anybody, but he's not the only one." He paused. "Sometimes I figure I'm mad at the whole world. I'd like to kill Quantrill with my bare hands, but I'd also like to blow up at Ma and Pa for dying on us and the war for killing James and Jedidiah. Then there's Rev. Fisher. I guess mostly at me for walking out and leaving Mrs. Greer with that snake when I knew he was going to hurt her."

He picked up a stick, broke it, and threw it in the fire. "I reckon I'm even mad at God."

"That's a powerful lot of mad, JJ."

"I'm afraid I'm going to hurt somebody one of these days. When I pointed that rifle at Mr. Greer, I wanted to kill him."

"What stopped you?"

"Pa. I remembered how he treated them rebel soldiers, and I couldn't do it. I don't want to be this way."

"You didn't pull the trigger."

"I know."

"Let's make a vow, JJ."

"What kind of a vow?"

"We won't ever hurt anybody no matter what happens, unless it's to protect someone or in self-defense."

Joshua thought it over. Pa always said a man doesn't break his word. He looked at his brother and knew he wouldn't let him down. With Jonathan's help, he'd be able to keep his promise. If he didn't, the anger would destroy him.

Chapter Seven

After a couple of months on the trail, the road ended in a town called Hunt's Peak near a stretch of mountains in Colorado.

They stabled their horses and asked directions to Hunt's Peak's only hotel. After entering through the heavy wooden door, Joshua nudged his brother and pointed to the big mirror behind the long oak counter. His ma had a looking glass, and there was a mirror at the general store in Lawrence, but he'd never seen anything like this. The mirror was at least as big as he was.

They stepped to the counter, and a stocky man behind the desk with a striped shirt and leather vest greeted them.

"We'd like us a room," Joshua said.

"Aren't you a little young?"

"We're old enough." He pulled some coins out of his pocket. "And we have money."

"Room three at the top of the stairs." The clerk handed him the key. "It's a dollar a day. If you want a bath, it's an extra fifty cents."

Joshua smelled under his arms and smiled. "Oh, we want baths." It was worth an extra dollar to get cleaned up.

"The bath room is the last door to your right." The clerk pointed down the hallway. "I'll let you know when it's ready."

Joshua scrunched up his nose. "I don't want a public bath."

"I assure you, there is only one bathtub and a lock on the door. You'll have one hour each."

Joshua face flushed, and he changed the subject. "Do you know of anybody hiring around these parts?"

"Yes, but I doubt they'll hire you," the desk clerk said. "You're too young. Maybe the saloon, they need a couple of bucket boys."

After they made their way to their room, Joshua unlocked the door and stepped into the hotel room. The room wasn't big, but it was large enough. A wood frame bed sat in the middle of the far wall. The sheets and faded green and blue patch quilt didn't smell very fresh, but at least they looked clean. A pine bureau with scratches and a missing handle on the bottom right drawer sat on the wall next to the door. A commode and chamber pot stood beside it. Two oak rocking chairs sat in front of an open window with a clear view of the main road and the mountains just outside of town.

Jonathan plopped his saddlebag in the corner. "It may not be much, but at least we have a bed to sleep in, and it's bigger than that shed."

Joshua laid his saddlebag on one of the rockers. "And we have chairs to sit on instead of the floor."

They unpacked their few belongings and emptied them into the top bureau drawer. Joshua hid the Henry rifle under the bed and covered it with a horse blanket.

Jonathan hid Mr. Greer's handgun in the drawer under their clothes. "Just think, a real bath. We haven't had one of them in almost two years."

"Yeah, I've been meaning to tell you how bad you smell." Joshua chuckled then stretched. He ached from the long days in the saddle and cold nights on the ground, and he was sure his brother would feel the same way. A warm bath would do them both good. "You take your bath first."

"You're the one who ordered them."

"The way you stink, you need it more." Joshua yanked off his boots and plopped on the feather mattress. "Kid, do you think we ought to try for those jobs in the saloon?"

"Ma and Pa would turn over in their graves if they knew we were working there. Pa always said evil lurked behind saloon doors."

He winced at the thought. "Sometimes you have to do things you don't want to. It's not like we're going to gamble or drink. We won't even look at the pretty girls."

"Ma always said, 'You can't lie down with fleas without getting bit.'"

"Yeah, well they aren't here, are they?" Joshua cringed at how harsh his words came out and softened his tone. "I don't know what to do, Kid. A dollar a day for this room, not to mention meals and livery costs, and our baths. The fifty dollars we took from the sugar bowl isn't going to last forever."

"Let's try to find decent work first. If we can't, we'll do it your way."

"We probably should buy another gun and some bullets."

Jonathan's mouth opened. "You planning on holding up a bank or something?"

"Of course not." Joshua flustered. "Look at it this way. We're two kids out here on our own. We need to be able to defend ourselves."

Jonathan leaned back in his chair. "Well, if we're going to carry guns, we need to practice. Except the couple of rabbits I shot on the trail, neither one of us has shot a firearm since Pa died."

"So, we'll practice."

Joshua and Jonathan entered Freeman's General Store and stepped over to the middle-aged man and woman behind the counter where a jar of rock candy sat. Rows of shelves lined the walls with various items including canned goods and sacks of flour, sugar, and salt.

The balding man with a well-trimmed beard raised his eyebrow. "What can I do for you?"

"We're looking for work, Sir," Joshua said. "We're hard workers, and we can read, and write, and do figuring."

"Why, you're just boys," the heavyset woman said.

The man folded his arms. "Where are your folks?"

"Dead," Jonathan said.

The woman splayed her fingers over her mouth.

"We really need this job, Sir." Joshua winced at his pleading tone, but he couldn't help it.

"Would you excuse us for a moment?" The woman led the man to the back corner, and they whispered to each other. Joshua caught a little of what they said. "… don't need orphans… might steal us blind… too young…"

They stepped back to the counter. "I'm sorry, boys," the man said. "I'm afraid we can't use you."

"Thank you, anyway, Sir." Joshua set a penny on the counter. "A penny's worth of rock candy, please."

They left the store and drifted down the dusty road eating their candy with their shoulders slumped.

"They can't all be like that." Jonathan grabbed another piece of rock candy. "Let's look some more."

They spent the next week searching for jobs. The men at the livery stable, the restaurant, the mill, the stagecoach depot, and the miners all said the same thing. "We need grown men for this job, not boys." They tried some nearby ranches and farms to see if they were hiring. Nobody was.

Jonathan even asked the sheriff if he needed a couple of

deputies. Sherriff Porter didn't say anything, just chuckled under his breath.

Joshua wanted to point out that he was only five years younger even if Sheriff Porter was well over six foot and looked like he could carry a tree trunk through town without breathing heavy.

After a week with no results, Joshua slumped into the chair in his hotel room.

His brother eased into the rocker beside him. "Maybe we could go to a church and see if they could help."

The muscle in his jaw twitched. "Kid, have you seen one church in this town?"

"No." Jonathan looked out the window as if checking to make sure one hadn't sprung up in the last hour. "How can a town not have a church?"

Joshua shrugged. "I don't think they're the churchgoing type, do you?"

"I guess not."

"You ready to try the saloon yet?"

"I don't like it." Jonathan rubbed his hand through his curls. "How much money do we have left?"

Joshua counted the money. "We've already gone through twenty dollars."

"Then we have time. I'm not going to work in a saloon unless we don't have a choice."

Joshua stood and paced. "We've tried everywhere. There isn't any other work."

His brother crossed his arms and gave him a steely glare, and Joshua gave in. "We'll keep looking."

They spent the next month and the rest of their money looking for employment somewhere before Jonathan finally gave in.

When they entered the saloon, Joshua's heart fluttered. Pa had said evil lurked behind saloon doors so many times, he didn't know what to expect. Somehow they managed to make it through the swinging doors without being struck dead or waylaid by the devil.

A scrawny man in a blue and white striped shirt played a fast song on the piano. Joshua had never heard it before, but he liked it. It had a lively beat.

A couple of girls wearing satin dresses barely long enough to cover their knees loitered around him. Their face paint made them look a little like the clowns he'd seen when the circus came through

Lawrence. Their skin had a pasty white look making their cheeks and lips too red.

A man with a handlebar moustache and wearing a red plaid shirt, a bowtie, and red suspenders stood behind the bar wiping out glasses with a towel. Behind him, a painting of a naked woman hung on the wall. Blood rushed to Joshua's face. He darted his gaze away.

The piano player stopped, and he and the girls stared at them as if they'd grown extra heads. Joshua fidgeted and wiped his sweaty palms on his trousers. Maybe Jonathan was right. Maybe they shouldn't be here no matter how much they needed the money.

"Boys, I don't serve children," the man behind the bar said without looking up.

"We're not here for drinks." Joshua dared one more glance at the painting and felt his face turning red. "We're here for a job. Man at the hotel said you were looking for a couple of boys."

The bartender raised an eyebrow. "How old are you two?"

"Sixteen." Joshua's stomach knotted. His pa always stressed the importance of telling the truth. *A man is only as good as his word.* Another one of Pa's famous sayings. He didn't like lying, but they needed the job. "My brother's fifteen. He looks young for his age. We need the work, mister."

"You look young for your age too, son. Hard to believe you're sixteen. I figure maybe about twelve or thirteen, and you two don't look like brothers."

Joshua pressed his lips together. Maybe he was lying about their age, but he hated someone not believing Jonathan was his brother. "I favor our pa. My brother looks like our ma." He paused wondering if he should admit all of it. "I'm fourteen. Jonathan's twelve."

A saloon girl with a royal blue dress sashayed over to him. "Ah come on and give them the jobs." She put her arms around him. "They're cute."

Joshua took in a strong whiff of lavender musk and pulled away. The saloon girl chuckled and strolled to the piano. He tried not to watch her, but he still noticed the way she sashayed and wrapped her arms around the piano player. He didn't know how the man kept playing without missing a note.

The bartender poured himself a drink. "Names?"

"I'm Joshua Jackson, and this is Jonathan."

"My name's Eli Hanson. We'll see how you do. You can stay in the room upstairs, and I'll pay you a dollar a week and give you meals and drinks for free."

Jonathan's eyes narrowed. "We won't be needing the drinks, Mr. Hanson."

Eli chuckled. "Well if you ever do, they'll be here waiting on you, and call me Eli. If you want extra money, you can take beer out to the miners at lunchtime. I'll give you five cents a bucket."

"Thank you, Mr. Hanson," Joshua said. "We'll sweep up now, and we'll take the jobs as bucket boys too."

"You can call me Eli. We don't follow the rules of polite society here, as you can imagine." He handed them a couple of brooms and strode to the room in the back.

"See, Kid." Joshua swatted the broom at his brother. "I told you it wasn't going to be that bad."

"I don't know. I still have a bad feeling in my gut."

Chapter Eight

A man in a tattered blue uniform pushed his brown hair under his army hat and marched down Vermont Street in Lawrence, Kansas. He passed the new buildings lining the dirt road as people gathered to watch him.

Mr. and Mrs. Miller whispered to each other and followed him. When Mrs. Hoover came out of the General Store, she dropped her handbag and ran back inside like she'd seen a ghost. A moment later, both Mr. and Mrs. Hoover ran out and stared at him as he strode by.

The man kept his eyes fixed straight ahead. He almost stopped to greet these neighbors he had known all his life, but he had business to attend to first. He'd been trying to get home to take care of it for over two years now, but God had other plans.

He ignored the stir he caused and strode on until he reached his destination, the Methodist Church. Had it been five years since he'd been there? At eighteen, he'd left Lawrence to go to Oberlin College and study theology. Three years later, he quit school and enlisted in the Ohio Seventh Volunteer Regiment. Since then, so much had happened. He stepped into the church.

Rev. Fisher entered from a side door and gasped.

The man chuckled and crinkled his eyes. "Didn't ever expect to see me again, did you?"

"No, Jedidiah, I surely didn't," Rev. Fisher said when he recovered his voice. "You're supposed to be dead."

"I'm very much alive." Jed Jackson cleared his throat. "I was wounded at Missionary Ridge and was transported to the army hospital in Chattanooga. When I recovered, they sent me home, but on the way, I was captured by the enemy. I've spent the last year in a Confederate prison camp. Been trying to find a way home since the war ended and I was released, but it's taken longer than expected."

"Thank God. I just hope it's not too late."

Jed's chest tightened. "What's too late?"

Before he got his answer, Mr. and Mrs. Miller burst into the church. Mrs. Miller cried, and Mr. Miller ran up to Jed and gave him a bear hug.

"I can't believe it. You're alive." Mrs. Miller took hold of his hands and lowered her eyes. "I'm guessing you know about the raiders."

"Yes." Jed's voice caught. "I heard the whole town suffered loss."

Mr. Miller slapped his hat down on the pew. "You got that right. Those blackhearts killed almost two hundred men and boys. They even planned on killing Rev. Fisher, a man of the cloth."

"Only reason I escaped is 'cause my wife hid me," Rev. Fisher said.

"They killed Rev. Snyder from the United Brethren Church down the way," Mr. Miller said. "And they gunned down Doc Griswold after telling him if he gave himself up, it would save the townsfolk. What kind of snake murders a doctor after lying to him to get him out in the street?"

Jed drew a fist to his mouth and let up a prayer for strength to forgive the men who killed his family.

Mr. Miller picked up his hat and twisted it in his hands. "The newspapers say Quantrill didn't kill any women, but we know different. Even if he didn't use a gun to kill your ma, God rest her soul, he murdered her just the same. Pushing down a lady as fine as Rose Jackson. God forgive me, but I was happy when I heard he was gunned down."

"I don't hold any hard feelings." Jed breathed a long breath as he tried to keep the anger from flaring up again. He'd spent a year in that camp trying not to hold hard feelings, but it hadn't worked. "The war is over now." Time to get on with his life. "What I really want to know is where my brothers are. I stopped by the farm, and they weren't there. I'm here to collect them."

Mr. Miller exchanged glances with Rev. Fisher. "I think it's time me and the missus head back home." He and his wife hurried out of the church.

Jed's shoulders tensed. "Now I can see there's something you need to tell me. Joshua and Jonathan are all right, aren't they?"

"I don't know." Rev. Fisher hung his head. "I hope so."

🤠 🤠

The sound of gunshots shattered the silence in a clearing at the base of Hunt's Peak Mountain as Joshua and Jonathan practiced their fast draws.

Joshua watched Jonathan draw his new Colt army revolver and shoot off six bullets, hitting the target every time. He wished he was that good. He stepped up and fired, unloading his Volcanic pistol a little slower than Jonathan and only hitting four of the six cans they used for targets.

"You're getting better, JJ."

"Not as good as you. You're a gunman to the manner born. I was thinking we should start carrying them, you know, for protection." He loaded his gun and shot six more rounds. This time, every bullet hit where he was aiming.

"That's a stupid idea. If we do that, folks will start to get an idea how good we are."

Joshua thought of that, seeing the sense in it even if he didn't want to admit it. They'd strayed far enough without trying to become gunslingers. "Kid, how come you had that beer, last night, when you were so dead set against drinking?"

"Got tired of all the teasing. There isn't a man there who doesn't have something to say about me having a baby face or how I'm not old enough to shave yet. They're all calling me Kid now. I figured if I have a beer sometimes, they might not bother me."

"Do you want me to stop calling you Kid?"

"Na, when you do it, it's all right. Besides, don't think it would make any difference. They'd still go on."

"How'd it taste?"

"It was all right." Jonathan scrunched up his nose. "I'd rather have buttermilk or sassafras, but it'll do."

Joshua stood quiet for a moment, almost tasting the buttermilk Ma brought them when they worked in the fields. So long ago. Having an occasional drink to forget the past might not be so bad.

"JJ, you ever reckon we'd be doing the things we're doing?"

"What do you mean?"

"We work in a saloon, we're practicing our quick draw, and now I'm drinking. We're not going to church, or praying, or nothing like that. Can you imagine what Ma and Pa would do if they could see us now?"

Joshua grinned. "I don't figure neither one of us would be sitting down for at least a week."

"You got that right."

"I'd give anything for them to give us a good going over, but they aren't here. If they were, we wouldn't be doing what we're doing."

"True enough," Jonathan said. "Still, maybe we shouldn't be

doing it."

Blood rushed to Joshua's face. "What do you want us to do, go to the nearest church and repent? There is no church in this town, in case you forgot. Maybe we should go to the sheriff's office and tell him we stole from Mr. Greer. Then we wouldn't just be getting a trip to the woodshed, we'd be in jail."

Jonathan drew his gun and shot six times. Cans pinged and jumped with every shot as the air filled with smoke.

Joshua looked at his feet. "I don't like it any more than you do, but we don't have a choice, now do we? We're doing the best we can 'til we get ourselves a stake. Then we can leave town and go someplace where we can get honest jobs."

"How're we going to get a stake working at a saloon for a dollar a week? Even with the extra money we pick up being bucket boys and collecting the spilled gold dust we sweep up, it barely pays our bills."

Joshua rubbed his hand over the back of his neck. As hard as he tried to take care of his brother, it was never enough. He needed to find a way to make more money. "I could play poker."

"Poker? JJ!"

"Now hear me out. I've been watching the men play. I can pretty much figure out the odds on getting the right cards 'cause of the cards already dealt. Besides, I can see when somebody's bluffing. They always do something, even if it's something small, to give themselves away."

"But what if you lose?"

"I'll be careful, but if I'm good and keep winning, we could move back into the hotel. I hate that tiny room over the saloon. We could even get out of this town with money in our pockets."

Jonathan crossed his arms.

"What's wrong, Kid?"

"We keep getting in deeper. Probably end up robbing banks and trains before we're done."

"I'm worried about them," Rev. Fisher said. "The way they acted, I knew they were headed for trouble, but I couldn't keep them here."

Jed tramped down the dread tying his stomach in knots. "So, they just rode away, and nobody's seen them since?"

"Mr. Miller saw which way they went. They used the road leading to Colorado."

"What makes you so sure they were headed for trouble?"

"The look in Joshua's eyes. It sent a chill right through me. Even though your brothers got into mischief at times, they seemed to be on speaking terms with the Lord. The Sunday before all this happened, they even went up front to dedicate their lives to God, but when they came back… I think that's over now."

Jed set his jaw. "I have to find them."

"And how are you going to do that? It's been going on four months."

"I have to try."

Rev. Fisher placed a hand on his shoulder. "Seems unlikely you could catch up with them. Maybe if you stay put, they'll come back. You were studying for the ministry before you joined up. I could put in a good word with the district to appoint you as a circuit rider."

"No, I'm going to travel that path myself." Jed let out a deep sigh and paused for a moment to silently ask God to direct him. "I'll stay on the road they took until I find them."

"It would take months, maybe years. What if they turned off somewhere? How will you live?"

"Sold my folk's farm. With that and my back pay from the war, I'll make do." He stuffed his hands in his pockets. *Lord, guide my steps.* "I can always stop along the way and work if I run out."

"It's foolishness, Son. You ought to leave your brothers in God's hands."

"Rev. Fisher, I can't do that. Doesn't Jesus teach if a man has a hundred sheep and loses one, he'll leave the ninety-nine to search for the one? These are my brothers. I have to try."

Even as he said it, hair lifted on the back of his neck. What if they were in trouble or dead? He couldn't think that way. It might take a miracle to find them, but he served a God who did miracles.

Chapter Nine

It had been a year since Joshua and Jonathan came to Hunt's Peak. Joshua sat at the poker table in the saloon and observed the reactions of the three grown men sitting at the poker table with him. "Call."

The man to his left with the mole on his chin tensed, but Joshua ignored it and hollered out to the bartender through the smoke-filled room, "Eli, how about another round back here?"

"Got a pretty good hand." The man to his right, who looked and smelled as if he spent most of his time mining in the mountains, threw in a Liberty gold piece. "I'll raise you twenty."

"Too steep for me." The man across from him with a missing front tooth threw his cards on the table.

The man with the mole threw his cards face down and raised his hands as if surrendering. "I'm out."

Joshua kept his face expressionless. "I'll call."

Mountain man laid his cards face up. "I got me three sevens." He reached for the pot.

"Not good enough, friend." Joshua showed his cards and grinned. "Full house–tens over aces." He swept the money toward himself.

The man grabbed his arm with the strength of a bear. "I think you're cheating."

"I'm not cheating." Joshua's smile faded, but he didn't dare show any fear. No matter how hard his heart was beating, he had to appear tough no matter how young he was. "With you, I don't have to."

Eli grabbed a shotgun from behind the bar. "Is there a problem?"

The man released Joshua's arm, knocked over a chair, and shoved through the crowd as he stormed out of the saloon.

Joshua shook his head, let out a silent sigh of relief, and forced a smile onto his face. "So, who's up for trying to win back your money?"

Later that night, the brothers strolled past the locked doors and dim storefronts and crossed Miner's Alley on the way to the hotel.

"How much you win?" Jonathan said.

"Biggest night ever. Think I come close to fifty dollars ahead."

Jonathan whistled, but before he could say another word, two men with bandanas over their faces stepped out of the shadows. One was burly and smelled bad like the mountain man. The other wore the same rabbit skin jacket as the man with the mole.

Joshua swallowed hard and shoved his brother behind him. It didn't do any good. The men dragged them both further into the alley and shoved them against the brick building.

"Give me your money," the mountain man said.

He hated giving into these bullies, but what choice did he have? He and Jonathan couldn't have defended themselves against one of them, let alone both. If only they had their guns. He reached into his pocket and pulled out a change bag full of coins.

Mole man snatched the money and tucked it in his trousers.

Mountain man grabbed them both by the scruffs of their necks and pushed them both further into the alley. "Now it's time we teach you boys a lesson," he said. "Don't be cheating grown men out of their money. Oh, and boys, this lesson's going to hurt."

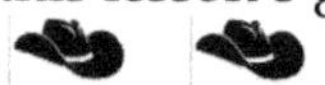

Joshua squinted. The images of the doctor and the sheriff become clearer. He groaned and put his hand to his head. He hadn't hurt this bad since Mr. Greer had horsewhipped him. He tried to sit up, winced, then groaned and lay back.

"We didn't think you were ever going to wake up," Dr. Smith said. "You gave us a scare."

"You remember what happened?" Sherriff Porter stood over him with his bulging arms, large chest, and tin star pinned to it.

Joshua closed his eyes for a moment and tried to shake the fog from his brain. "Two men stole our money and gave us a walloping. Said they were going to teach us a lesson."

"Did you see their faces?"

"No, had their faces covered with bandanas, but I'm sure they were the men I played poker with last night. One was a mountain man, think his name was Sam or Seth, something like that. Don't rightly recall."

"If you didn't see his face, I don't expect there's much I can do."

Jonathan moaned.

"Glad to see you're awake, son," Sheriff Porter said. "I got some advice for both of you, and if you're smart, you'll listen."

Joshua took a deep breath. He was too tired and sore to have the sheriff scold them for something they couldn't help.

"What in the Sam Hill are you two doing playing poker in a saloon at your age? If you had folks, I'd take you home so they could clean your plows." His tone lowered. "What you're doing is dangerous. One day, you'll run across somebody who wants to shoot his gun to settle the score, and I might not be around to stop him."

Joshua shot a look toward his brother.

"So, nothing I've said is getting through?"

He didn't bother to answer. Neither did Jonathan.

The sheriff threw his hands into the air and stormed out of the office.

"You can stay here a day or two," the doctor said. "I want to make sure you're all mended before you leave."

"Thanks, Doc." Joshua closed his eyes.

A couple of days later, when the boys felt well enough to go back to their hotel room, they fastened their gun belts and loaded guns around their waists.

They never left the hotel again without their guns.

"What're we going to do?" Kid fired a round of bullets shattering six glass jars set on a log thirty feet in front of him. "Winter's coming in a couple of months, and nobody will play poker with us."

"I don't blame them," JJ said. "We've gotten real good at it over the last year, and everybody knows it. Maybe we should be getting out of town."

"We can't run off. We owe the hotel five dollars, not to mention the livery stable. If it weren't for Eli giving us food, we'd starve. We don't have enough of a stake to win it back even if we were to find somebody we could hornswoggle into playing with us."

"I've been pondering on that."

That twinkle in JJ's eye gave Kid indigestion. "What are you planning?"

JJ paused. "We won't take much, just enough to get us to the next town."

Kid gasped. "You want to steal? Who from?"

"Now who's the richest man in this town? Who could afford to spare us some money?"

Kid clasped his hand over his mouth. "You want to rob

Freeman's General Store? JJ, what if we get caught?"

"We're not going to get caught. I have it all figured out. I won a lock pick set from a gambler a few months back, and I've been working on picking locks and such."

"You've been working on what? You crazy?"

"Well, I had to do something while you were practicing your fast draw all the time. Aren't you good enough yet? You have to be the fastest man in town. You hit everything you aim for."

Heat rose to the back of Kid's neck. "If I'm going to carry this gun and back you up, I need to be faster than anybody else. Even more so if we're going to take up robbing stores."

JJ grinned.

Kid rolled his eyes. Why did he even try? He always went along with his brother. Only now, he might follow him straight to jail.

JJ pulled out his lock pick kit, examined the different picks and chose one. A thrill rushed through him as he stuck it in the door of the Freeman's General Store and moved it around in the keyhole, trying to get it to catch.

The first time he turned it, nothing happened. The second time, he could feel the pressure from the lock and turned it, but it slipped. Wiping the sweat off his forehead, he tried again. Slowly he turned the lock with the pick, heard a click, let out his breath, and opened the door.

Kid followed him in and propped himself by the door. He watched out the window with his hand on the butt of his gun.

JJ found a candle on the counter and lit it. It brightened the whole room and cast glimmers of light on the window shade. Uh oh. They could probably see it clear to the sheriff's office. He found a box and placed it in front of the candle. He studied the shade. The box seemed to shield the candle okay.

Kid hadn't moved from his post, so JJ lurked through the store checking every shelf for a cash box. Each step he took squeaked on the floorboards, but his heart pounded louder.

Exhilaration burst through him like it did when he held a winning poker hand or when he used to get into mischief back in Kansas before his folks died. Except now, the excitement coursing through him burned stronger than when he poured pepper in the punch bowl at the church social or when he drew to an inside straight and won. Every sound, every breath, every heartbeat stirred his senses.

"Wait," Kid said. "I hear something."

JJ crouched behind a crate. Footsteps shuffled outside. They stopped. He was sure his heart paused as well. Steps softly padded again, this time growing fainter, until they drifted into the night.

Kid peeked through the corner of the blind before nodding.

He went back to work searching under the counter. He lifted a crate out of the way. A black safe with the words Silas C. Herring & Company etched on the front in big letters was behind the counter.

His heart sank. "Oh no."

"What?"

"I can't pick a safe."

"Let me see." Kid stepped to the counter. "It's just a little one. Maybe you could try to open it. I mean, since we're already here."

"You mean like listening for the tumblers?" JJ tilted his head. "I could try." He knelt in front of the safe, pressed his ear against it, and listened as he turned the combination lock. "They're real faint, but I can hear the tumblers. I might be able to do this."

"You keep working." Kid took his place at the window. "I'll let you know if we're running out of time or if somebody comes."

JJ turned his attention to the safe and turned the dial. Something dropped. He could barely hear it. Turned it the other way. Again, a slight clanking sound. Two numbers. Only one to go.

He tried for the third number. When it dropped, his stomach fluttered, and he turned the lever. Nothing happened. He looked at his brother and blew out a sigh.

Kid shrugged. "Maybe it has more than three numbers. The bank in Lawrence had five."

"How'd you know that?"

"Pa and I were in the bank once, and I watched them open the safe."

JJ grinned. Pa always said Kid had the brains in the family, that he could figure out things and remember stuff normal folks couldn't. JJ thought so too.

A twinge of guilt went through him. Kid was so smart and could have done a lot with his life if JJ hadn't been leading him into trouble. Even though he'd only been ten when they quit school, Kid had already been doing tenth grade work.

Maybe they should have stayed in Lawrence. JJ could have

farmed the land, and Kid could have gone back to school.

He let out a sigh. Too late for regrets now. Might as well see if he could open the safe.

Clearing the spinner, he dialed in the first three numbers. He turned the knob again and heard another click. "You're right. It has more than three numbers." He tried for the fifth number. "Blazes." He sat back on his feet and thought for a moment. "Maybe it's only got four numbers."

He tried the numbers and pulled the lever again. This time the safe opened. An urge to let out a yell was almost stronger than the common sense to squelch it. He pressed his lips tight, pulled out the bundles of money, and threw them in a sack on the counter.

With this much money, they could get to another town, one with a school. Kid could have all the money he needed to get some schooling and make something of himself. He emptied the safe, closed it, and blew out the candle.

Kid inched his head out the back door and nodded. They ran to their horses tied to the hitch post.

A man stepped out the back door of Hunt's Peak Hotel and lit a cigarette. JJ set a hand on Kid's shoulder to warn him not to move. He dared not take a breath, hoping the man wouldn't look their way. The man took his time enjoying his smoke.

Kid's horse whinnied, and the man started toward them. "Hey, you there, stop!" Two more men rushed out onto the porch, one trying to pull up his suspenders.

JJ mounted his bay. "Let's get out of here quick."

Chapter Ten

Rain plummeted to the ground, making it difficult for the horses to have sure footing. Kid shivered as the water soaked through his coat and dripped off his hat. Next time he and JJ robbed a store, he would insist they take a couple of slickers.

He nudged his sorrel further along the narrow path along the mountainside. Why was he even thinking like this? There would never be a next time.

At least the deluge stopped anyone from riding after them. A man would have to be crazy as a loon to ride in this. Even if the sheriff did come after them, he doubted Porter could find any hoof prints not washed away.

He took off his hat, dumped water out of the brim, and squinted to see where the path led. The darkness and cloud cover hid the trail farther than a couple of feet in front of them. Lightning flashed and illuminated a cave opening in the cliff. He pointed it out to his brother.

After setting up camp and taking care of the horses, they sat around the fire near the entrance. It wasn't really much of a cave, just an opening in the rock on the side of the mountain, but it kept them out of the rain. At least they didn't have to worry that some bear had made his home here.

JJ dumped the money out of his saddlebag and counted it. "Three hundred and forty-five dollars and sixteen cents."

Kid whistled.

"I heard Denver City's real nice," JJ said. "They've got fancy hotels, and saloons, and such. And churches. Lots of them. We said we would go to church when we got a stake."

It sounded good even though they had to steal to get this chance. "We could live on this money for a good, long spell." In a big place like Denver City, they would be able to get decent jobs and change their ways. Maybe he could even go back and finish school. "Were you scared?"

"Sure was, excited too. I'd never thought it, but I had fun."

Kid wanted to chide him and tell him they shouldn't have enjoyed robbing people, but he had to admit, it was a little fun. "When you opened that safe, JJ… That was blame amazing."

"I didn't think I could do it." JJ's face grew serious. "But we're never doing this again, right?"

Kid caught the glint in his eyes, and hoped he meant it.

They trotted their horses along Front Street in Denver City. JJ stretched his neck as he passed brick buildings lining one side of the street and the creek flowing on the other.

A commotion of people bustled past on wooden sidewalks in a flurry of activity, and horses and carriages crowded the roads. He turned, glimpsed a four-story brick structure, and pointed. "Have you ever seen so many brick buildings in all your born days?"

"Nope," Kid said. "I've never seen this many stores bundled up in one place before, let alone brick ones."

They climbed off their horses in front of a three-story lodging with a porch large enough to fit a house. The white sign with green lettering read *Overland Hotel.*

JJ tied his horse to a hitching post. "At least this town has churches. I counted three on the way in."

"Yep, looks like we can go in the morning."

"We passed two saloons, not that we're going to pay them any mind." JJ grinned to himself. He sure would like to play poker in Denver City. A shame to lose out on all those winnings. Maybe he could talk to Kid about it later.

He headed to the door of the hotel, but he couldn't help staring at everyone with his mouth hung open like a farm boy from Kansas. It was all so big and exciting. And expensive. He tipped his straw hat as he brushed past a group of ladies on the porch.

They didn't respond, but they eyed him like he had the pox. After a week on the muddy trail, with the stench coming from him, he understood their disgust.

Maybe he could use a little of the money they stole to buy baths. Then they could go to one of those fancy stores and buy a bowler or even a slouch hat, maybe even some better clothes. If they didn't look so ragged, it might be easier to find jobs.

They entered the spacious foyer, and JJ couldn't help but gape. Grand paintings and mirrors hung on the walls, and settees and balloon back cushioned chairs sat around a fireplace. A multicolored rug led the path to a large oak counter in the center of the room.

He and Kid set their saddlebags down.

The man behind the counter turned his nose up at them like they were nothing, just like the ladies outside. "Can I help you?"

"We need a room with two beds and two baths," JJ said, "and directions to the livery stable."

The clerk raised one eyebrow. "I'll need payment in advance."

Heat traveled up JJ's back, but he didn't say anything. Instead he pulled some coins out of his pocket. "We have money."

An accommodating grin crossed the clerk's face. "Room seven's available, Sir. It's upstairs to the right." He handed the key to a bellhop, a young black boy who couldn't have been more than ten years old.

At least carrying people's bags was better than carrying buckets of beer to the minors. He hoped the boy got paid better than they had.

The clerk gave JJ a pen and turned the registrar book so it faced them. JJ dipped the pen in ink and signed his name.

"I'll see your horses are taken care of right away. We have a hotel stable in back. And I'll have two baths prepared. The bath room is down the hall from you. We could call you when they're ready."

"We can both have baths at the same time?" Kid dipped the pen and signed the registrar.

"If you would like," the clerk said. "There are two tubs."

"Sounds fine," JJ said. "How much do we owe you?"

"The rooms are five dollars a day. The baths are one dollar apiece. That's six dollars for the first day, Sir." The clerk slurred the sir as if it stuck in his throat to have to be polite to them.

Kid's jaw dropped. "Seems awful steep."

JJ looked around and swept his hand sarcastically. "That's 'cause it's such a fine hotel. Besides..." He delivered the clerk a glower. "We can afford it." He handed the man a $20 Liberty gold piece. "This should take care of things for a few days."

The clerk's eyes widened. "Yes, Sir." His condescending tone was gone. "If there's anything else I can do for you, please let me know. I'll be happy to–"

Kid interrupted. "Is there someplace we can get something to eat nearby?"

"Yes, Sir," the clerk said. "The People's Restaurant's a short lope from here. Blake Street next to the drugstore. I could have a cab waiting for you if you like."

"How much for the cab?" JJ said.

"One dollar."

"Have it ready in ten minutes. We'll have our baths when we get back."

"Yes, Sir."

The bellhop grabbed their saddlebags and led them up the stairs to their room. The boy unlocked the door and placed their bags on a small table before giving them the key.

JJ perused the spacious room. A large poster bed with a feather comforter stood in the middle of the room. Across from the bed was a fireplace. On one side, two chests of drawers sat. On the other side, a settee and two chairs made a sitting area. The nicest room he'd ever seen, even in Lawrence.

Kid jumped on the bed and rubbed his hand along the comforter. "Look, we even have two matching bureaus. Isn't that mahogany wood?"

"I reckon so. Looks expensive." JJ plopped down on the settee.

Kid slipped behind a screen in the corner of the room and chuckled.

JJ joined him where he found a porcelain chamber pot and commode with orange butterflies painted on them. "Looks like we can do our business private like." He tried to look serious but couldn't keep the corners of his mouth from turning up. "This'll do fine."

"Wahoo, you said that right, but we have to find someplace cheaper soon, or we'll run through all of our money before we have a chance to look for jobs."

"We can at least stay a couple of days." JJ sighed. Maybe he could win enough money at poker so they could stay longer.

"Let's go get something to eat, and then we can take those baths."

JJ rubbed his hands together. "Since the restaurant's right next to the drugstore, let's get us a couple of fancy cigars too."

"But JJ, we don't smoke."

JJ and Kid sat in copper bathtubs holding their cigars.

"Ah, this the life," JJ said.

"Sure is." Kid took a puff on his cigar and suppressed a cough. "Tomorrow's Sunday. We said we'd go to church."

"I know." JJ rubbed his chin. How could he tell Kid he didn't want anything to do with church or God? Not since that day in Kansas.

Kid took a puff on his cigar and coughed spastically. Clearing his throat, he rasped out, "What're you scheming?"

"Well, if you don't want to do this, we can go to the original plan."

"Do what?"

"Once we get religion, we'd have to give up gambling and hanging out in saloons." He set his cigar down and tried to ignore the queasiness it caused.

"Yeah, so?"

"Why don't we take some of the money we... come by and go to the saloon, first? We could probably double our profits."

"We only stole it so we could go someplace where there's a church. Doesn't seem right not going."

JJ set his cigar down and flashed Kid a smile he hoped didn't look forced. "If we played poker first, we wouldn't have to fret about money. Maybe we could even make enough for you to go back to school instead of us both working."

Kid tilted his head, a far off look in his eyes. "I would like that." He shook his head." But we only gamble for a week, then no matter how much we have, we go to church. Right?"

"Oh, right. We can always repent later – after we win some money." JJ tried to hold back another coughing fit. He didn't like lying to his brother.

Kid didn't say anything for at least five minutes. "JJ, we're not going to be stealing anymore, right?"

"Of course not." *Not unless we need to.*

Chapter Eleven

Jed entered the Hunt's Peak sheriff's office. It had just enough room for a beat-up desk, two chairs, a cot, and a box stove with a pot of coffee brewing on it. Wanted posters hung on the wall behind the desk. He heard some of the names before, men like Musgrave and Jack Slade.

Two names made his teeth grind. Jesse and Frank James had ridden with Quantrill when his family was killed.

On the back wall stood two bear cages serving as jail cells. The small window with bars on it allowed the only light into the room, giving it a dismal fog-like appearance even though it was the middle of the day.

The sheriff was a tall muscular man who could probably wrestle a bear and win the fight. "Something I can do for you?"

"Jed Jackson." He extended his hand. "I'm looking for my brothers. They're fifteen and thirteen. Joshua, the older one, has dark hair and eyes. Jonathan, the younger one, is fair with curly hair and blue eyes like mine."

The sheriff's eyes narrowed. "Joshua and Jonathan Jackson?"

Jed's heart leapt. "Have you seen them?"

"Name's Sheriff Drew Porter, and yep, I've seen your brothers all right, but I don't have a notion of where they are now."

"I've been looking for them since I came home from the war." Jed slumped into the chair. "This is the first place I've come to where somebody's heard of them."

"If I knew where your brothers were, they'd be in one of these jail cells." Sheriff Porter motioned to the cages with a tilt of his head.

"My brothers?" Jed looked at them half-expecting to see them there. "What'd they do?"

"Robbed the general store, a few days ago, and took off with over three hundred dollars."

A lump formed in Jed's throat. That couldn't be. They would never do something this bad. "Are you sure it was them, Sheriff?"

"I'm sure." Porter poured a cup of coffee and handed it to Jed. "Let me tell you a little about those brothers of yours. They rode into town a little over a year ago and took jobs at the saloon."

"A saloon." They would never set foot in a place like that. The sheriff had to be mistaken.

"Yeah, they swept up around the place, but then they started gambling, that is until they were winning so much money from the townsfolk, nobody would play with them. Some said they were cheating, couldn't prove it though."

Heat seared Jed's face. They would have never gotten into this much trouble if he'd been able to get home in time to take care of them. He realized the sheriff had stopped and was waiting for him to get hold of himself. "Go on. I need to hear it all."

"After a few months, they looked like a couple of gunmen, wore their guns in holsters tied down like they knew how to use them."

Jed cleared his throat. "They didn't shoot anyone, did they?"

"Didn't have to. One night, some wrangler came into the saloon and lost a lot of money. He said JJ cheated and challenged him to a gunfight. The younger one, most folks call him Kid. Anyway, he stepped in and told him he would oblige him. As soon the man reached for his gun, the boy had his revolver pointed at the man's chest. Never saw that wrangler around here again."

"Why didn't you arrest Jonathan?"

"The man started it. He had a right to defend himself, but it still troubled me. He's a sight faster than me."

"He's only thirteen years old. If the man threatened him…" Jed wiped his neck with his hand. "I still don't see why you think they robbed the store."

Sheriff Porter's tone softened. "On the night of the robbery, a man stepped out on the back porch of the hotel to have a smoke and saw them sneaking around behind the store. He figured they were up to no good and chased them off. When he heard the store was robbed, he hurried right in and told me about it. He said they were riding a bay and a sorrel. Those are the horses your brothers ride. They didn't let the hotel clerk or the livery stable know they were leaving, left unpaid bills at both places. By the time we knew what happened, it was too late to send a posse. Rain washed away the tracks."

Robbing a store? "Thank you, Sheriff. When I find my brothers, I'll bring them back here to face up to what they've done. You can be sure of that."

"They'll be a hundred miles away by now."

Jed stood. He wished everyone would stop trying to talk him out of what he needed to do. "I'm planning to stay the night and tomorrow being Sunday... Could you direct me to the local church? I didn't see it when I rode in."

"We don't have a church," Porter said. "This is a mining town, and most folks here aren't the church-going type. There is a prayer meeting outside of town by Hunt's Peak Lake, ten o'clock."

Jed tipped his hat on the way out. He would need all the prayer he could get.

Golden leaves crunched under Jed's feet as he approached the clearing with his Bible under his arm. Hunt's Peak Mountain towered over him with green pines and yellow aspen dotting the side of the landscape and a clear blue sky hovering above.

It looked different than the mountains he'd seen during the war. They sort of rolled into each other, high peaks and deep valleys. Hunt's Peak sprang almost straight up with flat rock at its base. It took his breath away.

A few men stood talking, and some women and a handful of children sat on blankets by the lake. Jed walked over to them. "Good morning. Is this where the prayer meeting's being held?"

A man and woman in their early thirties greeted him. "Welcome. It's not much, but it's the only church we have." The man shook Jed's hand. "Name's Lucas Brewster. This here's my wife, Amelia." He pointed to the five children sitting on the blanket ranging from twelve to three years old. "These are my young'uns."

By then, an older couple and two young women walked to where Jed was standing. Both girls were fair with blond hair and freckles, obviously sisters. The younger one, around the age of his brothers, still had her hair in braids. The older one, only a bit younger than Jed, wore a smile that rivaled the sun in its brightness.

"We're Mr. and Mrs. Freeman," the older man said. "These are our daughters, Grace and Hannah."

Jed shook the Freeman's hand. "My name is Jedidiah Jackson. You can call me Jed, if you like."

Mr. Freeman raised an eyebrow. "Any relation to JJ and Kid Jackson?"

Jed's muscles tensed. "Yes, they're my brothers."

"Mr. Freeman owns the general store the boys robbed," Lucas said.

"I heard about that." Jed turned to Mr. Freeman hoping he'd see his sincerity. "I'm sorry for what my brothers did. When I catch up to them, I'll make sure they own up to it, but first, I have to find them."

Mr. Freeman placed his hand on Jed's shoulder. "Why don't you sit and tell us a little about yourself?"

Jed followed the others to the blankets and sat beside Grace, Mr. Freeman's oldest daughter. Maybe it would help to talk about it.

"I received the call to preach when I was ten. I studied at Oberlin College in Ohio. When the war broke out, I set my studies aside and joined up. A couple of years later, I received word my whole family was killed. Joshua and Jonathan were the only ones who survived."

Grace touched his arm. "How did it happen?"

"I'm from Lawrence, Kansas–Quantrill's raiders."

Her green eyes teared up.

"When I finally got back home, my brothers were gone. They were headed west, and I've been looking for them ever since. They think I died in the war."

"I'm sorry," Mr. Freeman said. "Let's pray for them right now."

After prayer time, Jed shared a little from what he was reading in the Bible. "No matter how far the prodigal son strayed, the father continued to look for him until he returned." He paused and gazed at the geese swimming in the lake.

"You're thinking of your brothers, aren't you, Rev. Jackson?" Grace asked.

"Yes, I suppose I am, and please call me Jed. I don't even know where to look for them."

"We planned to use the money the boys stole to hire a preacher from back east," Grace said.

Jed swallowed hard. His brothers stole money meant to hire a pastor and build a church? How could he make amends for that? "I'm sorry. I'll do whatever I can to repay…"

Glace blushed. "It's just if you have the call, maybe you could be our preacher."

"I can't." The muscle in his jaw twitched. "I have to find my brothers."

"In the prodigal story, the son came back on his own," Mr. Freeman said. "Who knows? God might have sent you here to start a work."

Jed rubbed his cleft chin. "You've given me a lot to think about, but I haven't finished my studies. I had a year left when the war broke out."

Grace snickered. "Do you know how hard it is to get any preacher out this way? Degree or not, we want the preacher God was good enough to send our way."

Later that day, the prayer group crowded around the Freemans' kitchen table, eating dessert and drinking coffee.

Lucas dismissed his children to play outside. They hurried out the door, knocking into each other as they each tried to be the first one out. Hannah stood back and waited until they all made their way through before she followed them.

"They're fine children." Jed ate his last bite of peach pie.

Yes, they are." Lucas put his arm around his wife. "Amelia's done a good job raising them. It isn't easy in this godless town."

"That's true enough," Mrs. Freeman said. "You won't believe what the men in this town are guilty of: drinking, gambling, fornicating. It's disgraceful."

Mr. Freeman patted his wife's arm. "It's been hard living among so many sinners."

Jed resisted the temptation to point out that gossip was also a sin.

Mrs. Freeman grabbed the pot and filled the cups with more coffee. "I hope you'll be staying on, Jed."

"Don't go pestering the boy," Mr. Freeman said. "He said he would pray about it, and I know he will."

"I noticed you don't have a church building." Jed set his fork on his empty plate. "There's already a chill in the air. You can't meet outside much longer."

"We meet in my father's store." Grace dished him out another slice. "It gets a little crowded and stuffy, so when it's nice out, we meet in the clearing."

Jed smiled at Grace and nodded. "Is there any building in town larger than the store?"

"Only one." Lucas took a sip of coffee. "But it won't do us any good."

"Why not?"

"Because, it's the saloon."

Jed devoured the last bite of his second slice of pie. "Won't they let you meet there?"

Mrs. Freeman set her cup down. "We would never ask such a thing."

"Seems to me," Jed said, "a saloon would be a good place to meet for church, kind of like being a light in the darkness."

"It doesn't matter. Eli wouldn't allow it," Mr. Freeman said.

Jed held up his hand when Grace tried to dish out a third piece. "Who's Eli?"

"Eli Hansen," Lucas said. "He's the one who gave your brothers work when they arrived in town."

"Work, hmmm." Mrs. Freeman plunked the coffee pot on the stove. "He corrupted them. If it weren't for him, they might not have ended up the way they did."

"Now, Edna." Mr. Freeman set down his cup. "We're just as much to blame as he was."

Jed's jaw tightened. "What do you mean you're to blame?"

"You might as well know the truth of it." Mr. Freeman let out a gusty sigh. "The boys came to us looking for jobs. We turned them away."

So, they tried to find honest work first, and the Christians in the town turned them away. He swallowed hard and tried to keep his voice calm. "Why would you do that?"

"Lots of no-accounts come here to mine gold dust, and we didn't want to take a chance these orphans might steal us blind." Mr. Freeman wrapped his hands around his cup. "I've asked God to forgive me for my part in this. I'm sorry."

Heat rose up the back of Jed's neck. Two young orphans came to town and the only help they could get was from the saloon. No wonder they turned to crime.

He stuffed down his anger, knowing what the Lord expected of him. "I forgive you." Later that evening, he would ask God to help him truly forgive. For now, he wanted to get away from these good Christians who had turned away his brothers.

Patting his stomach, he stood. "If I stay much longer, I'm going to bust from all that pie. Grace is a mighty fine cook."

Grace blushed. "Thank you, Rev. Jackson."

Jed raised an eyebrow. "Rev. Jackson?"

"Rev. Jed."

"Just Jed. I haven't said I'd take the job yet." He said his good-byes. A short time later, he traipsed through the leaves on the path beside the lake. He needed time to think before he headed to the hotel.

A white-tailed deer headed toward the mountain. A monarch

butterfly flew past him and landed on a rock near the path.

He stopped and sat on a felled tree. Anger coursed through him. If they'd helped his brothers, Joshua and Jonathan might not be running from the law.

There was plenty of fault to go around. If he could have gotten home as soon as he heard about his family, he might have been able to stop this.

Then there was Quantrill, the man who killed his family.

Lord, please help me set aside this anger and forgive.

A peace swept over him. This town needed a preacher, someone who would disciple them to show God's love to those who were in trouble, but he wasn't that man. He needed to find his brothers.

Joshua and Jonathan did steal the money they were going to use to hire such a man. Maybe he owed it to them to stay and try to make amends.

But how could he abandon the search for his brothers?

Chapter Twelve

The next morning, Jed surveyed the inside of the saloon. It looked well able to seat up to fifty people comfortably if the tables were stacked to one side, and they wouldn't have to worry about music. They could use the piano in the corner.

As much as he tried not to, he glanced to the wall above the bar where the pulpit would be. The woman in the painting didn't have on a stitch of clothing. She was very attractive with her come-hither look, even though her face wasn't the first thing he noticed. He cleared his throat and looked down. *Sorry, Lord.*

His pa used to say evil lurked behind saloon doors. Apparently, he was right.

He kept his eyes diverted and strode to the man with the handlebar moustache behind the bar. "Are you Eli Hanson?"

"Saloon's closed. Come back 'round six."

"I'm not here for a drink, although a cup of coffee would be nice." Jed extended his hand. "Jed Jackson, Joshua and Jonathan's brother."

Eli raised an eyebrow. "I have coffee in the back."

Jed followed Eli to a small room with a rope bed, a box stove, a table and a couple of stools.

"It's a shame about those boys." Eli poured two cups of coffee and handed one to Jed. "Can't blame them for taking the easy way out."

Heat flushed Jed's face.

"Who knows what any of us would do if we were faced with the same thing at their age? I did the best I could for them, but I guess they figured sweeping up a saloon for a dollar a week and picking up a little extra being bucket boys wasn't enough."

Jed clamped his hands around the warm coffee cup. "Did they say where they were going?"

"No, I didn't even know they were leaving 'til they skedaddled with the general store's money. Don't much blame them. The good Christian folks in this town sure didn't help them."

"I appreciate what you did for my brothers, but that's not the only reason I'm here." Jed suppressed a chuckle. "I was wondering if you would let those good Christian folks use your saloon for church meetings on Sunday mornings."

Eli sprayed coffee out of his mouth. Jed pounded him on the back as he choked and spluttered. He caught his breath and wiped his face with a bandana. "Ha, you crazy? They won't go to a gospel mill held in a saloon."

"They will if I become their preacher."

Eli started coughing again. "You... you're one of them gospel sharps?"

"Well, I don't know about that, but I am considering starting a church here in Hunt's Peak if you'll let me use your saloon as a meeting place."

"I can't believe it, JJ and Kid's brother, a preacher. Forgive me for saying this, but you don't seem much like a man of the cloth. The ones I've known look like they've swallowed a lemon whenever I'm around."

Jed let out a snort. "I never have understood how someone who looks miserable can preach the good news. So how about it? Can we use the saloon?"

Eli shook his head. "You're out to sea about the religious folks around here. They won't set foot in this place even if it is a church on Sundays."

"Now that's my problem, isn't it?"

"I'll tell you what. You have yourself a deal." Eli flashed a big grin. "I'll even come. Be worth it to see the looks on their faces as they darken the doors of my establishment."

Jed stood and shook Eli's hand. "Thanks so much. One more thing."

Eli raised an eyebrow. "What?"

"During church meetings, would you mind taking down the painting hanging behind the bar?"

Eli slapped him on the back. "Sure will."

Jed said his good-byes and pushed through the saloon's swinging doors.

Mrs. Freeman came out of the cobbler's shop, and his eyes met hers. She marched in Jed's direction with the sour expression Eli had described so well, her dark blue dress rustling in the wind.

She stepped in front of a chestnut horse trotting down the road.

"Look out," Jed said running toward her.

Mrs. Freeman either didn't hear him or ignored him, and the rider pulled the reins bringing the animal to a stop just in time.

Jed let out a sigh of relief.

Mrs. Freeman barely noticed she'd escaped being trampled and placed her hands on her hips. "What were you doing in a saloon?"

"Good day, Mrs. Freeman."

"You didn't answer my question."

"I was doing the Lord's work." He tipped his hat and strolled toward the hotel before she could say another word.

Let her stew on that for a while. He resisted the urge to glance back to see if she was still standing in the middle of the street, glowering at him. If he became their preacher, they'd need to get rid of that holier-than-thou attitude. It not only kept them from ministering to his brothers, it pitted them against the whole town.

He shook his head. He was acting like he'd already decided. He had always wanted a congregation of his own and had planned to come out West after college, but would it be right to do this? What if his brothers strayed farther? How could that be in God's plan?

Jed collided with a flash of yellow calico that fell with a thud. He barely managed to stay on his feet.

Grace, clothed in a yellow calico dress, lay sprawled in the middle of the dirt road.

He reached his hand out to her. "I'm so sorry. I didn't see you."

She grabbed hold and pulled herself up. He noticed the smudge on her face and grinned.

"What?"

"You have dirt on your face."

She took her handkerchief and tried to wipe it, but smeared it more.

"Here let me help." He took his bandana and dipped it in the horse trough on the side of the road before dabbing her face with it.

She was different than the others he'd met. Her compassion showed in everything she did, but that wasn't what he noticed at the moment. Her beautiful green eyes were the color of Hunt's Peak Lake.

He stepped back. "The dirt's gone now."

"Thank you."

Jed watched her glide away and felt an overwhelming urge to stop her. "Grace, wait."

She turned toward him. "Yes?"

"I was wondering…" He stuck his hands in his pockets. "Since I practically accosted you in the street…"

Grace stared at him, not saying a word.

He wished she'd blink or something. He couldn't think clearly. "I was just… well… I thought the least I could do is take you to the diner and buy you lunch, that is, if you're free."

She tilted her head. "I'd be happy to have you escort me."

Jed's stomach fluttered. He had to stop this. He hadn't decided if he was staying. He couldn't allow himself to have feelings for her until he made his decision.

He walked with her to the only restaurant in town, a diner that served breakfast and lunch to the miners. They made their way through a group of men eating outside on the porch and stepped through the doors. It was crowded with tables, most already filled with men eating their lunches.

They squeezed through the throng to an unoccupied table. A drone of noise filled the small front room. The proprietor, an older man with a full beard, served as waiter and cook. He hurried between the kitchen and tables carrying plates of food and filling coffee cups.

Jed and Grace both ordered chicken noodle soup. The only other choice was Kentucky Burgoo, but the cook warned them the stew was a week old.

While they were eating, Jed couldn't help chatting away. Grace was so easy to talk to. She not only listened to his every word, but offered her own insights. Before he knew it, he had told her his life story.

Jed sipped his coffee. "I suppose you think it's crazy riding across the West, searching for my brothers."

"Not at all." Grace set her cup down. "If Hannah had gone through what your brothers did, I would search to the ends of the earth for her."

Jed smiled, relieved she understood.

"God won't let your brothers go. You must know that?"

He rubbed his hand across his chin. "Yes."

"Excuse me," the owner said. Jed glanced up. "We're closed. You need to pay your bill and leave."

Grace chucked.

"I didn't realize." Jed flushed as he checked his pocket watch. They'd been there for almost three hours. "Of course. May I escort you home, Grace?"

"No, I'm meeting my ma at the store. I was supposed to be there an hour ago."

"I'm sorry I detained you so long."

"Not at all. Ma will understand."

Jed doubted Mrs. Freeman would be that amiable about it.

The next morning, Jed entered Freeman's General Store. Lucas and his youngest boy stood by the counter as Mr. Freeman talked to him in whispers. Jed caught their attention, and Mr. Freeman stopped short. It didn't take much to figure out Mrs. Freeman had wagged her tongue to everyone who would listen.

"Mr. Freeman, Lucas." Jed set a penny on the counter. "I'd like to buy a licorice stick." He turned to Lucas' son. "What flavor do you like, Clint?"

"I like the red, Sir."

"Red it is." Jed gave the licorice stick to the boy.

"Clint, take your candy outside," Lucas said.

The boy obeyed his pa.

"Jed." Mr. Freeman leaned on the counter. "Were you at the saloon yesterday?"

"Yes, I was."

Mr. Freeman's brow wrinkled. "Why were you there?"

Lucas leaned forward to hear the answer.

"I asked Eli Hanson if we could hold our church services there."

"You shouldn't have bothered." Mr. Freeman put his hand on Jed's shoulder. "We warned you he'd say no."

"He said yes." Jed crossed his arms, giving them what his captain during the war called his preacher look. "He said he'd even come."

"He can't come to church." Lucas' lips pressed together. "He owns the saloon."

"Let's get something straight before this goes any further." The muscle in Jed's jaw twitched. "If I'm your preacher, sinners – all sinners – are going to be welcome in God's house. Makes no difference if they own a saloon or if they robbed the general store. No other lost souls are going to come into this town and not find Christian charity to help them on the right path."

Mr. Freeman glanced at the floor. "I guess we deserved that."

"Yes, you did, and I won't hold back the truth of God's Word in any of my sermons or in my Bible studies, so if that's a problem, you can find somebody else."

"So, does that mean we can count on you to be our preacher?" Lucas asked.

Jed blew out a short breath. How could he give up on his brothers? A verse came to his remembrance, Exodus 13:14. He could see it on the page: *Fear ye not, stand still, and see the salvation of the LORD.*

Part of him wanted to ignore it, to go after his brothers no matter what the Holy Spirit prompted him to do. He'd come this far. It didn't make sense to stop now.

He let out a sigh. It never did do any good arguing with God. Hadn't he learned that often enough during the war? Besides, he didn't even know where to look.

Lord, I trust You with them. That wasn't completely the truth, but it was all he could muster for now.

He shook Mr. Freeman's hand. "You won't have to wait any longer for an answer. I'll stay."

Grace stepped into the store in time to hear Jed agree to stay. A warm glow passed through her. Hoping her face wasn't as red as it felt, she kissed her pa on the cheek. "Rev. Jackson."

A dimple bored into Jed's right cheek. "Now, Grace, I told you before, call me Jed."

"I can't. Since you're our preacher now, it would be disrespectful."

"I don't hold much with formality. In the army, my regiment would call me Chaplin Jed or Preacher. Folks here can call me Rev. Jed or Preacher. I'll answer to any of them."

Grace nodded. "Okay, Rev. Jed."

Jed turned to her pa. "The saloon has a piano, so we can have hymns during church. Do you know anyone who can play?"

"Grace plays," Pa said, "and sings."

"That's wonderful." Jed turned his steel blue gaze on her, and she thought her knees might give way. "Maybe we could get together later and talk about it."

If he turned that look on his congregation, he would make a good minister. "I do play, but it's been a while. I haven't had a piano since we came out west."

"You can practice in the saloon. There's a piano there."

The vein in her pa's neck throbbed. "Look here. I've agreed to having church in the saloon and you going by Rev. Jed instead of being addressed properly, but my daughter's not playing for drunks and gamblers."

Jed's lips pressed together. "Do you really think I'd subject your daughter to practicing piano while they're open?"

"No, I suppose not."

"I'll find out when we can go there without exposing her to any evil influences." Jed gave Grace a hesitant smile. "And I'll stay with her while she practices."

Pa wiped his hand over his face. "I suppose, if Grace is willing."

She nodded. "It's important for the church to have hymns."

"Great. I'll let you know when. Good day to you both." Jed tipped his hat and walked outside.

Pa gawked at the door. "He's got some strange notions for a preacher."

"Really? I hadn't noticed." Grace tied her apron around her waist and started stacking canned goods to distract herself from the fluttering in her stomach.

Those strange notions were what made her want to be his wife someday.

Chapter Thirteen

JJ shivered from the cold air blowing through the crack in the window of the only boarding house in town cheap enough for them to afford. He counted their last three dollars for the fifth time. How did they manage to go through it all in only a few months?

The peeling paint made the walls look dirty. The room didn't have chairs or a bureau, just an old rope bed with a missing wedge, a broken mirror, a cracked commode and a slop jar.

It was so small there was barely a foot on each side of the bed. It gave JJ that closed-in feeling he hated when he was in cramped spaces. If he didn't figure out something soon, they wouldn't even have that.

He crawled under the blankets next to Kid to keep warm. "We're almost out of money."

"I don't get it," Kid said. "We did good at poker in Hunt's Peak, but when we go against those dandy type players here, we just can't win. Do you think they cheat?"

"Some might, but that man I played with last night won our last ten dollars fair and square. He was blame amazing. I couldn't even tell when he bluffed. I think we're outgunned here, at least at poker."

"Maybe we could look for a job, tomorrow."

JJ cupped his hands to his face to warm them with his breath. "We might have to sell our horses."

"I hate to do that."

"Something will come up. Let's get some shut-eye. I'm all played out."

He tried to sleep, but instead, he stared at the crack in the ceiling illuminated by the moonlight coming through the window. He didn't want to worry Kid, but there was no way they could find jobs in the middle of winter, and if they sold the horses, they wouldn't have a way out of town if the need arose. The money they had wouldn't last two weeks even in this dump, and then they'd be living on the street.

There was only one choice. JJ would go to the saloon tomorrow and use that last three dollars to win a little money to keep them going. If he watched for a while, he was sure he could spot someone who wasn't that good.

The next morning, ice encrusted the window. All JJ could see was snow coming down in sheets and shapes of the buildings under the white blanket encasing the city, and his heart sank. There was no way the saloon would be open today.

"I don't reckon we're going to be looking for work today." He pulled a blanket around himself. "We're not going anywhere."

Kid looked out the window. "Be a good day to build a snowman."

"Don't think they'd like us building no snowman on Blake Street?"

"You're right. Besides, we'd need warm coats and gloves and warm hats if we wanted to do that."

JJ paced to the door with the blanket still wrapped around him. It wasn't right. Kid was only fourteen, and he never got to have any fun. Six steps to the window. Now this blasted snowstorm hit, and they couldn't even build a snowman 'cause he wasted all their money gambling. He stopped and grinned.

Kid flashed a steel blue glare. "All right, what's the plan?"

"There's a store two doors down. I doubt it'll be open with all this snow. We can let ourselves in through the back door and get what we need, then we can build a right proper snowman. What are they going to do, come out in this weather to stop us?"

"I thought we weren't going to steal anymore," Kid said.

"We're just borrowing the coats. When we're done, we'll take them back."

"JJ, what if somebody checks on the store? They'll be able to follow our tracks real easy."

"Nobody's stupid enough to be out in this weather."

JJ and Kid had just finished the snowman when JJ reached down, formed a snowball, and hit his brother in the back of the head.

Kid laughed and swooped up some snow. His eyes widened, the snow fell out of his hand. JJ turned to see what had caught his attention.

A man wearing a sheepskin coat headed toward them. "All right, boys. You better come with me." The tin marshal's star was pinned to his coat.

The knot in JJ's stomach grew with each step as they trudged to the marshal's office.

When they stepped inside, heat from the potbelly stove in the corner of the room swept over him. At least they would have a warm place to stay and food to eat. But being locked in a tiny jail cell…

"All right, boys," the marshal said, "take off everything you stole."

They removed their outer clothing, hats, gloves, scarves, boots, socks, and wool coats.

"Remove the gun belts very slowly, boys," the marshal said, "and toss them over here."

JJ"s chest tightened. He'd forgotten about the guns. He unbuckled his belt, careful to show the sheriff he meant no harm, and tossed it on the floor. Kid did the same.

"All right, take a seat." The marshal motioned to the two chairs in front of his desk.

They followed the marshal's instructions. JJ barely dared to take a breath. He just wanted Kid to be able to have a little fun, but that wasn't the whole truth. He tried to convince himself he was doing it for his brother, but he wanted the thrill he had when they robbed the general store. He'd really gotten them into trouble this time.

The marshal leaned on the edge of the desk. The corners of his mouth turned up a little. "The next time you want to steal clothes from the Blake Street General Store, I suggest you don't leave a trail to where you're building a snowman in the middle of the street. When Mr. Cooper reported the robbery, I didn't have any trouble finding you."

"Not one of your better plans, JJ," Kid said.

"How'd I know anyone would check that store in the middle of a snowstorm?"

"I told you they might."

"You went along with it," JJ said.

"I'm Marshal Cook. Your names?"

"Jonathan Jackson, Sir."

"I'm Joshua." JJ tilted his head toward Kid. "His brother."

"Not anymore."

"What's that supposed to mean?"

"Enough!" Marshal Cook roared. "Now, who are your folks, and where do you live?"

"We live at the Eyser Boarding House next to the saloon," JJ said. "Our folks died during the war."

Marshal Cook wiped his hand over his face. "I'm sorry."

JJ gave Kid an apologetic gaze and exhaled a deep breath. "How long a jail term will we get for this, Marshal Cook?"

"Oh, I'd say anywhere from one to six months."

JJ took slow breaths to keep calm himself. He didn't like the idea of being crammed in a small cell, but it could be worse.

"Of course, that's if you aren't wanted anywhere else, in Colorado. Anything I should know about?"

All the air left JJ's lungs. He wiped his hand on his trousers and barley squeaked out, "No, Sir." They weren't going to get out of this with only six months in jail.

Marshal Cook stood and strode to the jail cells. He opened a barred door and motioned to the boys.

JJ rose. Everything inside him wanted to run, but he followed Kid in. The noise of the iron cell door clanging shut vibrated through him. Brick walls, six-by-six feet, two rickety cots. Not much better than the boarding house room, but there he could always leave.

When the marshal left, Kid turned to him, his face scrunched up with anger and fear. "You know they're going to find out we robbed the store in Hunt's Peak."

"I know."

"And when they do, they're going to lock us up and throw away the key."

JJ let out a sigh. "The fault's mine. You didn't want to rob anybody."

"I didn't see you pointing a gun at me."

"Maybe it's best we were caught now before we get in too deep," JJ said, trying to convince himself it was for the best. "Ma and Pa would have wanted us to tell the truth and pay for what we've done."

Kid nodded. "Let's just acknowledge the corn about Hunt's Peak and get it over with."

JJ leaned back on his cot, the heaviness lifting from him now that they'd made the decision. If only there were some way he could get his brother out of this. Kid's only crime was going along.

A few minutes later, the door creaked open, and a draft came in the room. They stepped to the bars. Marshal Cook came in, accompanied by a bearded man in his forties with smile lines and twinkling brown eyes. The man held a bundle wrapped in a blanket.

"I'm Mr. Cooper. I own the Blake Street General Store." He unwrapped the bundle to reveal their clothes. "I assume these are yours."

JJ groaned. "Yes, Sir."

"Were you planning to retrieve them?"

"Yes, Sir," JJ said. "After we played in the snow for a bit, we were going to bring back the clothes we borrr… stole."

"I see," Mr. Cooper said. "Who picked the lock?"

JJ looked at the floor and muttered, "I did."

"Marshal Cook told me about your situation. Do you two have jobs?"

"Not at the moment, Sir," Kid said.

"My customers have told me other things about you too," Mr. Cooper said. "Gambling, drinking, carrying guns with you everywhere you go. Word gets around."

JJ stared at his feet. The storekeeper wasn't likely to let this go.

"I won't press charges if you agree to a few conditions," Mr. Cooper said.

"Such as…" JJ couldn't imagine there was much they wouldn't agree to if it would keep them out of jail.

"Give me your words you won't steal again."

No problem there. Stealing had only led them into this mess. "I give my word."

"Me too," Kid said.

"Can you boys read, and write, and do figuring?"

"Yes, Sir," JJ said.

"You're going to work for me. You can keep the coats you stole, and I'll take half of your salary until they're paid for."

A job? That was more than he'd hoped for.

"No more gambling or drinking. That's going to stop, or I'll march you back here in no time."

JJ nodded. Gambling wasn't working out for them any more than stealing had. If they had jobs, they wouldn't need winnings to pay their bills.

"You'll come to church every Sunday."

JJ pressed his lips together. Kid wanted to go to church, and he'd put him off. He still didn't want anything to do with God, but it was better than jail.

"Okay," Kid said.

"And you're going to stop wearing those guns."

JJ's chest tightened. "We need them to protect ourselves."

"Son," Mr. Cooper said, "if you carry those guns around like you intend to use them, you'll attract all sorts of trouble."

"You don't know what it's like for a couple of orphans out on our own. We're not getting rid of them."

Mr. Cooper drew his forefingers to his mouth. "You can keep them, but you're not wearing them. If you don't agree to this, you won't be able to have them in jail anyway."

JJ took a short breath. What choice did he have? He nodded.

"Well, Marshal Cook, let them out," Mr. Cooper said.

The marshal unlocked the cell and returned their guns. The boys put on their new coats and carried their gun belts over their shoulders.

JJ whispered to Kid, "I wish we'd met somebody like him in Hunt's Peak."

The marshal raised an eyebrow and wrote something on a piece of paper on his desk. It was obvious he'd heard him. Hopefully he wouldn't check them out.

Chapter Fourteen

Grace's heart raced when Jed walked into the store to talk to her pa. It had been almost a year since he'd come to town, and she wanted to spend the rest of her life as Mrs. Jedidiah Jackson, working alongside him in ministry. She was beginning to think he didn't feel the same way.

She snuck into the storeroom before he saw her and listened at the door. She'd ask his forgiveness later, after he proposed.

Jed's voice. "Sir, you wanted to see me?"

Then her pa's. "That's right. There's a matter we need to discuss."

"Go ahead."

"I gave you permission to court my daughter because I believed your intentions were honorable."

There was a bang, and she dared to peek through the crack in the door. Jed had knocked over a display of canned meats and was trying put them back in their place.

He finished with the display. "Sorry about that." He motioned toward the cans. "But why would ever you say that about my intentions? Of course, they're honorable."

"I'm not so sure." Pa crossed his arms. "You've been courting her for well over six months now. You've done well with the church, and the town has given you a parsonage and provided you with a salary."

Jed pressed his lips together. "The town has been more than generous."

"Are you toying with my daughter's affections? You haven't even approached the subject of marriage yet."

Heat rushed to Grace's face. If Pa had to force Jed into proposing, then she didn't want him anyway.

"Isn't that between Grace and me, Sir?" He started to lean against a display of farm tools, paused, then leaned on one leg.

"Normally, I'd say yes, but my daughter isn't getting any younger." Pa flattened his hands on the counter and glared at Jed. "She turned twenty-four last week."

She groaned. It wasn't like she was an old maid yet.

Her father continued. "If you aren't planning on marrying her, then own up to it and clear the way for another gentleman to court her."

Jed stuffed his hands in his pockets. "I want to marry her."

Grace's heart skipped a beat.

"But I don't know if I should."

Her pa's voice roared, "Why not?"

When Jed spoke again, he was so quiet she opened the door a crack to hear him. "What happens if I find out where my brothers are? Where would that leave Grace? She wouldn't want to leave her family to pursue two boys she'd never met. It wouldn't be fair to her."

Grace banged the door open. "How dare you!"

Jed stared at her with those piercing blue eyes of his.

She blinked so he wouldn't see her cry. "I told you I understand how you feel about your brothers. Do you think so little of me?"

Jed held out his hand.

Grace brushed it away. "Don't! If I were your wife, I'd follow you anywhere to find your brothers. You think I'm so shallow I wouldn't stay with you because I wouldn't want to leave my family.... Ugggh."

She stomped out of the store, slamming the door behind her and half-walked, half-ran down Freeman Road, wiping the tears off her face.

"Grace, wait up."

She spun on her heels. Jed's face drooped like a lost puppy.

She almost relented. "Leave me alone, Jed. You leave me be." She turned and ran.

When she reached her house, she glanced back, almost hoping he'd followed her, but he didn't. She pushed the door open and darted inside.

Sheriff Drew Porter sat at the corner table of Eli's Dining Hall with Jed and Eli.

Eli and Drew had both given their hearts to God within six weeks of Jed starting church services in the saloon, and they'd been having breakfast together ever since.

It had been a year, and so much had changed since then. Shortly after Jed started the church, the gold ran out, and the miners left.

Within a couple of months, the saloon had a much bigger crowd on Sundays than any other day of the week. Eli had closed it and had opened the dining hall across the street.

Within a few months, the new church had been built, and now the town was working on a schoolhouse. The new teacher from Denver City was expected on next week's stage.

Drew let out a sigh. He would miss these weekly Bible study breakfasts most of all.

Jed said, "We're starting Ephesians today."

"Before we get started," Eli said, "I have something important to tell you."

Jed leaned back in his chair. "Go ahead."

Drew swallowed. "Hunt's Peak doesn't need a full-time sheriff anymore."

"What are you saying?" Jed asked.

"There isn't much crime to speak of. We don't even get the Saturday night drunk to lock up anymore."

"Well, I can't say I'm too surprised," Jed said. "So what are you and your wife going to do? You planning buying a farm?"

"No, I'm a lawman," Drew said. "It's my calling every bit as much as preaching is yours. Amy and I are heading out for Bear River in Wyoming Territory. I got a job as sheriff there."

"Congratulations on your new job." Eli sipped some coffee. "When are you leaving?"

"End of the month." Drew hated good-byes. Time to lighten the mood. He crossed his arms and delivered a smirk toward Jed. "I guess I'll be missing your wedding. That is, if Grace don't marry somebody else while she's waiting for you to ask her."

Jed's shoulders slumped. "Probably won't be a wedding. She's so angry she won't even speak to me."

"Why?"

"She heard me talking to her pa. I told him it wouldn't be fair to expect her to travel all over the territory looking for my brothers."

Drew drank a sip of coffee. "That makes sense."

"That's what I thought." Jed leaned back in his chair. "The thing is, I really do love her. When she stood there shouting at me, with passion in her eyes, telling me she'd follow me anywhere… Well, I wanted to swoop her up and marry her right then and there."

Eli grinned. "You sure about this? She sounds stubborn."

"I want a woman with some fire in her, a godly woman who will tell me the truth even when I'm in the wrong. My ma was like that."

"What are you going to do?" Eli ate a bite of eggs.

"I'm meeting with Mr. Freeman tomorrow to ask for her hand in marriage. Of course, then I have to ask her, and that's not going to be easy, considering how angry she is." Jed furrowed his brow. "I'm still not sure what I did wrong."

Jed arrived early the next day. He didn't want to be late when he asked Mr. Freeman for his daughter's hand in marriage. He still wasn't sure she'd say yes. Grace hadn't said a word to him for two days.

When he saw the house up ahead, he pulled out his pocket watch, twenty minutes to go.

He leaned against a tree and waited. A few minutes early was one thing, but he didn't want to be this early. A scurrying sound caught his attention, and he turned in time to see a fuzzy black animal with a white stripe dart away.

The stench burned his eyes and assaulted his nostrils. At least, the skunk didn't spray him straight on. Maybe if he moved away from the area… He crossed the road and wet his bandana with water from the pump. He almost wiped his face with it, but the smell attacked his nose, and he threw it down. He was hit. At least his clothes were.

If he hurried, he'd have time to bathe and change. He ran back to the parsonage, filled two buckets with water, and dumped them in the tub, not bothering to heat them. He stripped off his Sunday suit and threw it outside. Shivering in the cold water, he scrubbed his skin with lye soap until it was raw. Still the stench lingered.

Maybe the smell was in his nose. It might not be on his skin. He dressed in clean clothes and ran as fast as he could to the Freemans' house. Ten minutes late. He groaned and knocked on the door.

Mr. Freeman opened the door and scrunched his nose.

Jed could feel his face turning red. "Good day."

"Guess I don't have to ask you why you're late."

"No, Sir. I expect not."

"We can talk outside." Mr. Freeman chuckled. "But don't stand too close, and make sure it's downwind."

"Yes, Sir." Jed's shoulders slumped and he followed Mr. Freeman away from the house.

"All right, talk, and make it quick. Standing near you is making my eyes water." He said it as if it was the funniest joke he ever heard.

Jed would remember this moment as the most embarrassing of his entire life.

Mr. Freeman moved a few steps upwind. "Get on with it."

"I would like your permission to ask for Grace's hand in marriage."

"I figured that's what you wanted. You have my blessing, but I'm not sure what Grace will say. She's still madder than a hornet's nest."

Jed looked at the ground. "Yes, Sir."

"You can ask her when you get rid of that stink." Mr. Freeman's chuckles turned to roaring laughter as he held his sides. It took a couple of minutes before he could speak again, and when he did, it was through chortles. "You've waited... this long. You can... wait... a few more... days."

Jed nodded. "I understand."

Mr. Freeman finally got hold of himself. "I'll set some jars of tomatoes outside my store for you to pick up later today. That should cut the smell some." He doubled over, laughing hysterically again as his face turned as red as those tomatoes he'd mentioned. "Now... Jed... I'm going to... ask you... to leave."

Jed opened his mouth to say something but couldn't think of the words. He didn't find this funny at all.

Five baths with tomatoes and three days later, Jed was fairly sure the smell was gone. At least, after church a few hours ago, people had stood near him to shake his hand, then laughed about him getting sprayed by a skunk. Mr. Freeman apparently could spread gossip as quickly as his wife.

Grace had pushed past the line on the way out without saying a word or even looking his way.

So, here he was again at Mr. Freeman's door with a bouquet of buttercups and fairy slipper orchids he'd picked at the base of the mountain earlier that day. Considering how she acted in church, he doubted this would go well.

A dryness settled in his mouth. If she said no, he wasn't sure how he'd live his life without her by his side.

Grace opened the door. "Rev. Jackson."

"Ah, come on, Grace. When are you going to forgive me?"

"You must be mistaken. I don't hold anything against you."

Jed blinked. "You called me Rev. Jackson."

Grace laughed and motioned him inside. "I guess you've been through enough, being sprayed by a skunk and all."

He groaned. His stomach twisted as if a swarm of birds fluttered around in there as he looked into Grace's green eyes. He couldn't think of what to say.

She tilted her head toward the flowers. "Are those for me?"

He nodded and handed them to her. When she reached for them, their hands touched. Warmth shot through him. "Could we talk?"

Grace set the flowers in a vase on the table. "Of course."

"I'm sorry about what I said. I know you'd stay by the side of any man blessed enough to marry you." The birds in his stomach took flight. "I was just hoping… I want to… Grace, will you marry me?"

"I'd be honored."

For a moment, Jed stared at her, wondering if he heard right. When the words sank in, he let out a holler, wrapped his arms around her, and swung her around. He set her down and leaned in toward her parted lips.

Before their lips touched, he pulled back and cleared his throat. "I love you, Grace." The scent of soap coming from her hair made him woozy.

"I love you too." She tilted her face toward him.

Jed leaned forward, tenderly touching her lips with his, then allowed the kiss to become more passionate.

He pulled back. *Please Lord, don't take her away too.*

Chapter Fifteen

Mr. Cooper stepped through the door. "Early again, boys?"

Joshua glanced up from a stack of canned goods. "You know how it is. We need to get these crates unpacked."

"It's been four months today," Mr. Cooper said. "That means you're no longer in debt to me. All the money you make from this point on, you can keep."

"Thanks, Sir," Jonathan said.

"I need to go to the bank, boys," Mr. Cooper said. "Mind the store for me until I get back."

"Sure thing," Joshua said.

Mr. Cooper left.

A short time later, a man, dressed in a frock coat and black dress trousers, entered the store. He wore a ruffled white shirt and a blue satin vest and cravat. The black dress gloves covering his hands wrapped around a gold-tipped walking stick. A black derby hat sat on his head, and instead of boots, he wore black shoes.

Joshua suppressed a chuckle and nudged his brother. "There's a dude if I ever saw one."

"You got that right. I wonder what he's doing this far west."

"Only one way to find out." Joshua approached the man. "Can I help you?"

"Yes, I believe you can," the man said in a New England accent. "I've inherited a horse ranch, and I need supplies. If you two fine young lads could help me decide what to buy, I would appreciate it."

"Could you excuse us a moment while I have a word with my brother?" Joshua asked.

"Of course," the man said.

Joshua motioned Kid to the back of the store where they couldn't be overheard. "We have a chance here to really help Mr. Cooper after all he's done for us."

"How?"

"That greenhorn doesn't know anything about what he needs to run a ranch. We could sell him a whole bunch of stuff and make Mr. Cooper a good profit."

Jonathan's eyes widened. "But that's cheating?"

Joshua gave his brother a sideways grin. "If you don't think we should…"

"If it'd help Mr. Cooper, let's do it."

An hour later, the greenhorn paid Joshua. "I'll be back in an hour for all of my supplies. If it hadn't been for the two of you, I wouldn't have purchased half of what I needed. Your help was invaluable." The man left.

Joshua studied the list in his hand and chuckled. "Boy, we sure pulled one over on him."

"Yeah, I reckon we could have sold him the whole store if we wanted to."

"You got that right."

Mr. Cooper tromped up to them and snatched the list out of Joshua's hand. "I see you boys haven't given up on robbing people!" The vein in his neck bulged. "I thought you had changed your ways. I trusted you. Was I wrong?"

Joshua backed up a step, not knowing what to say. He'd never seen Mr. Cooper angry before, and it startled him.

"Answer me!"

"Mr. Cooper, Sir." His voice came out scratchy. "That man could afford all this stuff."

"And you told him he needed it."

"Yes, Sir," Jonathan said, "but we were only trying to help you."

"By lying and cheating?" His lips pressed in a straight thin line. "It's stealing. I'm ashamed of you both. If I was your pa, I'd take you out back and give you a licking you'd never forget. I can't abide liars and thieves."

Heat rushed to Joshua's face. "Well, you're not our pa. Our pa's dead." He rushed out of the store, ran into the street, and avoided a cart headed his way before tramping toward the nearest saloon.

Jonathan glanced at the door and back toward Mr. Cooper. "I'm sorry… I have to go."

He rushed out the store and ran after Joshua. He finally caught up with his brother in the saloon.

Joshua strutted up to the bar and banged a coin down. "I want whiskey."

The bartender handed him a glass, and he plunked down at a nearby table, gulped down his drink, and set his glass on the table a little harder than necessary.

Jonathan sat beside him. "Why are you so mad?"

Joshua raised his glass to let the bartender know he wanted another. "Why do you think?" A blond saloon girl with a pink dress brought another glass, and he took a sip and waved her away. "He's got a lot of sand, saying what he'd do if he was our pa. Our pa would have thanked us."

"No, he wouldn't." Jonathan rubbed his hand across his mouth. "Our pa was a good Christian man, and he would have been ashamed at what we've become. Mr. Cooper was right. We cheated that dandy, and you know it. I've never known you not to own up when you're in the wrong before."

Joshua stared into his whiskey, but he didn't drink any more.

"You're riled up 'cause he reminds you of Pa."

His voice thickened. "I miss him."

"I know." Jonathan placed his hand on his shoulder. "We have a chance here. Mr. Cooper's the closest thing we'll ever get to having a family."

Joshua's features softened, and he pushed away the half-empty glass of whiskey.

"So, you ready to go face him?"

Joshua nodded. "You know, he can't abide liars and thieves and we're both."

The guilt about what they'd done soured Jonathan's stomach as it had every time he thought about it. "We should tell him about Hunt's Peak. Better he hear it from us than find out another way."

"Yeah, we should. Someday. We have enough to fret about after what we did today."

Jonathan stuffed down the regret. "Yeah, someday." He didn't really want to tell Mr. Cooper anyway.

They meandered back across the street and into the Blake Street General Store.

Mr. Cooper stood by the counter with his arms crossed.

Jonathan swallowed hard. "I'm mighty sorry, Sir."

"We were wrong," Joshua said. "We deserved you blowing up at us. I'm sorry, too."

"I know you were trying to help me, but what you did was the same as stealing." He let out a gusty sigh. "I guess I shouldn't have acted like I was your pa, but I'm starting to think of you that way."

Joshua stuck his hands in his pockets. "I miss my pa." He cleared his throat. "But you're the closest we'll ever have to family. If that means you get on us when we've done wrong like Pa would have, we'll take it."

"In that case," Mr. Cooper said, "you're going to refund that greenhorn's money and tell him what you did. Then you can sell him what he really needs if he still wants to buy from us."

"Yes, Sir," they said almost at the same time.

"And if you really mean that," Mr. Cooper said as he leaned in and smelled Joshua's breath, "I'm going to have to come up with some punishment for you drinking."

"Yes, Sir." Joshua's voice cracked. "Whatever you decide."

Mr. Cooper laid his hand on Joshua's shoulder. "That's fine, Son."

"Now remember, boys," Mrs. Cooper said, "no later than five o'clock."

Seventeen-year-old Joshua unloaded a box of canned goods onto the store shelves. It had been a year-and-a-half since they'd come to live with the Coopers. "We'll remember."

"Isn't there anything we can do to help?" Jonathan had grown as tall as Joshua but was twenty pounds skinnier. "We want to make sure this day is special for him after all he's done for us."

"You make sure you're on time," Mrs. Cooper said. "You being there is enough of a present for Mr. Cooper's birthday."

She turned to leave. "Mind you're not late." She walked out the door.

"I don't believe she has much faith in us to be on time," Joshua said.

"Why would she? We're always late for supper."

"That's not our fault," Joshua said. "We have to finish up at the store, don't we?"

"Well, we aren't going to be late today."

An hour later, Mr. Cooper strolled up to the counter. "It's kind of nice having two hard-working men to rely on while I go out for lunch with my wife. I could get used to this."

"Sir," Joshua said, "we were wondering if we could take off just a bit early today."

"I guess that would be all right," Mr. Cooper said. "You boys have plans, maybe sparking girls?"

"Yeah, we have plans," Jonathan said.

"Well don't fret about the store. I'll stay and finish." Mr. Cooper took two boxes from behind the counter. "As a matter of fact, I have presents for you."

Joshua shook his head. "It's your birthday. You're supposed to get presents, not give them."

"Since it's my birthday, I can do whatever I want, like giving my sons presents."

"Thank you," Jonathan said.

"Aren't you going to open them?"

Jonathan grinned. "Which one's mine?"

"The one on the right."

Jonathan opened his box and pulled out a brown, slouch cowboy hat with a silver hatband around it shaped in a rectangle pattern. He held it in his hand and turned it. "I've never had a hat so fine in all my born days." He tried it on. "Fits perfect."

"Well Joshua, your turn."

He opened the box and pulled out a black gambler's cowboy hat lined with a silver hat band in a diamond-shaped pattern, and choked up. "Thank you." He'd admired that hat since they started working there a little over a year ago. He placed it on his head.

"Now, throw out those old straw hats you wear," Mr. Cooper said. "I can't have my boys walking around town without decent hats, now can I?"

Joshua grabbed the straw hats and threw them in the trash box. He swallowed back his emotions. "Thank you and not just for this."

"You're welcome," Mr. Cooper said. "I couldn't ask for two finer sons."

Joshua couldn't think of anything to say that wouldn't sound too mushy. Maybe it was time to confess everything about Hunt's Peak. He wanted to make things right, and Mr. Cooper would know how.

He'd talk to his brother about it later. It wasn't like Jonathan hadn't mentioned telling him everything at least once a month for the last year. It was time.

Ruining Mr. Cooper's birthday wasn't a good idea, but they could tell him everything the next day.

Jonathan ran into the house. "He's coming." He was as excited as he would be if it had been his birthday.

"All right, everyone, take your places," Mrs. Cooper said.

Everyone hid behind sofas, under tables, and in closets. When there weren't enough places to hide, the rest of the company scurried into the hallway.

The door opened, and Mr. Cooper entered.

Everyone jumped out from their hiding place and yelled, "Surprise!"

Mr. Cooper startled and backed up for a second, placing his hand on his chest.

Mrs. Cooper ran to him and kissed him. "Happy Birthday, Sweetheart."

"I can't believe it," Mr. Cooper said. "Mary, how in the world did you keep this a secret with half the people in this part of Denver City in on it?"

"I have my ways," Mrs. Cooper said. "I also have two excellent helpers that make great sneaks."

Jonathan raised an eyebrow. Tomorrow when they told him the truth, he would know how big of sneaks they really were. "Happy birthday, Sir."

"You knew about this and kept it a secret?" Mr. Cooper said. "Amazing."

Jonathan smiled. Somehow, knowing they were going to come clean didn't ruin his appetite or his ability to enjoy the party. In a way, he felt relief. "Let's eat."

The party wore on until about nine o'clock when, one by one, the guests left. When the last guest departed, they stayed to help Mrs. Cooper clean up.

When the work was done, Mrs. Cooper turned to them. "It's getting late. I think you had better stay here tonight."

Joshua placed his new cowboy hat on his head. "Wouldn't hear of putting you out after you did so much work getting this party ready."

Jonathan reached for his hat. "Besides, it's a nice night for a walk."

"Now, boys, you know you're not any trouble." Mrs. Cooper put her hands on her hips.

"We know," Joshua said, "but we're not staying tonight. We have some business in town to take care of."

Mrs. Cooper raised an eyebrow. "What kind of business at this hour?"

"Oh, you'll find out tomorrow." Jonathan kissed her on the

cheek

They said their good-byes and left.

It didn't take long to walk back to the store. Jonathan looked around to see if anyone was around before Joshua unlocked the door.

Chapter Sixteen

When they arrived at the store early the next morning, Joshua opened the door. Overturned boxes and goods cluttered the floor. A lead weight dropped to his stomach.

His brother brushed past him and picked up the empty cash box lying on the floor among the rubble.

Joshua heard the door close behind him and spun to see Mr. Cooper walk in with the marshal.

"Hello, boys," Marshal Cook said. "I didn't expect to see you two here."

"Huh." Joshua turned to Mr. Cooper. "What happened here, Sir?"

"Boys, it'd be better for you if you come clean." Marshal Cook's tone hinted at anger.

He heard the words, but they didn't make sense, as if the marshal spoke some strange jargon. "You don't believe we would… We didn't do it."

Mr. Copper stood stoic, his brow furrowed, gazing at the overturned boxes.

"Weren't you here late last night, boys?" The marshal rested his right hand on the butt of his gun. "Before you answer, my deputy saw you."

Joshua glanced at his brother. "We were here. Yesterday was Mr. Cooper's birthday. We came back after his party to reorganize the storeroom. He's wanted to do it for a spell, and we thought we'd go ahead. Sort of like a birthday present."

"You rearranged the storeroom, all right," Marshal Cook bellowed. "You rearranged the whole store. You were here last night, you have a key to the store, and the lock box was picked open. Joshua, we all know you know how to pick a lock. Now quit trying to wiggle out of it."

The muscle in Joshua's cheek twitched. Mr. Cooper had to know they wouldn't do this.

Mr. Cooper walked in front of them, facing Marshal Cook. "I believe them."

"They were at Hunt's Peak before they came here," the marshal said. "I planned on sending a message to them a year ago, but I plum forgot. I'll telegraph the sheriff there. If they check out, I'll give them the benefit of the doubt for now."

"You'll see," Mr. Cooper blustered out. "They're good boys."

The marshal glared at them until it became uncomfortable. "Stay put until I get back. Don't make me chase after you." He tromped outside.

Joshua wiped his sweaty hands on his trousers. Everything in him wanted to run.

"Don't fret, boys." Mr. Cooper placed a hand on his shoulder. "When the marshal hears back from Hunt's Peak, this will all be cleared up."

"Sir." Joshua grabbed a broom. "We'll go back to the storeroom and start cleaning up." He followed his brother into the back room and closed the door.

Jonathan spun toward him. "We should have had the sand to tell the truth before now. They're going to believe we did this."

His shoulders slumped. "Only one way out of this. We have to tell Mr. Cooper everything. If we confess what we did in Hunt's Peak before the marshal gets back, he might understand."

"What if he doesn't believe us?"

Joshua let out a sigh. They had made peace with it when they decided to tell the truth, but having to face jail with the Coopers thinking they might have done this... He set his jaw. "Best be getting it over with."

They headed to the next room where Mr. Cooper was sweeping up shards of glass.

"Mr. Cooper." Heat flushed Joshua's face. "Sir."

"Now boys, don't fret. I know you wouldn't rob me."

"No, we didn't." He cleared his throat. "We would never steal from you after all you've done for us, but we were in trouble at Hunt's Peak, and we figure you ought to hear about it before Marshal Cook returns."

Mr. Cooper's Adam's apple bulged. "What kind of trouble?"

Joshua exhaled a deep breath. "We robbed the general store in Hunt's Peak of almost three hundred and fifty dollars."

At first, Mr. Cooper's expression was blank. Then a glint of understanding registered in his eyes, and a vein in his neck pulsed. "You robbed the general store! What'd you do, pick the lock on their strong box too? Is that why you learned to pick locks, so you could rob stores?"

"Yeah… I mean… no." Joshua resisted the temptation to look away. "We did rob a store, but we wouldn't steal from you."

Mr. Cooper slammed his fist on the counter. "After what you did in Hunt's Peak, you expect me to believe this wasn't you?"

Joshua winced as if he'd been slapped. "We don't do that anymore."

"I took you into my home. I gave you jobs. I treated you like my own sons."

"This wasn't us. I give my word." Jonathan placed his hand on his heart.

"You give your word? You betrayed me." Mr. Cooper grabbed them by their collars and led them to the door. "You march yourselves to the marshal's office and tell him everything. This time I'm pressing charges."

Joshua grabbed his stomach to hold back the terror lodged there. "But we didn't–"

"Get out! When I meet you at the jail, you better have told the truth, all of it. Now go."

They staggered out of the store. Gunshots fired in the distance, and Joshua jumped as if he'd been the one who was shot. He broke into a run toward the boarding house with his brother at his heels. They rushed into their room and locked the door.

"What are we going to do, JJ?"

Joshua threw his belongings into his saddlebags. "We're going to get out of here." He took his gun belt out of the drawer where it had laid for the last year-and-a-half and strapped it on.

"I knew he'd blow up. We deserved it." Jonathan grabbed his gun belt. "But I never thought he wouldn't believe us."

Joshua placed his hand on his brother's shoulder. "Pa would've believed us and stood by us even if he did march us to the marshal's office." His voice thickened. "I wanted Mr. Cooper to be like Pa, but he's not." He wiped his face with his hand. "Nothing we can do about it now."

They finished packing their saddlebags and, grabbing their new hats on the way out, hurried to the livery stable. After saddling their horses and tying down their saddlebags and bedrolls, they mounted and rode out of town. Joshua pulled back the reins.

Jonathan came to a halt beside him. "Where we headed now?"

He thought for a moment. To the left, the foothills of the Rocky Mountains headed to Hunt's Peak. To the right the prairie traveled back to Kansas. Ahead of them, a dirt road led north. "How about Wyoming Territory? Maybe we can stay on the right side of the law there."

At the Denver stagecoach station, Jed took Grace's hand and strode toward a middle-aged woman in a green dress and bonnet standing beside a bearded man with grey hair.

When Marshall Cook had contacted the town about his brothers, he'd asked for any information about them. Mr. Cooper had written him and invited them to Denver City.

So, a month later, here they were. "Are you Mr. and Mrs. Cooper?"

Mr. Cooper nodded. "You must be Rev. and Mrs. Jackson. Let me take your bags and put them in my buggy. My house isn't far away."

"That's all right, Mr. Cooper," Jed said. "We wouldn't want to cause you any trouble. We'll stay at a hotel."

"Nonsense, we wouldn't hear of it," Mrs. Cooper said. "You'll stay with us. We insist."

Mr. Cooper and Jed set the bags on the back of the nearby buggy.

As the buggy rolled along the streets of Denver City, Jed wanted to plunge right in and ask a million questions about his brothers, but he squelched the impulse knowing it would be wiser to wait until they got to the house.

Instead he surveyed the stores they rode past to occupy his mind. "Why are all the buildings made of brick?"

"A fire back in sixty-three burned all the wood structures," Mr. Cooper said. "Since then, there's been a brick ordinance."

"We're a growing city," Mrs. Cooper said. "We already have four churches, a seminary, two theaters, and a couple of banks, not to mention the train coming through here. Soon Denver City's going to be the largest city in the West, next to San Francisco."

Jed leaned forward and pressed his hands on his legs as if to urge the horses on. The road was too busy for the buggy to go any faster. "Do you like living here, Mr. Cooper?"

"Truthfully, it's getting too big for me. We came here in fifty-nine, when it was small. Mary and I keep talking about selling out and buying a store in a smaller community."

"My pa owns a general store in Hunt's Peak." Grace placed her hand on Jed's.

"Then he's the man the boys stole from," Mrs. Cooper said.

"Grace's pa dropped the charges as a wedding gift." A shiver went through Jed. If his brothers still believed they were wanted, they might head into even greater trouble.

"Denver City has two bodies of water, Cherry Creek and South Platte River," Mrs. Cooper said. "Our house is on Cherry Creek."

Jed nodded, grateful she changed the subject. As they rode on, they continued to share information about the city. He feigned interest and asked a few more questions even though all he could think about was his brothers.

"Mrs. Jackson," Mrs. Cooper said. "You and Rev. Jackson look so young. How long have you been married?"

Grace smiled. "Not long. Less than a year."

"Most ministers your husband's age are still circuit preachers. You must be proud of him having his own church."

Jed shrugged. "No great accomplishment. God brought me to Hunt's Peak looking for my brothers when they needed a preacher. I was available."

"He's being modest," Grace said. "The church is doing very well, and my husband is a gifted pastor."

Jed patted Grace's hand. "And my wife thinks I can walk on water."

Grace's elbow nudged his ribs. Normally he would have chuckled and teased her some more, but he couldn't muster his sense of humor.

The buggy pulled up to a brick federalist house on the edge of the creek. The men helped their wives down from the buggy and escorted them inside.

"You must be tired after your journey," Mrs. Cooper said. "Sit in the parlor, and I'll make us coffee."

"I'll help," Grace said.

"No, you won't," Mrs. Cooper said. "This trip had to be hard, you being in the family way. You rest."

Grace's mouth dropped open. "How did you know?"

"You have that glow," Mrs. Cooper said.

Grace blushed and sat on the settee. Jed scooted in beside her and put his arm around her shoulders. He had a warm feeling about these strangers who had helped his brothers. It was as if he'd known them all his life.

"I told her she should stay home in her condition." Jed winked at his wife. "She wouldn't hear of it. Said her place is by my side."

Mrs. Cooper chuckled. "I'll get the coffee."

A short time later, Mrs. Cooper carried in a tray with sandwiches and cups of coffee. As they ate, Mr. Cooper told them what had happened since he met Jed's brothers.

"I could see they were troubled." Mr. Cooper's entire body slumped into the cushion of the chair. "I have a temper, and sometimes I say things I don't mean. I wouldn't listen even when Jonathan gave his word they didn't betray me. I believed them, but I was so angry I couldn't admit it."

Jed wrapped his hands around his coffee cup. He'd been so close to finding them, and now this. He didn't blame Mr. Cooper, the only man who had lent them a hand since this whole thing started. He was angry at them too. If only they'd stayed put. "How did you find out they didn't rob your store?"

"Marshal Cook spotted a member of the Musgrove Gang on the way to the telegraph office." Mr. Cooper wiped his face with his hand. "He followed him to the Overland Hotel where gunfire was exchanged. When the marshal searched the man's room, he'd found everything stolen from me."

Mr. Cooper reached for his coffee cup, and it rattled. "I tried to find your brothers, but it was too late. This is all my fault."

"Don't blame yourself." Jed swallowed a gulp of coffee to try to wash down the lump in his throat. "You helped them when nobody else would."

Grace put her hand on Jed's shoulder. "You asked God to let you know they're safe, and He did. You need to leave them in His hands."

"I'm working on it." A heaviness lay in the pit of Jed's stomach. His brothers believed they were wanted men. If he didn't find them soon, it might be too late.

Chapter Seventeen

Joshua pulled Jonathan to the side to avoid the horses clopping down the dirt road through the center of Cheyenne, Wyoming. Denver City had been crowded, but he couldn't remember working this hard to avoid disheveled cowboys filling the dusty walkways.

A hum of activity and piano music roared from the saloon. The smell of stale, dusty air mixed with horse droppings gave a foul odor.

Two men fell through the saloon doors and fought in the street. Joshua sidestepped one man who punched the other and almost fell into his brother.

They passed at least two more saloons and one brothel on their journey to the train station.

Joshua chuckled. "Looks like Cheyenne's a place where we can see the elephant."

Jonathan rolled his eyes. "All I want to see right now is food. Let's get some chow before we try for the railroad."

"You always thinking of your stomach?"

"I can't help it," Jonathan said. "We haven't had anything since breakfast, and it's way past lunch."

"You know that might cost as much as two dollars, and we still have to pay the livery and get a room."

"JJ, I have to eat." Jonathan stopped in the middle of the street and crossed his arms.

"Boy, when you got a bee in your bonnet, you don't let go. You know, the train depot's just two hoops and a holler from here."

Jonathan said nothing but stood with his jaw set.

"All right, let's find where we can get something to eat."

Jonathan unfolded his arms and pointed next door. "There's a place right there."

Joshua chuckled and followed his brother into the restaurant.

After they had spent two of their last twelve dollars on pot roast with boiled potatoes, carrots, and cornbread, they left the restaurant and hurried to the train depot.

A middle-aged man in a grey suit stood behind the counter. On the wall, a flyer was posted with large letters across the top. *HELP WANTED.*

Joshua strolled closer to read the smaller print. "Expressmen.

We're both good shots. We could do that."

"JJ, you couldn't beat our grandma to the draw."

"You know I'm fast. Can't help it if I'm not the fastest gun in the West, like you. Besides, we haven't practiced in over a year. Maybe you're not that good anymore."

Jonathan lifted an eyebrow. "I'm still better than you."

"Let's go ask about those jobs."

The man behind the counter glanced up. "May I help you?"

"We're inquiring about the expressmen jobs," Joshua said.

"You'd have to be at least eighteen," the man said.

"Oh, we're both eighteen." The lie didn't stick in his throat the way it used to when he told a falsehood. Why should it? Even when he told the truth, nobody believed him.

The man raised an eyebrow at Jonathan and muttered, "You look more like fifteen."

Joshua placed his hand on his brother's shoulder. "He's just skinny. He's eighteen all right."

Jonathan's eyes narrowed. "Please, mister, we need the job."

"You swear you're eighteen?"

Joshua placed his hand in the air. "We swear."

"The name's Mr. Griffin. Let's go out back and see if you can shoot."

Six bottles sat on a log outside about twenty feet away. Joshua strode to his place.

"You have to hit all six bottles as quickly as you can," Mr. Griffin said. "Anytime you're ready."

He drew his Remington revolver. A succession of six shots hit the bottles, breaking them into glass shards as they fell on the ground below.

When the smoke cleared, he smiled. "I'm a little rusty. Been a few months since I shot anything."

Mr. Griffin's mouth hung open. "Where did you learn to shoot like that?"

"My pa taught me, and I've practiced a lot."

"You're hired. What's your name?"

"Joshua Jackson and this here's my brother, Jonathan."

"Well, I've never seen a man draw that fast and hit what he was aiming at. Jonathan, your turn. Let's see if you're as good as your brother."

Mr. Griffin went to the log and placed six more bottles on it.

"Anytime you're ready."

Jonathan took his place and breathed in a deep cleansing breath. Joshua kept his eyes on Mr. Griffin, knowing what was coming next.

Gunshots and smoke filled the air. It was difficult to tell where one shot ended and another began. The smoke cleared, and all six bottles lay shattered on the ground.

Mr. Griffin swore. "You're not hired gunmen or wanted by the law, nothing like that?"

"Would we want honest jobs if we were?" Joshua wasn't exactly lying this time, just asked a question.

"You're hired. Ever since the Reno brothers took up train robbery, we've been trying to get a couple of guards on each train carrying over ten thousand dollars."

He'd read about the Reno brothers. Maybe he and Kid would come against some real live outlaws.

Two years later, the train chugged along the tracks, rumbling the walls of the payroll car. Nineteen-year-old JJ knelt in front of the safe with his ear pressed against the door. He spun the knob, tuning out the noise of the train and listening for that faint drop. There it was. Smiling, he turned the lever.

Kid darted to his side. "You did it again. Let's see what's in there this time."

He hauled the strongbox out of the safe, pulled a lock pick out of his pocket, and opened the box. He pulled the bundles of money and counted them. "I figure we have at least twenty thousand dollars here."

Kid whistled.

JJ placed the money in the safe, closed the door, and turned the knob.

"You're getting good at cracking them. Shame we can't keep that money."

"You know I just open safes to pass the time of day and add a little excitement to this boring job. Why do you always jabber on about keeping the money? You reading dime novels again?"

Kid grinned. "I read this one called *The Heroic Bandit of the Wild West,* and I figure we could do better than that man in the book. You can open every safe we lay our eyes on."

"Not every safe," JJ said. "A few of them have me beat, tumblers too quiet. I was reading about this rubber tube whim-wham some doctors have called a stethoscope, supposed to make it louder when they listen to somebody's heart. I've been saving up for it."

"Why, if we're not taking the money?"

"It's fun opening them, like one of those puzzle boxes."

Kid cleaned his new Smith and Wesson Model 3 revolver with a thin brush. Even though they didn't make much, he'd saved up for a year to buy it. "We should at least ponder on being train robbers like those fellers in the books. We've been working for the railroad two years, and we hardly have anything to show for it. I want the good life for a change like those big bugs that own the railroads and the ranches."

It was the third time this month Kid brought up the subject of robbing trains. JJ didn't know how to get through to him anymore. He'd led his brother down the wrong path early in life, but Kid used to be the one talking him out of trouble. Now all his brother talked about were dime novels and outlaws.

"I want the good life too, but think of how it turned out when we stole from a store. We still have to be watchful every time the train stops at Denver City. Can you imagine how they'd chase after us if we robbed a train? Besides, I don't like the idea of hurting folks and taking their hard-earned money."

"If we do it smart, nobody will get hurt." Kid glanced up from cleaning his gun. "It'd be as easy as licking butter off a knife, and we'd be rich."

Familiar temptations churned inside. Nothing exciting ever happened on this job. It would be nice not to worry about where the money came from. Better than sitting in a payroll car for hours a day, waiting for train robbers that never came.

Kid holstered his revolver. "We don't need to use our guns. We could just point them, and we know how to use the telegraph since we started working here. It would be easy to find out when shipments are coming through."

JJ shrugged his shoulders. The voices in his head battled. A part of him wanted to make things right, but the only way was to go back to Denver City or Hunt's Peak and face jail time, and he wasn't going to. Maybe Kid had a point.

"No, no, no, no, no! Get it out of your head, Kid. We'd be on the dodge the rest of our lives."

"We're on the dodge now."

"Maybe, but do you really want to stray that far?" The train brakes screeched. "It's not time for a stop yet." He leapt to his feet. "Wonder what's going on?"

Kid stepped to his side as they cracked the door open and peered around the edge. Three men on horses pointed guns at the conductor. "Road agents!"

JJ's heart raced. "There's only three of them. I'll see if I can get the drop on them."

"No, I'll go. I'm a better shot. You unbolt the door and wait here in case they make it past me."

JJ waited until Kid pressed out of the escape hatch before taking his position in the corner where the shadows hid him. The door screeched open.

A tall man tossed a satchel onto the floor, then raised himself onto the edge and made his way to the safe.

JJ pointed his gun toward the man. "Don't move or I'll shoot." The man froze in place. "Drop that bag on the floor."

The man's shoulders stiffened. "Not a good idea. It's filled with dynamite."

"All right, then. Slowly place it on the floor."

The man did what he said.

JJ grabbed his gun. "Now go sit against that wall over there. We're going to wait until my brother gets back with the rest of your gang."

The man spat. "I hope you're not too close to your brother. He might not be around much longer."

JJ's cheek muscle twitched.

"Best you let me go now. I'll see your brother comes to no harm."

"You better pray he doesn't." JJ cocked his gun. "Or you'll be joining him real soon."

The sound of a scuffle and footsteps neared the car outside.

Kid appeared at the open door and called back over his shoulder. "Get over here."

Two men shuffled to the car opening and raised themselves into it. The first man looked a little younger and was stockier and shorter and worked a wad of chewing tobacco with his jaw. The second looked more like a boy, maybe fourteen. He wiped his stringy blond hair out of his eyes and squared his shoulders, trying to look older than he was, the way Kid did when he was that age.

"Get over there with your friends." JJ motioned toward the tall man with his gun.

The coalman showed up at the door, and Kid barked at him, "Get some rope."

He took off and came back a few minutes later with the twine.

"How'd you manage it?" JJ said.

Kid tied up the first man. "It wasn't that hard. They didn't even put up a fight."

"I'm glad. I was afraid they might..."

"Stop babying me. I can take care of myself."

The coalman finished tying up the youngest outlaw, and JJ checked the ropes on all three.

Sam, the engineer, poked his head into the payroll car. "I telegraphed Marshal Cook. He'll be expecting them three yahoos when we stop in Denver City. Says he wants to congratulate the men who caught them."

A lump formed in JJ's throat. "Did you mention us?"

"Of course," Sam said, "Dang, I wasn't supposed to tell you. Said he knew you, and he wanted it to be a surprise. You'll act surprised, won't you?"

JJ gave his brother a sideways look. "Isn't that something, Kid? Our old friend, Marshal Cook's going to surprise us and meet us at the station."

Sam and the coalman slammed the door shut. The train jerked, and the engine hissed as it released steam.

"What are we going to do?" Kid whispered. The wheels turned, and the train moved along the tracks.

JJ put his finger to his lips and tilted his head toward the outlaws. There was no way out of this one. The decision had been made for them. He slumped against the side of the car, listening to the train rumble on its way to Denver City, the end of the line.

Chapter Eighteen

The train wheels chugged along the tracks and steam escaped the engine. Both sounds moved Kid and his brother closer to being arrested. He wouldn't go peaceably if he could help it.

The tall outlaw cleared his throat. "We've never done this before, and we had us a reason."

Kid ignored him.

"Name." JJ stood and stretched.

"Gus Franklin. These are my brothers, Bob and Pete.

"I suppose we all have reasons for what we do. Won't make any difference, but you tell it if you want."

Kid glared at his brother. "Don't we have bigger problems?"

"I could use something to keep me from fretting about those bigger problems."

"What are you bellyaching for?" Bob, the tobacco chewing man, chomped his wad. "I don't see how you two got cause to gripe when we're the ones hog-tied and headed for prison."

"Why don't you get to jabbering about those problems of yours," JJ said. "We're listening."

"Wouldn't make no never mind to you," Paul, the youngest, said. "You never had your pa and brothers murdered."

Kid shot a look toward him.

The muscle in JJ's jaw twitched. "Our folks were killed when we were just boys. Like I said, won't make a lick of difference, but we're listening."

JJ could listen to their hard luck story if he wanted. Kid couldn't understand why he would. Why didn't he try to think of a way out of this mess? Maybe his brother didn't mind going to jail, but he did.

It had been four years since they robbed Hunt's Peak, and they were just boys at the time. Hadn't they gone through enough when their family was killed? First, they had to escape a madman, then they lived from hand to mouth just to survive.

When they thought God had given them another family, and they were ready to tell the truth, Mr. Cooper turned on them. He set his jaw. No, sir. It wasn't fair, and he wouldn't do it no matter what JJ said.

"Sorry about your loss," Gus said. "After our ma died, our pa raised us and our older brothers. He mined the Wind River Mountains looking for gold a few years back. Didn't find much, but he unearthed enough to buy us a small ranch. We had a few head of cattle and were making a pretty good living 'til the railroad came through. Railroad man said we had to sell our land to them at pennies on the dollar. Law sided with the railroad, so we fought for our land and lost. Pa and our brothers were killed by the law."

Bob spat. "The law… bought and paid for by the railroad. Gus and me were shot, but we mended. We've been taking care of Paul and each other ever since."

"When we healed up, the railroad had already run us out," Gus said. "We went up in the hills, where we used to mine, and got to pondering. We couldn't let them get away with it. So, we decided to rob a train and get back what's ours."

Kid leaned forward. "How were you going to get the safe open?"

"Dynamite," Bob said.

"Don't have to use dynamite with JJ around." Kid clamped his mouth shut and shot a glimpse toward his brother. Yep, he was mad. Kid shrugged his shoulders. "Sorry."

"What do you mean by that?" Gus said.

JJ sighed. "I can open a safe by listening to the tumblers. Just do it for fun though. I don't rob trains."

"We ought to tie in together," Bob said. He and Gus sat up a little straighter.

"You untie us and show us how you can open that safe," Gus said, "and we'll split the money even. Nobody needs to know you took it. You could tell them we got away."

A gleam of hope shot through Kid.

JJ grunted. "Nobody's going to swallow that, you tied up and us holding guns on you? We're in enough of a fix as it is."

"We could hide out near that old mine in Wind River I was a telling you about," Gus said. "We probably know them hills better than anyone."

"We're not doing it," JJ said.

Kid's stomach hardened. He had to convince his brother soon or they'd both end up in jail. "Ah, could we talk, private like?"

"Sure." JJ followed him to the corner.

"We can't take them to Denver City. Marshal Cook will be waiting for us, sure as shooting."

"If we do this and get caught, we'll get twenty years instead of the few we have coming. It's not worth it. Besides, we have good jobs here."

"How long you think we're going to have these good jobs after Marshal Cook arrests us for thieving?"

JJ rubbed his chin. "I don't know. Twenty years? A lot more than we'd get for robbing the Hunt's Peak General Store."

"You're the smartest man I know," Kid said.

JJ shook his head, then started pacing. Six steps forward.

"You could figure it out so we don't get caught."

Six steps back.

"Think of what it would be like to finally live the good life, to have money to spend."

JJ paced a few more steps.

"It would be exciting, not like riding in this boring baggage car day after day."

He stopped and gazed at Kid. "I don't hold to stealing from common folks." He strode away again, turned back, and quirked an eyebrow.

"Come on, JJ." Kid blew out a sigh of frustration. "What choice do we have?"

"Stealing is one thing, but hurting or maybe killing anyone? I'd march into Marshal Cook's office myself before I'd agree to that."

"Who says we have to hurt anybody?"

"We don't know these men." JJ took his hat off and wiped his fingers through his hair. "They might not feel the same way."

Kid let out a gusty sigh. "If they were murderers, they would've tried to shoot me. If they had, I wouldn't have gotten the drop on them."

The gleam returned to JJ's eyes, and Kid knew he'd convinced him. "We could at least see what they say about it." They strode to the middle of the car where the outlaws were tied up. "Men," JJ said, "we're giving your offer some consideration, but we'd need to get things worked out first."

"Like what?" Gus said.

"We aren't going to steal from people who don't have enough as it is, and we don't want to go to a necktie party for killing anyone. We just want to get rich."

"Sounds right to us," Gus said. "We can rob trains and leave the passengers alone."

"One more thing," JJ said. "My brother and I will be in charge.

You aren't smart enough to keep us from getting caught."

"Now wait a minute," Paul said. "Who says we're not smart?"

"We did get caught our first job," Gus said. His brow furrowed. "All right. If you have a plan for getting us out of here, we're in."

"As a matter of fact, I do have an idea on that." JJ knelt and opened the safe. All three outlaws' eyes widened. JJ took the money out, stuffed it in a nearby sack, closed the safe, and twirled the tumbler. "Just a bit." He motioned for Kid to follow him to the corner of the car.

"Yeah?"

"There's another way than doing this. We could face up to what we've done. Might be the better way to go."

Kid set his jaw. "No, if we're going to be on the wrong side anyways, we might as well do it the way we want and get something for our trouble. Like I've been trying to tell you, I'm tired of having nothing."

JJ grunted. "Untie them."

Kid knelt and untied the ropes. He had gotten what he wanted, and he thought he'd be happy JJ agreed to it, but a heaviness rested on his chest as if he'd come to a fork in the road and had chosen the wrong path.

🤠 🤠

Jed strolled the dusty road toward Eli's Dining Hall when he heard a voice behind him.

"Rev. Jed." It was the telegraph operator who'd come to town a year ago. He never missed a Sunday at church and even taught a boy's Bible study.

"Hello, Adam, how's your family? I heard Betty's in the family way again."

"Preacher, this is important. I have a telegram for you from Denver City. Figured you'd want it right away."

Jed took the message and read it.

> *Joshua and Jonathan robbed payroll train to Denver-stop-Marshal Cook after them-stop-Prayers going up. George Cooper.*

His hand trembled as he crumpled the telegraph and stuffed it in his pocket.

Chapter Nineteen

Kid didn't see the hideout entrance until they were almost upon it. The narrow pass opened into a lush green valley with a creek flowing through it. The refuge had everything they needed: a large cabin, a corral for the horses, a smokehouse, and a nice size woodshed.

An elk drank from the creek and ran into the woods. As they unsaddled their horses, a monarch butterfly landed on a low-lying branch of a pine tree near the corral then flew away.

The cabin nestled against the base of a bluff in the Wind River Mountains. They stepped inside.

It had a wooden floor, four windows, and two rooms split by a wooden divider. The front room had a pantry, an oak table and chairs, a gun rack, and a potbelly stove. The larger back room had four wood frame bunkbeds with tick mattresses and a fireplace. It reminded Kid of a bunkhouse.

A couple of hours later, Kid sat at the table eating the beans and cornbread Bob made and drinking the coffee Gus brewed. He dished out his fourth helping.

"I'm surprised he's so skinny," Gus said. "Does he always chow down like that?"

"Why do you think we're taking up train robbing?" JJ said. "Have to find some way to pay for his food."

Kid looked up from his plate and laughed at being the brunt of the joke. He'd gotten used to his brother teasing him about his appetite.

"I've been thinking the last couple of days," JJ said, "and I have some ideas."

"Well, let's hear them," Gus said.

JJ cleared his throat. "First off, we should pitch in half of our first haul to buy supplies and get things ready for our outlawing careers."

"Careers?" Bob said.

Kid grabbed another corn muffin. "You know, your job."

Bob nodded.

"Now wait a cotton-picking minute." Paul glowered at JJ. "Who died and made you the biggest toad in the puddle? I know why Gus said you were the leader before when you had us all tied up, but you're in our pond now."

Kid tensed and set his muffin down.

JJ glared at Paul, and the vein in his neck pulsed. He spoke quietly with a hint of anger in his voice. "You agreed to this before we robbed that train. Are you backing down on your word?"

Kid stood. The boy couldn't see how dangerous it was goading his brother. Paul stood and rested his hands on the butt of his gun. JJ stood and pushed away from the table. Kid had to stop this. If JJ hurt the boy, he'd never forgive himself. He stepped in front of his brother.

"I can handle…"

Kid spun and glared at him. JJ's eyes flashed for a moment, but he backed off and sat at the table. JJ was right about one thing. They couldn't back down and show any kind of weakness now.

"Paul," Kid said, "if you take up with him, you're taking up with me."

The boy chuckled. "You keep going on about how you're so fast at the draw. Maybe we ought to see for ourselves."

Gus put his hand on Paul's shoulder. "We agreed JJ's the leader."

Paul brushed his brother's hand away and stepped toward Kid. "You going to put up or is your brother here going to back down?"

Kid walked away from the table, his chest tightening. "JJ's not backing down and neither am I." He didn't want to hurt Paul, he liked the kid, but he had to figure out something. "How about I prove how fast I am without us shooting?"

"How about you quit beating the devil around the stump and draw?"

Gus punched Paul in the jaw, and he landed with a thump.

"Sorry about my brother. Since our pa died, he's been all uppity like he doesn't have to listen to anybody."

Paul stood to his feet and rubbed his clenched jaw. A bruise was already beginning to form.

"I'm willing to put this behind us if you are." Kid extended his hand. Paul glared at him, and wouldn't shake his hand. "I'll tell you what," he said. "We could still find out who's faster without shooting each other."

"How?"

"We'll take the bullets out and do the fast draw. I'll even let you reach first. If I prove I'm faster, you're going to start obeying orders."

The corner of Paul's mouth hinted at a sneer. "And if I'm faster?"

"Then we back down."

Paul removed the bullets from his gun.

Kid did the same and rested his hands by his sides. "I don't have all day. We going to do this?"

Paul reached for his gun.

Kid drew and pointed his Smith and Wesson Model 3 in Paul's face before he had his gun out of the holster.

Paul's mouth opened wide. "Wow! I've never seen anything like that before. You have to be the fastest man alive. Appreciate you not killing me."

"No problem, figured we needed the extra man." Kid tapped his finger on Paul's chest. "You get too big for your britches again, and next time, I'll put you down."

Paul shuffled his feet as he sat at the table next to Kid.

JJ leaned back in his chair. "Now, can we get on with this?"

Paul nodded. Every time Kid glanced at him, he blushed and grinned.

"As I was saying, we need supplies. What's the nearest town?"

"South Pass City," Gus said. "They keep a blind eye toward any wanted men who might wander in, as long as they don't cause a bother and pay the sheriff for his hospitality."

JJ stoked his chin. "Do they have a telegraph?"

"Yeah," Gus said.

Bob spit a wad of tobacco in a can sitting by the stove. "What kind of supplies you looking at?"

"We should get stocked up on some basics in case the law comes around and we get stuck in here," JJ said. "At least six months' worth. We're also going to need a telegraph wire and key. Oh, and I need a stethoscope."

"What in tarnation for?" Bob poured himself a cup of coffee.

"The telegraph wire," JJ said, "is so we can hook into the telegraph line to South Pass City. We can find out about railroad shipments if we're patched in."

Gus threw a log into the stove. "What about that steth-o-whim wham? I never heard of such a thing."

"It's a rubber tube doctors listen to folks' hearts with," Kid said, "to make things louder. JJ wants it so he can hear the tumblers in the safe, makes it easier to open."

"We'll need red lanterns and two red flags," JJ said.

Bob snorted. "Why, we planning on opening up a brothel?"

Kid snickered.

JJ tugged on his ear and gave Bob a blank stare, then also laughed. "No, they're also used for letting an engineer know there's an emergency. How'd you stop the train?"

"We built a fire on the tracks," Gus said.

"This'll be easier," JJ said. "Just a bit more. We always act polite when we can."

Bob snorted. "Why? We're robbing trains, not going to a quilting bee."

"If we're polite and considerate, folks might not be as quick to want to shoot us, but that's not all," JJ said. "After this job, we'll give half of the money we steal to help those who need it. We'll do everything we can to get the people on our side."

"Great idea," Bob said.

Paul looked wide-eyed at Kid. "Sorry I acted up before."

Kid leaned forward. "Time you learned a man doesn't spout off like that."

"Yes, sir, Kid. It won't happen again."

Gus took a sip of coffee. "I figure we ought to add a bit more."

"What's that?" Kid grabbed another corn muffin.

"If it looks like we're going to get caught, we do whatever we can to escape, but we'll give up before we shoot any lawmen or anyone else for that matter. We all know what we're facing."

"I give my word," JJ said.

While the others agreed, Kid didn't say anything. He didn't want to hurt anyone if he could help it, but he'd do whatever it took to stay out of jail.

After ordering what he needed, JJ met the gang in front of the mercantile. "Man says it'll take at least two weeks, maybe even a month." He handed out bundles of money. "I'll take the rest over to the sheriff to pay him off. If I have anything left after that, I'll give it to a church or something."

Gus, Bob, and Paul nodded and headed to the saloon.

"You want to go with me, Kid?"

"Sure. You need someone to back you up just in case. How do you want to play it?"

"A strong show of force," JJ said, "just in case."

They arrived at the sheriff's office, then burst in with their guns drawn.

A skinny man about five feet tall jumped out of his chair and raised his hands. "What going on here?" he said in a squeaky, high-pitched voice.

JJ could hardly believe his eyes. "Are you the sheriff?"

"Yep, Sheriff Fife, but why the guns?"

As much as he wanted to laugh, JJ narrowed his eyes and glared at the sheriff for a moment. If the man thought they were hardened outlaws and killers, he might not be as eager to arrest them. "Well, sheriff." He tipped his hat back with his gun. "We heard you allow certain folks in your town who might not be welcome other places. We heard you're real friendly that way."

"Let's get to it." Sheriff Fife puffed out his chest and spat in a nearby spittoon, obviously not impressed with JJ's glower. "No questions asked, provided you pay me a percentage of your take, and you don't cause any trouble in town."

JJ pulled out all the money that was left. The bigger profit the sheriff made, the more likely he was to be cooperative. "That's the first payment. Enough?"

"It'll do. How long are you going to be here this time?"

"Two weeks, maybe as long as a month," JJ said. "We won't be any trouble."

"You better not be." Sheriff Fife rested his hand on his gun. "Another gang made the mistake of figuring they could rob this town. The whole town showed up for their lynching. Quite a shindig."

"Fair enough," JJ said.

"We'll be mindful of that." Kid holstered his revolver, and they turned and walked out.

When the door closed, JJ couldn't help but chuckle.

Kid shook his head. "Scrawniest lawman I've ever seen."

They headed toward the saloon.

JJ strolled in and fixed his eyes on a saloon girl with big brown eyes wearing a red satin dress with feathers pinned to her matching hat. An evening with a pretty girl might be just the thing to get rid of his restlessness.

Chapter Twenty

A couple of months later, JJ strode toward the White Swan Saloon to find Mercy. The nervous energy from his latest train robbery kept him on edge. He wanted to expend some of it spending time with the beautiful saloon girl he'd met when he'd first come to town. She took his breath away. When he gazed into her sad brown eyes, he saw… something.

Mercy strolled down the dirt road in the other direction. He followed her through town and over the footbridge to Willow Creek. She removed her shoes and stockings, baring her legs, and waded into the stream. He cleared his throat.

She spun toward him. "JJ, you startled me."

"I wanted to see you."

She looked even more appealing without face paint covering her subtle features. She traipsed out of the water and sat on a nearby tree stump. "I don't work on Sundays."

"That's funny," JJ said.

She grabbed a black stocking and pulled it up over her foot. "What's so funny about that? Lots of folks don't work on Sundays."

"Yeah, I know. My ma wouldn't let me do anything on Sundays when I was young. It's just you're a… you know."

"I've told you before, I serve drinks in a saloon, and that's all I do. If you want something more, find another girl." Mercy grabbed her shoes in her hands and stomped off toward the footbridge.

"Wait, I'm sorry." He chased her and placed his hand on her shoulder. She tensed under his touch, and he pulled back. "I didn't mean anything by it. You don't have to go. I will. Or I could stay, and we could talk."

Mercy twirled back toward JJ with fire in her eyes. "Talk? Right. You want more than that."

His cheeks burned. He had wanted more when he followed her there, but now he felt ashamed. "I figured just talking to a pretty girl might be… well, kind of nice."

She tilted her head for a moment and sat cautiously on the log with her back straight as if she were a soldier standing guard. "Okay, if that's all you want to do. What should we talk about?"

"I don't know." He flustered, and he didn't know why. He'd

been around saloon girls before, lots of them. "Maybe about you."

"No, I'd rather hear about you. What made you decide to become an outlaw?"

"I didn't set out to be one. My folks would pitch a fit if they knew."

"They don't know?"

He gazed out at the river as a flock of ducks swam to the edge. "They died when I was young."

"I'm sorry."

"Happened a long time ago. Anyway, there wasn't much opportunity for two young boys on their own.

She placed her hand on his. Her touch sent a tingle through him.

"How about you?" he asked. "I don't expect you dreamed about working in a saloon."

"No, I didn't." Her brow furrowed. "I wanted to be a preacher's wife."

"A preacher's wife?" She couldn't have surprised him more if she wanted to be a circus clown. "So, what happened?"

"A traveling preacher who came through town often seduced me when I was fifteen." She bit her lip. "When I ended up in the family way, he told me he was married, and nobody would believe he was the father. He warned me I better keep my mouth shut."

"I'm sorry."

"Don't be. I learned early what men are like." Mercy stood and walked to the edge of the creek. "Anyway, this is the only job I could get after my father threw me out."

JJ rubbed the back of his neck. If his pa were alive now, he'd march Kid and him to the nearest sheriff's office, but he would never stop loving them. "What happened to the baby?"

"Died at birth."

An ache welled up in his throat. He started to reach out, wanting to wrap his arms around her and comfort her, but she would misjudge his motives, and for good reason. Wasn't that why he sought her out? He pulled his hand back and rubbed it on his leg.

"Don't feel sorry for me. I have plans." She picked up a pebble. "When I save enough, I'm leaving South Pass City to go someplace where nobody knows me. Then I can buy a cabin, and plant a garden, and maybe earn a living doing sewing for folks." She skipped the rock along the top of the creek. "I like to sew."

"Sounds real nice."

She slipped into her shoes. "We've talked enough for one day. I'm heading home now."

"Mercy." He wanted to see her again. "I'm going to be in town all week. Can we spend time together?"

"You know where I work. Come around anytime you want a drink, and I'll serve it."

"No…" JJ stammered out. "That's not what I meant. We could do things together."

"I've told you before, I'm not a soiled dove."

"That's not what… I… I didn't mean that. I want to spend time getting to know you, you know, talking." He sounded like a kid, but he couldn't help it.

Mercy raised an eyebrow. "Just talking?"

He nodded. "Maybe we could take some walks together too."

"How about we meet here tomorrow at noon? I don't have to be at work until six. I'll bring a picnic basket."

"I'll be here." He stuck his hands in his pocket and watched her dart over the footbridge to the red-light district where she lived. Whistling, he strolled toward the Miner's Exchange, where he planned to meet Kid and play poker all night.

Kid raised an eyebrow. Ever since he met JJ in the saloon, his brother acted… well, he didn't act like himself.

Maybe it was the stupid mistakes he made at the poker table. He even drew to an inside straight. He would never make such a fool move if something wasn't wrong.

After losing seven hands in a row, he came away from the table two hundred dollars poorer. At this rate, he would go through his cut of the money from their last job in a week.

JJ met Kid at the bar and ordered two whiskeys. The bartender set the drinks on the counter, and JJ gulped his down. "Something wrong?"

"Yeah, something's wrong." Kid worked his jaw. "You. What's eating you tonight?"

"I don't know what you're talking about." JJ held out his glass. The bartender poured more, and he guzzled another swig.

"You never drink like that unless something's bothering you. And what's with the poker? I've never known you to play so bad."

"So, what are you, my ma?"

"The last I saw you were going to find Mercy. You know, if she didn't scratch your itch, there's other girls like her in town."

When the punch landed, pain shot through Kid's jaw, and he fell on the floor with a thud.

JJ galloped out of town across the path leading through Wind River Mountains, the breeze hitting his face as he rode. He'd pushed too hard. He slowed the sorrel to a trot.

He couldn't believe he'd punched Kid. He knew why he did it. Kid talked about Mercy like she was trollop. Wasn't that what he thought about her -- until today?

There was more, but he didn't want to think about that part, at least not yet. First, he had to make things right with Kid. He rubbed his jaw. His brother was probably going to want to return the favor. Well, might as well get it over with. Turning his horse around, he rode back to town.

He took a deep breath and pushed open the door to their hotel room at the Idaho House. Kid sat in the chair facing him as if he was waiting for him. His cheek was red and a little swollen. Looked like it was going to bruise.

JJ cringed at the sight. "Hi, Kid."

Steel-blue eyes glared.

"I went for a ride on that path west of town, you know the one. It's real pretty out there, Kid." He swallowed hard. "This is a real fine town to hide out in, with all the mountains around it and such."

Kid kept his gaze focused on him.

JJ wiped his face with his hand. "I'm mighty sorry. Really I am. If you want to flatten me, go ahead."

"Why'd you hit me?" His tone hinted at hurt more than anger.

"It's what you said about Mercy. I'm beginning to like her, and, well, you talked about her like she was a soiled dove."

"Well, she is a saloon girl, and a lot of them are. You never had a problem with that before."

"I know, but she's not like that. She's only working in a saloon until she gets enough to leave town and support herself."

"JJ, you could have told me to back off."

"You sure you don't want to hit me?"

"I don't want to hit you. I want to know what's eating you."

JJ let out a breath through his nose. "We burned our stinking bridges. We're never going to be able to fall in love, or get married, or raise young'uns, or anything like that. We'll never have what Ma and Pa had."

"That must have been some talk you had with Mercy."

"I like her. I want to spend time with her, and that's all it's ever going to be. Because of the choices we made, it can't ever be anything else."

"We knew that when we tied in with the Franklins."

"I know." JJ started pacing. "It just struck me when I was talking to Mercy. We should have turned ourselves in to Marshal Cook in Denver City that day. We gave up a lot to do this."

Kid's brow furrowed. "I don't know what to say. I talked you into it."

"What choice did we have? I didn't want to go to jail any more than you did."

Kid stood and set a hand on his shoulder, strong enough to keep him from pacing.

"Don't fret about it." JJ sank into a nearby chair. "I'll be all right." He knew that was a lie. The choices he had made smacked him in the face. No going back for either of them.

"You going to spend more time with her?"

"Yep, I'm seeing her tomorrow."

"Be careful."

"I'm sorry I hit you." JJ stood and prepared himself for the punch.

Kid rubbed his jaw. "So am I. Let's get some shut-eye."

"Okay." JJ let out a breath just as Kid's fist landed in his gut.

Chapter Twenty-One

It had been three years since Jed had received the telegram from Mr. Cooper telling him about his brothers robbing the train. Since then, he'd tried to find them, but every time he'd heard any news it was after they'd robbed a bank or a train.

Now, he burst into the house with his hope renewed, holding another telegram in his hand. A former member of his congregation had moved to a small farm near Bear River, last year, and had telegraphed he'd spotted Jed's brothers.

He hated leaving Grace after what she had been through over the last week with the influenza epidemic, but she'd understand how important it was.

They'd sent their two sons to stay with Eli when Grace's parents and sister came down sick, so he wouldn't have to worry about her taking care of them alone while he was gone.

Striding through the house, he hunted for her so he could share the news. He came to the bedroom where her sister Hannah lay in their bed. She wasn't there.

He called down the hallway. "Grace, Grace, where are you?"

"I'm here." Her voice sounded weak. She walked painstakingly slow into the bedroom, carrying a pan of water. "I'm here." Her green eyes, normally sparkling like the sea, looked dull and puffy. She gave him a grin so weary it hardly moved the corners of her mouth.

Although her parents were the only ones who had died, half a dozen people, including Hannah, had come down with the influenza.

There was worry about an epidemic especially since they didn't have a doctor. The council had just approved paying for a town doctor, but it wasn't soon enough.

School and church services had stopped, and Eli was considering quarantining Hunt's Peak.

Guilt swept through Jed as the smell of sickness assaulted his senses. He couldn't desert her, but how could he not do this? He might not have another chance to find his brothers.

Grace laid a wet cloth on Hannah's brow. "She's getting worse."

"I'm sorry." Of course, he couldn't go. He laid the message on the bureau.

"What's that?" His wife pointed to it.

"I received a telegram."

"Who from?"

"Joe Tanner. He saw my brothers near Bear River."

Grace bit her bottom lip and stroked Hannah's hair. "You have to go to them."

Hannah coughed, trying to catch a breath. The coughs weakened then subsided, and a gurgling noise came from her chest.

He wiped his face with his hand. "I can't leave you like this."

"You have no choice."

Hannah's breathing slowed. He stepped to Grace's side and wrapped an arm around her waist. He didn't know how long they stood there watching her sister suck in a couple of short raspy breaths, sometimes not breathing at all, then a minute later, breathing in again. Then she took five labored breaths and was gone.

Jed wrapped his arms around his wife.

Her dress was soaked in perspiration. She buried her face in his shoulder and sobbed. After a time, she wiped her tears. "I'll prepare her. Could you dig the grave?"

Jed nodded. He strode next door to the graveyard behind the church and started digging the grave.

After the burial, he would buy a ticket for the stage the next morning. If he waited, Hunt's Peak might be under quarantine, and he wouldn't be allowed to leave for weeks. By then, his brothers would be gone.

A few hours later, he said a few words over the fresh dirt lying next to Mr. and Mrs. Freeman's graves. Beads of sweat covered Grace's pale face. Caring for her family had taken a lot out of her. He helped her back into the house.

She turned to him. "You have to go. They're the only family we have left."

He nodded, headed to the bedroom, and packed a few essentials before rushing to the kitchen to kiss her good-bye. She grabbed hold of the table.

His stomach knotted as he reached for her. She collapsed in his arms. He leaned his face to hers. Heat emitted from her. She had the influenza.

Swooping her up in his arms, he laid her in the bed. He grabbed the wet cloth setting in the pan of water and placed it across her forehead. Tears filled his eyes. The lump in his throat nearly choked him. Out of the corner of his eye, he saw the telegram. He picked it up, crumpled it in a ball, and threw it in the fireplace. He would never leave her like this.

He didn't know what to do, but he did his best to take care of her. Staying up by her side all night, he listened to her labored breathing, gave her sips of water, and stroked her hair in case she needed him. He wouldn't have been able to sleep anyway.

The next day, Eli stopped by to hang a quarantine sign on their door, but he didn't come in. He did call through the door to let Jed know the influenza had been contained. Only a few other cases, and they weren't as serious. As relieved as he'd had been to hear that, why didn't God spare Grace or her family? His family?

Two days later, he was startled by a knock on the door. "Go away," he called out. "There's influenza here."

"Let us in," Mr. Cooper said.

He cracked the door open and leaned against the frame, unable to stand any longer on his own power. Exhaustion threatened to overtake him, but he fought it for Grace's sake. "You shouldn't have come."

Mrs. Cooper pushed through the doorway. "Nonsense. If you think you can keep us away when you're going through this trouble, you're mistaken. Where's Grace?"

"She's in the bedroom." Jed pointed to an open door off the main room.

"How about your sons?"

"Eli's keeping them until this is over. We can't risk them getting sick too."

"Get some sleep." Mrs. Cooper pulled bottles and packets out of her bag. "I'll see to her."

"If something happens…" Jed wiped his eyes. "She and the boys are all I've got left."

"You're not going to lose her." Mr. Cooper placed his hand on his shoulder. "What happened to your faith, Son?"

The lump at the back of Jed's throat threatened to choke him. He'd never been so scared, not even during the war when he learned his family had been killed. *I love her, Lord. Don't take her away.*

Sheriff Drew Porter stormed into his office in Bear River,

Wyoming and slammed the door.

Deputy Mark wiped his sandy brown hair out of his eyes. "What's wrong with you?"

"They did it again! It's bad enough them robbing this town three times, they had to destroy Green River."

"The Jackson gang?"

"Yeah." Drew threw his hat against the wall. "They robbed the payroll train headed to Green River again. That just about finishes Meg's family."

"Why don't you ask your sister and her husband to live here?"

"I already offered. They won't hear of it." Porter plopped into his chair. "The problem is Meg's husband. He doesn't want us around reminding him he should be taking care of his wife and children instead of going to the saloon every night."

"Sounds like Meg's been through the mill." Mark poured a cup of coffee and handed it to him.

Drew took a sip. "He's always kept a roof over their heads and food on their table until lately. Those robberies took their toll."

"That's too bad."

"I wish they'd trust God to help them through this, but it's hard when you haven't been raised that way."

"How'd you get religion?"

"You wouldn't believe me it I told you," Drew said.

"Now I have to hear the story."

Drew chuckled. "JJ and Kid Jackson's brother showed me the way down in Hunt's Peak, Colorado. My wife and I attended his church there."

Mark snorted. "No, that is hard to swallow."

"Yep, never met a more decent, God-fearing man than Rev. Jed Jackson."

"With a brother like that, maybe they'll get religion one of these days."

"Not likely," Drew said. "I knew them when they were between hay and grass, and they were already on the wrong road then."

Drew's jaw twitched. If he'd tried to help them when they were young, maybe they wouldn't have gone down this path. He let out a sigh. He couldn't change what happened in the past, but he tried his best to learn from it.

Now he and Amy made a point to reach out to boys headed for trouble, even adopted a couple of them. Amy was thrilled by each new addition to their family since they'd never been able to have children of their own.

It was too late for the Jackson boys, though. All he could do now was to try to catch them and make sure they didn't hurt anybody else.

Chapter Twenty-Two

After climbing out of his oldest son's bed, Jed staggered into the hallway. His head spun as he fought the grogginess, but he followed the sound of the voices in the bedroom.

Mr. Cooper's voice reached through his fog. "Jed's lost so much in his lifetime. He can't lose Grace too."

The muscle in his jaw twitched. He hurried to the bedroom where his wife lay, pale and unmoving. He had to know. "How is she?"

"Her fever's down a little, and she's resting." Mrs. Cooper took Jed's hand in hers. "But the grippe is in her chest. She has pneumonia."

He rubbed his other hand over his face and tried to fight the despair rising up, gripping his heart. "Why didn't you wake me? I can't lose her. I can't."

She placed her hands on his shoulders and squeezed. "Stop it. She needs your strength."

"But pneumonia…" Jed slumped into the nearby chair.

"It hasn't come on strong yet. She's a healthy woman, and she still has a good chance. Sit here with her while we make another mustard plaster."

The next few days passed as a blur. Mr. and Mrs. Cooper continued with the mustard plasters and vapor treatments, but Grace didn't seem to get any better.

Jed knelt beside the bed, fought back tears, and begged God to save her. The God who took his family. The God who allowed his brothers to wander further into trouble. The God who took Grace's parents and sister.

He knew he would continue to serve Him no matter what happened. Where else could he go? But he didn't believe he would be able to bear the loss.

Hadn't he preached a week ago that God never promised He wouldn't give His followers more than they could bear, only that He'd walk through it with them? Harder to apply the sermon to his own life than to preach it to others.

"Please, God."

A hand on his head startled him.

"Hi," Grace said in a raspy voice.

"Hi." He reached to feel her forehead. The fever had broken. "Halleluiah!" *Thank You, Lord.*

She stroked his cheek with the back of her hand. "Did you find them?"

"Find who?"

"Jed…your brothers."

He stroked her hair and chuckled for the first time in a week. "No, I had something a little more important to do, like take care of the stubborn woman the Good Lord gave me."

"Jed, why? You might have missed your chance to catch up with them."

"I'm done trying to find them," he said, amazed that this time he really meant it. If God saved Grace from certain death, He could take care of Joshua and Jonathan without his help. "They're in the Lord's hands now."

Drew arrived in Bear River, discouraged and frustrated. He'd planned to head straight home, but decided to check in at the office first.

Mark caught his eye. "I'm glad you're back. The Jackson Brothers robbed the payroll train coming into Bear River again."

Drew clenched his jaw. "Did you send a posse after them?"

"Not right off," Mark said. "We got a telegram the train was delayed."

"So, do you reckon it was them who sent it?"

"Could be," Mark said.

Drew threw his chair across the room and heard the crunch as it hit the floor. He started to the door.

"Where are you going?"

"I need to let my wife know I'm back. After that, I'll try to square things with the mayor. I expect he's all fired up about me being out of town every time they rob the train. When he's done blowing up at me, I'll go to the church and pray."

"You think prayer will help you catch them?"

"I don't know. It never has before." Drew slammed the door behind him.

JJ waved a red lantern at the approaching train. The brakes

screeched as the Iron Horse slowed, and a familiar excitement made his heart race. The train rolled to a stop.

He dashed to the engine, pointed his revolver at the engineer, and grinned, happy to see the familiar person.

The grimace on the engineer's face showed he wasn't as pleased. "You robbing my train again, JJ?"

The roar of horses' hooves signaled the arrival of his gang.

"Howdy, Sam." Kid tipped his hat. "Good to see you."

"Well, I'm sorry I can't return the sentiment. You've robbed my train six times in the last two years. Starting to feel like you're picking on me."

JJ holstered his gun. "Now, you know you're our favorite railroad engineer in the whole Union Pacific, but we have a job to do, and this train carries the largest cache." He nodded to the gang.

Paul trotted his horse to the passenger car and called out instructions. "Now, folks, this train is being robbed by the Jackson Franklin Gang. We're not stealing from any of you, so sit tight, and nobody gets hurt. Do as you're told, and you'll have a story to tell your grandchildren someday."

Bob took his position near the front of the car and pointed a rifle at the engineer.

Kid and Gus followed JJ to the payroll car.

JJ knocked. "Open up in there."

"No, Sir," a voice from inside the car sounded out. "I'm not opening this door."

Kid grinned. "That you, Zeke?"

"Yeah, it's me," Zeke said. "I have a rifle in here, and I'll shoot you dead if you try robbing me again."

JJ pushed his hat back. "Why do you have to be so all fired stubborn about this? If you don't open that door, you know we'll have to use dynamite."

He tried the door again and shot an exasperated look at Kid. "Probably make the big bugs at the railroad pretty mad if they have to replace another payroll car. Why don't you just open up?"

"I'll blast you to kingdom come."

JJ nodded to Gus, and Gus pulled a stick of dynamite out of his saddlebag.

"You know you're not going to shoot us. You wouldn't hurt anybody over the likes of some big bug's money." JJ banged on the side of the car. "Open the door."

"Nope," Zeke said.

JJ placed the stick of dynamite in the car door where it would do the most amount of damage.

"You make sure you get behind that safe so you don't get hurt." JJ backed away.

Gus lit the fuse. "Take cover."

They dove behind a fallen tree and stuck their fingers in their ears as the dynamite exploded.

JJ peeked up. The door had been blasted off the payroll car. A dazed Zeke staggered to the opening with a rifle in his hand.

Kid ambled toward Zeke with his Smith and Wesson drawn. "You're not going to do anything with that rifle, are you?"

Zeke looked at the Winchester, groaned, and set it down. "I wouldn't shoot you after you paid for my wife's operation and all."

Kid grabbed the gun. "How is Sally?"

"Doing fine thanks to you."

"Come on," Gus said.

Zeke jumped out of the car, followed Gus to the engine, and scrambled up to where Bob had a Henry rifle pointed at Sam and the coalman. Gus joined Paul in the passenger car.

JJ climbed into the payroll car. A Holmes and Butler safe. They used cast iron to insulate these safes, and it made it harder to hear the tumblers. This would take some time.

He pulled out a stethoscope. Taking a deep breath to quiet his heartbeats, he placed the stethoscope on the safe and turned the spinner to the right.

A faint click. "Forty-three." Then to the left. No click. He spun the dial again and turned it to forty-three. He tried for the next number.

He heard something faint but wasn't sure. Then to the right again. No click.

Letting out a sigh, he tried again. He knew he could easily get it open with dynamite without damaging the money inside, but he wouldn't let another Holmes and Butler beat him.

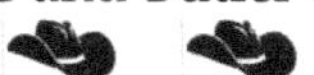

Kid sat on the edge of the car door with his feet dangling. He hated waiting for JJ to open the safe. The posse could ride up on them any minute. He suspected his brother didn't want to use dynamite because he had a hard time admitting a safe had beaten him, but JJ would cut things too close if he let him.

He shot a look back. "You done? Been an hour."

JJ waved his hand at him and continued to turn the knob. A moment later, he stopped and smiled.

Kid stood, his heart racing.

His brother turned the lever and opened the safe.

"You did it."

JJ took a sack and filled it with the money. "There has to be five thousand dollars here. Nice since the last three hauls weren't worth the trouble of robbing."

Kid checked his pocket watch. His chest tightened. "Let's go."

Gus, Bob, and Paul climbed onto their horses.

JJ turned to the engineer. "Good seeing you again, Sam, Zeke." He tipped his hat. "Keep an eye out, now. There's outlaws in these parts."

Sam scowled. "You're the only outlaws I've seen. You best get moving. We should have been in Bear River a half hour ago."

"I wouldn't fret," JJ said. "I hear they expected you to be late, something about a buffalo on the tracks."

"Not fretting a bit." Sam flashed a sideways grin. "Just don't want to see you boys hurt when you're arrested and sent to prison. You can't outrun the law forever."

Sheriff Drew Porter arrived with a posse of ten men. When he spotted the stopped train, he nudged his horse forward.

Sam ran to him. "How'd you get here so quick?"

Drew raised an eyebrow. "I got a telegram you were running late." He shot a look back to Deputy Mark. "Now that I have it figured out, they won't evade capture for long."

Sam scratched his head. "Have what figured out?"

Drew sat back in his saddle. "Never mind about that."

"They headed that way." Sam pointed toward the hills.

Drew and the posse rode into the mountains tracking the outlaws.

Chapter Twenty-Three

A rumble sounded behind JJ, and he glanced back to see a dust cloud moving in their direction. His heart skipped a beat.

"Posse," Kid yelled as he nudged his horse to the front of the group.

JJ waited until the others rode past before taking his place at the rear. The thunder of the horses' hooves filled his ears. He rode fast, leaning forward in his saddle and pulled his bandana over his face, but it didn't keep him from swallowing dust as he held tight to the reins of his galloping bay.

Trying to think of a plan to evade the pursuers, he swatted his horse, urging it to go faster. Maybe the approaching darkness would discourage them. He and his men rode through the night, but Porter's men never weakened their chase.

At dawn, they reached the mountains. The lawmen were still close behind. The horses couldn't take much more without a rest. He couldn't see any way out of it this time. Another hour at most.

The only way any of them could escape was for him to be a decoy. He'd be caught, he was sure of it, but at least the rest of the men would get away.

He rode to Kid as the gang edged out of view of the posse. "Hide out in that canyon over by those rocks 'til your horses are rested. I'll lead them away."

"You won't be able to manage it alone," Kid said. "I'm coming with you."

JJ didn't like the idea, but he knew Kid was right. He nodded.

Gus wiped his face with his bandana. "You crazy or something? They'll catch you just short of an hour."

"They won't catch you." JJ furrowed his brow. "You want Paul to go to prison? He's only eighteen."

"Guess we have no choice." Gus extended his hand to them. "Good luck."

JJ untied the sack from his saddle horn and threw it to Gus. "If we get caught, it won't do us any good. If we make it to the hideout, we'll split the money there."

Gus secured the sack, and he, Bob, and Paul rode into the mountains. They turned and tipped their hats before riding toward the canyon.

JJ turned to his brother. "You ready to give them a good chase?"

"Yep."

They waited for the posse to crest the hill, then rode in the opposite direction from the Franklin brothers. JJ glanced back, and as he expected, the dust cloud trailed them. Good so far.

The clouds ahead darkened the sky. "Looks like a storm brewing," JJ said. "Might be able to get lost in it."

"Worth a try. What do we have to lose?"

"About twenty years in prison." He grinned sideways at his brother as they rode off in the direction of the storm.

A few hours later, JJ adjusted in his saddle, drenched and miserable, and gazed at the flooded riverbank. "Looks like we lost them. Now if we can keep from drowning…"

"Look." Kid pointed to the river.

One lone rider, Sheriff Porter, sat at the edge of the river and nudged his gray stallion forward. The current rushed by him as he urged the mount on until the water reached his waist.

Kid groaned. "He's going to get himself killed."

The horse stumbled, and Sheriff Porter fell into the rushing deluge.

JJ clenched his jaw and watched the sheriff fighting to keep his head above water. "Come on."

They rode to the river where Porter struggled against the current.

"Sheriff Porter," JJ called. "Give your word you won't try to arrest us this time, and we'll help you out."

"Need favor," Porter spurted out.

"What's that?"

"Deputy. Mudslide. Your word, help find him. Won't arrest… this time."

JJ dismounted his horse, grabbed a rope, and threw the end to the sheriff. Porter clutched it, and he tied the other end around his saddle horn. "You have my word."

Kid inched as close to the bank as he dared. "Mine, too. Pull."

JJ tugged on the reins. The horse backed up the bank. Sheriff Porter drew closer to the edge. Kid gripped Porter's arm and dragged him out of the water. The sheriff lay on the ground, gasping for air and coughing up water.

"You're a stubborn man." Kid plopped on the wet ground

beside him. "Is catching us worth your life?"

JJ nudged his horse to the bank, waiting to hear the sheriff's answer.

"I'll keep my word." Sheriff Porter coughed up water. "Don't fret about it."

"Why?" The vein in JJ's neck pulsed. "We never hurt anybody. We only stole from the railroads and banks, and they can afford it. Why are you so all fired anxious to catch up with us? Is it the reward? Is five thousand apiece worth your life?"

"It's not the money," Sheriff Porter said.

"Then, what?"

The sheriff delivered a piercing glower. "I have a sister who lived in Green River with her husband. She was with child. You remember Green River, don't you?"

JJ shot a look toward Kid.

"When you robbed the bank, a little over a year ago, Meg and Frank lost their life savings. That wouldn't have been so bad, but the payroll train you held up had the money to pay the railroad workers. Frank worked for the railroad."

Sheriff's Porter voice deepened. "Still, that wasn't enough for you, was it? You robbed the payroll train two more times in the next month. The town might have recovered if, when they found a way to sneak the money in, you hadn't robbed the bank again."

The clouds covering the mountain range had blown away with the tempest, but the storm lodged in JJ's gut.

Kid crossed his arms and studied the blue horizon as if he were looking for an answer to Porter's accusations.

The sky was clear except for a lone hawk, a predator that preyed on innocents.

"The whole town suffered from what you did," Sheriff Porter said. "My sister lost her baby during a difficult birth 'cause they couldn't pay a doctor. Her husband went plum crazy from the shame of not being able to take care of his family and hanged himself. Their oldest boy found him, but you don't hurt anybody, do you?"

"You're not putting all that on us." Heat rose up JJ's spine. "The banks and railroads could have helped them, if they were a mind to."

Sheriff Porter snorted. "You don't think you have any part in this?"

JJ got within inches of the sheriff's face. "He's not the only one who ever came on a hard spell!" He backed up and cleared his throat.

"Let's go find your man, so we can all go home."

"Which one of you do I ride with?" Sheriff Porter walked to where they straddled their horses.

Kid extended a hand, and Sheriff Porter pulled himself up.

"Where'd you see him last?" Kid asked.

"A little ways down the river. He made it to the other side, but a flood of water came down the mountain and caused a mudslide. I don't know if he's trapped or not. I couldn't cross there, so I went farther up the river to find a place. That's where you came in."

JJ nudged his horse through the mud.

After a short ride, Porter pointed ahead. "There, that's the place."

Kid pointed to an area against the mountain that curved in. "It looks like the mudslide covered up a cave entrance."

A chestnut and a gray horse stood in a clearing beside the mountain. Kid turned to Porter. "His horses?"

"Yep, his and mine."

"Probably in the cave." JJ dismounted his horse and grabbed a long piece of wood. "Let's try to dig him out."

They dismounted and started digging. An hour later, saturated with mud, Sheriff Porter poked his hand through a small hole. "Mark, you there?"

"I'm here, and I'm doing fine." Mark said. "I knew you'd find me."

Sheriff Porter dug out the opening until his deputy could squeeze through.

"It wasn't me." Porter tilted his head toward JJ and Kid. "They figured it out."

Mark reached for his gun.

JJ's chest tightened, but he resisted the urge to draw his revolver.

"Don't!" Sheriff Porter grabbed Mark's arm. "They saved my life. I gave my word if they helped me find you, I wouldn't arrest them."

"Still," Mark said. "Doesn't seem right letting them go."

"I'm not breaking my word."

JJ let out the breath he was holding, but a moment later, Sheriff Porter thumped him on his chest with a pointed finger. "Don't think this changes things. I aim to see you behind bars."

"You have to catch us first," JJ said, "And we mean to make that mighty hard on you." He mounted his bay and rode as fast as his horse could carry him, his brother trailing behind. If only he could ride away from his guilt as easily.

Later that day, the rain ceased, and the sun shone through the clouds, leaving a double rainbow arching over the mountains. They camped at Wind River and started a fire to warm themselves. Indian paintbrush plants dotted the riverbank with red flowers. A monarch butterfly perched on one of the leaves.

JJ hunched near the campfire and looked at his black hat. With the caked-on mud, it would never come clean. He poked his finger through the hole in the front. Beyond repair. "I suppose we need new hats."

"I guess." Kid tried to brush the mud off his but only smeared it.

"I'll keep mine a little longer. I just need to clean it up a bit."

Kid raised his eyebrow. "You're not getting rid of that hat no matter how beat up or dirty it gets 'cause Mr. Cooper gave it to you."

"I know."

A rabbit wandered close. Kid shot it and picked it up by its hind feet. "No jerky tonight."

The butterfly still perched on the red leaf. Even the sound of gunfire hadn't disturbed it. JJ stared at it in amazement.

He and Kid worked together to get dinner ready. After years on the trail together, each knew instinctively what the other was going to do. They huddled around the fire and ate, each lost in his thoughts.

Kid broke the silence. "What do you think about what Sheriff Porter said?"

"You mean about Green River?"

"Yeah."

"We never meant to hurt anybody."

"It looks like we hurt them anyway," Kid said. "Remember what Pa used to say."

"Which saying? He had a lot of them."

"Sinning is like ripples in a pond. It keeps getting bigger 'til it disturbs the whole pond."

JJ's voice grew thick. "We should have known we couldn't backslide as far as we did without causing some suffering, but I sure didn't aim to."

The butterfly flew away.

Kid picked up a stick and poked at the fire. "I don't want to do this anymore."

"Me either." JJ cleared his throat. "It's going to be hard though. We need money to hide out the rest of our lives."

"How much do we have?"

"After all we owe for supplies, not much. I can't go back on the rule that half of it goes to charity just 'cause we're quitting. We should figure a way for the money to go to Green River or maybe to Sheriff Porter's sister."

"Yeah, I guess." Kid warmed his hands over the fire. "We could do one more job, a big one. After that, we'll have enough to quit."

"Let's not tell the others 'til we have something lined up."

Kid unwrapped his bedroll. "You ever think about what would have happened if we hadn't run out on Mr. Cooper?"

"Yeah, I do." JJ broke a stick and threw it into the fire. "But we can't undo that any more than we can fix our hats."

Chapter Twenty-Four

As soon as JJ arrived in South Pass City, he looked for Mercy. She wasn't at the saloon, so he tried the footbridge by Willow Creek. He found her there, splashing the water with her feet.

He strolled to her. After greeting her, he went right to the point of why he sought her out. "I'm quitting outlawing."

"Quitting? Can you do that?"

"We'll do one more big job, and then go someplace nobody knows us, maybe change our names. We want to live decent lives, maybe raise families."

She stared at the ground. "So, I guess this is it. You'll be riding out soon."

He wrapped his arms around her and pressed his lips against hers. Warmth flooded him as she parted her lips and leaned into his kiss. He pulled back. "There's something I need to ask you."

She bit her lip. "Yes."

"I'm not making any promises." He touched her cheek with the back of his hand. "But if it all works out..." His chest tightened. "What I mean is... will you marry me?"

Her eyes filled with tears, and she turned away. "You don't want to marry a saloon girl."

"And I'm an outlaw." He placed his hands on her shoulders. "I love you, and I want to be with you. Nothing else matters."

"If things go all right, you come get me. If they don't... I'll be ready."

Kid rode to the hideout, jumped off his horse, and left it saddled as he rushed into the cabin.

JJ stomach tightened. "Something wrong?"

Kid gasped to catch his breath. "I found us a job. Eighty thousand dollars is going to be delivered at the Bear River Bank, next week. There's some big cattle drives coming through, and they need the ready cash. This is it, the big haul." He slapped JJ on the back and let out a howl.

"Security will be tight."

"Yeah, but we'll manage."

"Sheriff Porter knows us."

"That's the best part," Kid said. "He'll be out of town taking two prisoners to Cheyenne. He telegraphed another lawman to watch the town 'cause he's worried about us robbing it."

JJ chuckled "Well, let's not disappoint him."

"Are we going to let the gang know we're quitting after this?"

"Yep," JJ said. "It's time."

They met the rest of the gang at the bunkhouse, and JJ told them about the robbery plans for Bear River. "So, any questions?"

"No," Gus said. "Seems like an easy job."

Something didn't set right. Maybe it was too easy. JJ shook the thought away. "There's something else. This is going to be the biggest haul we ever made, and Kid and I were kind of…"

Bob raised an eyebrow. "Yeah."

"We want to quit," JJ said. "With all this money, we can go somewhere and get lost. Maybe we'll head to Texas or Arizona. Just thought you'd want to know."

"I can't believe it." Gus stood up. "Why do you want to go and do a fool thing like that? We're famous. We have dime novels written about us."

"And every posse in Wyoming looking for us," Kid said.

"We could get a lot richer than this," Bob said. "Why now?"

JJ wiped his hand across his mouth. "You wouldn't understand, but we've made up our minds."

"If you want to quit, fine." Gus leaned his palms on the table. "There are others who'd love to take your place. You with me, Bob, Paul?"

Bob slapped Gus on the back. "I'm with you. No way I'm quitting when we're on top."

Paul pressed his lips together in a straight line.

"How about you, Paul?" Gus crossed his arms. "You're awful quiet."

He stared at his feet. "I didn't ever figure I'd have a chance, but…" He looked up. "I'm going to quit too."

"Suit yourself," Gus said. "You're a man now."

JJ let out a sigh. He hoped Paul would make that decision. Leading the boy into a life of crime when he was so young was one of the ripples in the pond he regretted. "If you want, you can ride with us."

"Na, I'll go off somewhere on my own," Paul said. "I'm only

eighteen. I have my whole life ahead of me. Besides, I've been thinking on it a lot since I heard that circuit rider preacher last month in South Pass City. He made a lot of sense."

JJ nodded. He hoped Paul would have that chance, but he had an uneasy feeling in the pit of his stomach.

JJ rode into Bear River and rented a room under the name of Joshua Reddinger, an alias he often used. After taking a bath, he changed into a white shirt, gray frock suit with gray stripped trousers, black vest, and burgundy cravat. He slicked his hair back, placed a derby hat on his head, and headed for the bank.

The bank president motioned him into his office. "My name is Mr. Hanford. I'm the president of the Bear River Bank. And you are?"

"Mr. Joshua Reddinger, the Third." JJ extended his hand. "Good to make your acquaintance."

"Is there something I can do for you, Mr. Reddinger?"

"Yes, sir, there is." JJ smiled. "I have holdings in the area – silver mines. I'm looking for a town where I can open an office as a home base. You're centrally located, and the railroad comes through here, which is another plus."

"You're right." Mr. Hanford chomped down on his cigar. "With the railroad making regular stops, this would be an ideal location."

"Before I can make a final decision, I must know what security measures your bank has taken to ensure it will not be robbed."

"Of course." Mr. Hanford opened the door to his office. "The railroads and the cattle buyers deposit large amounts of cash, from time to time, without worry. As a matter of fact, we have a large shipment in our bank right now. Let me give you a tour."

"I would appreciate that."

Mr. Hanford pointed out the features. "We have bars on the windows, and at night, we have a steel door that closes over the entrance. Nobody can get in this bank once it locks up."

"What about daylight robberies?"

"We have two security guards posted at all times, and a deputy makes regular stops to check up on the bank day and night. The sheriff's office is right across the street."

The tour ended with a view of the safe, a Diebold Safe & Lock Co, 1870. JJ grinned. The Diebold 1870 was known for its reinforced steel, but the company didn't worry about making the tumblers quiet. This would be an easy job.

"I want to thank you for a most enjoyable visit. Your security measures are indeed noteworthy." He shook Mr. Hanford's hand. "I'll let you know the board's decision, but I must say I am very impressed. I foresee no difficulties in convincing them Bear River would be a perfect location."

Early the next morning, JJ let the members of his gang into his room. They snuck in, one at a time. JJ and Kid sat in the chairs by his dresser, Gus and Bob sat on the bed and Paul on the floor.

"All right, Paul," JJ said.

"The horses are ready. The livery stable is near the back alley that runs behind the bank. The barber says a shipment got here yesterday. Said it was a hundred and fifty thousand dollars, another man said only eighty."

Kid swore. "Still a lot of money either way."

"You stay with the horses tonight, Paul," JJ said. "Make sure they're ready when we need them. What about the extra horses?"

"They're waiting right where you said," Paul said.

"How about you, Gus, Bob?"

"Didn't hear nothing we didn't already know," Gus said. "Sheriff Porter's not due back 'til next week sometime, and the lawman the sheriff sent for isn't expected until tomorrow."

JJ stood and paced as nervous energy took over. He had a strange feeling gnawing at him. What was he missing? "All right, Bob, you be a lookout at the general store. Gus, you're in front of the hotel. You both should have a clear view of the bank." He stopped pacing and spun toward Kid. "When do they make their rounds?"

"Every two hours. We should have a clear shot after eleven-thirty."

"There's a tree at the rear of the bank we can climb. We'll go through the roof," JJ said. "Once we break in, it shouldn't take too long. They have a Diebold, 1870. We'll take our places around midnight."

The church bell struck midnight. The road was empty with only a half moon lighting their path. JJ waited a couple of minutes to make sure the rest of the gang was in place before he and Kid started toward the bank.

"Hold it right there."

JJ froze. The voice was Sheriff Porter's, but he wasn't even supposed to be in town. He swallowed the lump in his throat and turned slowly.

Porter, Deputy Mark, and a dozen other men stepped out of their hiding places behind wagons, in alleys, on roofs, and in doorways, all with their guns drawn. JJ raised his hands.

"Gus, Bob," Sheriff Porter called out. "Get over there with JJ and Kid."

They did as they were told.

Sheriff Porter drew closer, his peacemaker in hand. "Where's the younger one, Paul?"

"Sick," Kid said. "He left for home this morning."

Porter smirked. "We figured out you were listening on the telegraph, so we used it to trap you."

JJ groaned. Something inside had told him this was too easy, but he thought he was being so smart. His own arrogance had tripped him up.

Mr. Hanford stepped toward him, looking like a pigeon the way he puffed out. "That's right. There isn't any eighty thousand dollars. We were all in on it."

An explosion near the livery shook the ground. Some men turned toward the barn and looked in all directions. Others fell to the ground and covered their heads or jumped behind water troughs, crates, and wagons.

Paul appeared through the dust, struggling with their spooked horses. JJ and the gang rushed toward him and leaped in the saddles, and the five of them rode off as fast as they could.

The sound of gunshots whizzed past JJ's ear. Gus jerked, fell off his horse, and lay motionless in the dirt. Then Bob fell and sat in the street holding his arm. JJ pulled hard on the reins to turn his horse back.

"Go!" Bob yelled. "Nothing you can do."

JJ spun his colt again, but in the corner of his eye, Paul's chestnut fell to the ground. Paul jumped up, but men surrounded him before JJ could get to him.

They galloped away from the barrage of bullets. JJ felt sick at the thought of leaving his men behind.

Chapter Twenty-Five

Sheriff Drew Porter bellowed, "Stop." He ran in front of the men who were shooting. "That's enough. We don't want to kill them."

A dirty man with rotten teeth ran up to him, a Winchester rifle in his hands. "Speak for yourself, Sheriff. They ruined me, and I'm going to make them pay."

Drew grabbed the rifle from him. "Mark, saddle two horses quick. If they get to the river, we'll lose their trail."

Mark ran to the livery stable.

Drew rushed to Gus and leaned down. "This one's dead. Steve, get him out of the street." He waved toward Bob and Paul and threw a key to another man. "Ben, get them over to the jail, and get the doc to look at them."

Mark brought out the horses. They spurred them in the direction JJ and Kid had taken.

Drew kicked his horse to a gallop to get to the river in time.

JJ and Kid rode as fast as they could out of town. JJ's heart still hammered in his ears as they reached the canyon wall.

They dismounted, hit the horses on the rump and yelled, "Yaaah." The horses ran off toward the river. Edging backwards around the side of the canyon, they brushed the ground with a tree limb until they got to a clearing with five saddled horses waiting for them.

JJ patted his bay and rested his head on the mane. "I know we can't help them, but I have to know what happened, especially to Paul."

"It's a powerful risk," Kid said.

"It's dark. They won't see us if we sneak in from the side and get to the back of the jail. After we know, we'll leave."

Kid nodded and they rode to the outskirts of town, tied up their horses, and lurked through the side alley near the jail.

JJ started to peek in the jail window when he heard a commotion coming from Main Street in front of the bank.

They skulked into the shadows near where the alley intersected the street. A crowd pressed toward the bank. Lanterns and torches cast an eerie glow on the storefronts. JJ took a step back so the crowd wouldn't spot them, but he was sure he didn't have to worry. They were all focused on something else.

He took a risk and stepped a little closer, but the crowd blocked his view. All he could see was a few feet down the street where Gus' bullet-riddled body posed next to the undertaker's.

All the holes in Gus' chest reminded JJ of that day when his family was killed. His throat ached. By next week, a photograph of Gus' corpse would be in every newspaper in the West.

A low roar of voices filled the air as more people pressed in, all facing the bank and stretching their necks to catch a glimpse of whatever was happening. Kid stepped out of the shadows and stood beside him. The noise stopped.

The bank manager called out loud enough to be heard by everyone. "Bob and Paul Franklin, we, the vigilante committee of Bear River, find you guilty of bank robbery and sentence you to hang by the neck until dead."

The crowd cheered.

A lead weight hit JJ in the gut.

Kid started toward them.

JJ grabbed his arm and pulled him into the shadows. "There's nothing we can do. We can't save them. We'll get hanged too."

"Maybe it's what we deserve," he said thickly. "Paul's only eighteen. They never killed anybody."

"I know, Kid, but all we can do is watch."

"Maybe we could ride out and get Sheriff Porter. He'd stop this." Kid took his hat off and threw it to the ground. "I don't care if we go to jail."

"He's too far out by now." JJ's throat felt tight as if the noose were around his neck. "We couldn't get him here in time."

Two hangmen's ropes were flung across the scaffolds sticking out of the roof of the bank. Bob and Paul were lifted onto something. Hands placed nooses around their necks.

"No, this can't be happening." Kid's Adam's apple bulged. "This isn't fair."

JJ's voice choked up. "So, when's life ever been fair?"

Another voice came from the crowd. "Paul, do you have any last words?"

Paul stood there, his jaw set, with the rope around his neck. "I'm guilty, no getting around it. Lord, forgive me. I wish I'd made the decision to serve You before now, but I know I'll be seeing You soon."

Paul jerked and fell. He hung from the rope, his feet kicking.

"Nooooo." Kid groaned as he turned his head away.

Paul's body twitched, feet still kicking, until the jerking finally stopped. The crowd cheered.

Bile rose in JJ's throat. He wanted to look away, but he forced himself not to. He owed it to them to witness what was happening.

The banker bellowed again. "How about you, Bob? You have any last words?"

"It's not right, you doing this." Bob's eyes darted around. "We never hurt anybody. We just stole money from them who could afford it. It's not right. It's not right."

Bob's body fell, then jerked and hung from the rope with the same jolting motions.

JJ didn't wait for it to stop this time. He'd seen enough. He wiped the back of his hand across his mouth. "We have to get out of here."

Kid nodded and picked up his hat.

As they made their way to their horses, JJ heard the cheers.

JJ moved his fork through his eggs but didn't manage to latch onto a bite. He and Kid had arrived at the cabin the night before, but neither of them slept or talked.

A monarch butterfly perched on the windowsill.

"Did you hear what Paul said?" Kid pushed his plate away. "He asked God to forgive him."

"Yeah, I heard." JJ took a sip of coffee to keep his throat from crackling.

Kid's voice thickened. "Do you think God did?"

"Yeah, I do."

"Do you think God would forgive us if we asked Him?"

Tears formed in JJ's eyes. He wiped his face to keep them from being shed. "You remember what Ma used to say?"

"No… No, I remember a lot of what Pa said, but I only remember Ma tucking me into bed at night and singing. She had such a pretty voice. So long ago."

"Ma said, 'If you ever stray from the right road, God is merciful. Turn to Him, and He'll direct your paths.'"

Kid covered his face with his hands.

"I believe Ma." JJ fell on his knees and sobbed for the first time since his parents died. "God, forgive me. This is all my fault. I was so angry when they died. I've sinned and turned from You. Please, forgive me."

Kid dropped to the floor.

A flood of warmth, forgiveness, and love filled JJ's emptiness, guilt, and grief. He stayed on his knees as a peace he'd never known swept over him. Tears flowed, and he surrendered everything to God.

After a long time, he wiped his eyes with his sleeve and turned to Kid. "I don't know what to do. We're still wanted, but we can't ever go back to outlawing again."

Kid's Adam's apple bulged. "Who says we have to do anything for a while? There are enough supplies to last a year. Why don't we stay put for a spell before we figure all that out?"

"We don't have a Bible," JJ said. "We need a Bible."

"We can buy Bibles in South Pass City, maybe even go to church Sunday." Kid pulled himself to his feet and offered JJ a hand. "You going to have a talk with Mercy while we're there?"

"Yeah." JJ swallowed the lump in his throat. "I have to tell her what happened."

"It's a hard thing. I know you love her."

"I do. That's why I have to tell her good-bye."

JJ gulped back his nervousness as he and Kid stepped into the South Pass Holiness Church and slipped into the back row. The church looked a lot like the one he used to attend in Lawrence when he was a boy: wooden benches to sit on, a Franklin stove, a piano, an anxiety bench, and a wooden pulpit in the front.

People wandered in, and JJ twiddled his thumbs as they greeted each other. He remembered how Ma and Pa used to get on him for fidgeting in church and placed his hands in his lap. His foot started tapping, and he forced himself to stop that too. Try as he might, he couldn't sit still. He didn't know how his brother managed it.

A couple of men dressed like cowboys greeted them with a handshake and a smile. JJ was grateful for their kindness since most of those who came in turned their heads and walked by without saying anything. He didn't blame them. Everyone in town knew who they were.

The preacher glided to the pulpit with his black robe swaying. He wore a stern look on his face and kept his focus on the front of the church. When he reached the pulpit, his eyes locked onto JJ's.

JJ had been an outlaw for years now and had perfected a look of striking fear in the hearts of others. He now knew what it was like to be on the receiving side.

The preacher marched toward them. "You're not welcome in my church."

"I understand your concern," JJ said, feeling more like a scolded child than a dangerous outlaw. "We're not here to cause trouble. We got right with God a week ago."

"Are you planning on turning yourself into the law?"

"No… maybe… I don't know."

"Until you're ready to receive the punishment for your sins, you haven't really repented, and I don't want you here." The preacher crossed his arms. "If you don't leave now, I'll send for the sheriff."

They collected their things and stumbled out the door. Guilt weighed JJ down like a tree had fallen on him. He couldn't catch his breath. Every sin he ever committed pointed him in the face.

He ambled to his bay and buried his face in the mane. "You think there's a church in town that will have us?"

"They all know who we are and what we've done," Kid said. "Seems like God's more forgiving than some church folk."

"I don't blame them. We sinned so much it's hard to believe God saved us from all of it."

"I believe He chased us down until we stopped running."

Peace swept over JJ as he considered that. "Come on. We still have some things to take care of."

They strode to the general store.

Brian, the clerk, nodded in their direction. "What can I do you for today?"

"Not much today," JJ said. "We want a couple of Bibles."

"Bibles?" Brian raised his eyebrow. "You two?"

JJ grinned, a little embarrassed. "Yep, we got right with God. We're giving up outlawing."

"Well, isn't that something," Brian said. "My wife is always saying she's praying for you two. She says you're too kind and polite to be outlaws."

"Thank her for us, and tell her to keep praying."

"Here." Brian handed them two large Bibles. "No charge. Good luck to you both."

JJ nodded.

"Thank you," Kid said.

They left the store and placed the Bibles in their saddlebags.

Mercy ran toward JJ and threw her arms around him.

Kid excused himself and walked his horse toward the road back to the hideout.

JJ pulled her in close and leaned his face into her hair. He tilted his face toward hers and kissed her, knowing it would be their last.

She pulled back and gazed into his eyes. "Did you get the money?"

"Mercy." He struggled to find the words. "It was an ambush. We barely escaped. The others didn't make it."

"No." She splayed her hand over her chest.

"We're leaving town. We'll probably end up turning ourselves in to the law."

Her eyes welled up. "Why would you do that? You got away."

He glanced down. He wanted to tell her he loved her. He wanted to marry her, but he couldn't. "We made things right with God."

She pulled away. "I see how it is now. You don't want me anymore because you became one of those holier-than-thou church goers, and I'm still a saloon girl. I told you this would happen." Her words were as sharp as barbed wire.

"No." He grasped her hands.

She tried to pull them away, but he wouldn't let her.

Somehow, he had to make her understand. "I'm the one in the wrong here. I'm sorry for hurting you, but I don't have a choice. You won't ever have a chance of a better life if I let you come with me, and I love you too much to let you do it."

She pulled away and wiped the tears from her face.

He didn't want to leave her like this, in this town, with no hope of ever getting out. *Lord, how can I help her?* He took the money sack from his saddlebag and stuffed it in Mercy's hand.

Leaning forward, he kissed her cheek lingering near her for a moment longer than he should. "Take this and make a new start where nobody knows you. Trust God to help you."

She looked in the bag. "This is a lot of money in here, enough to run off together where nobody's ever heard of you."

He wiped a tear off her cheek with his thumb. "It's too late for that."

She wrapped her arms around herself pulling the bag close to her chest. "Even if you don't take me with you, please don't turn yourself in."

"I'll miss you." He wanted to tell her he would never stop loving her, but he didn't have the right. He turned and walked to where Kid held the horses.

"You know that's all the money we have left," Kid said.

"I know." JJ glanced back to where she stood in the middle of the street watching him, tears streaming from her eyes.

Kid placed his hand on his brother's shoulder. "I'm glad you gave it to her. Didn't feel right keeping money we stole anyhow."

JJ squelched the longing to run back into Mercy's waiting arms. Making things right wasn't easy.

Chapter Twenty-Six

Kid ran his hand across his new Bible and opened it to the first page. The smell of the leather binding stirred his insides. He was grateful for the forgiveness he received from God, but he had a hard time figuring what this meant for him and his brother.

JJ thumbed through the pages. "Pa always said it's easier to start with the New Testament."

"Fine by me."

JJ stared at the page. "Do you think that preacher's right, that we need to turn ourselves in?"

"Maybe." Kid hoped not. "When I fell on my knees a week ago, I know God heard me and forgave me. It felt… I never had a feeling like that since that Sunday before Ma and Pa died."

"Me, either." The muscle in JJ's jaw twitched. "We deserve prison."

"Maybe God's going to give us better than we deserve."

"Whatever He wants is fine by me."

Kid's stomach knotted. He wanted to surrender his fate to God, to obey Him, but going to prison for twenty years?

Months passed as they stayed in the cabin and had daily Bible studies. The weather grew colder.

Kid stood at the window. Leaves on the aspen trees had turned yellow and many had fallen to the ground. Wind gusts blew them across the field in front of the cabin. Dark clouds loomed over the mountain. A squirrel scurried up one tree with a nut in his mouth.

Kid sat at the table across from his brother. "Looks like a snowstorm's brewing."

He opened his Bible to Philippians, but he couldn't concentrate on the verses. He had prayed every day for God to help him accept whatever happened, but every time he thought he'd won the battle, a gust of doubt would blow in, and he'd start praying for God to get him out of this.

JJ cleared his throat. "You know how it says in Philippians, 'I am apprehended of Christ?'"

"Yeah," Kid said.

"Well isn't that another word for arrested?"

Heat rose to the back of his neck. Arrested by God. Twenty years in prison. He headed for the door. "I'm going for a walk."

"Wait," JJ said.

Kid flashed him an icy glare.

"You forgot your coat."

Kid grabbed his sheepskin jacket off the hook and slammed the door on his way out. The brisk air burned his cheeks as he marched toward the creek. A breeze blew the yellow leaves on the path in front of him. He watched the storm clouds closing in.

A blast of cold air shot through him, and sheets of snow fell. Blizzards like this one brewed quickly in the Wind River Mountains, but he wasn't about to go back. He was too angry.

He shook his fist at the sky and shouted, "I'm not going to be arrested by You or anyone else. I don't want to go to jail."

A gust swirled around him, and he fastened his jacket. It was stupid to leave without a muffler and some gloves. Turning toward the cabin, he squinted to make out the image through the whiteout but couldn't see it through the snow. He cupped his hands over his mouth to warm them, stuck them in his pockets, and headed back.

A short breath burned his lungs. He tried to get his bearings, walking straight ahead, one foot in front of the other. His fingers grew numb, and his cheeks stung. This had to be the right way. If he walked in a straight line… he couldn't tell. He might have veered off course.

He couldn't feel his hands and cheeks anymore. One foot, then the other. The snow grew deeper, and each step weighed him down a little further. Was he going the right way?

"God, please help me." It felt foolish to be calling out to the God he had been yelling at a few moments earlier.

He heard something above the roar of the wind. Very faint, then louder. Gunshots. He moved a little faster now despite the burning in his toes until he collided with the cabin. He felt his way against the walls until a hand pulled him through the door.

He stumbled over to the fireplace and plopped onto the floor.

JJ holstered his gun and grabbed a quilt. "You need to get out of those wet clothes."

Kid removed his boots and undressed. JJ wrapped blankets around him, and he shivered by the fire trying to get warm. The sound of the crackling blaze and the wind howling outside were the only things that disturbed the silence.

JJ sat in the chair, rocking, his lips pressed together in a thin line.

Kid's voice slipped through chattering teeth. "Go on. Say it."

"You could have been killed straying that far from the cabin with a storm brewing. What's gotten into you?"

"I was mad."

JJ grabbed another blanket and wrapped it around him, then poured him a cup of hot coffee and handed it to him. "Why?"

Kid cupped his hands around the mug and took a sip. It felt good going down his throat. "When you read that part about God arresting us… I'm still trying to figure a way out of it."

"Prison?"

The shivering started to calm. "I'm not proud of what we did, but… How come you're not squawking about it?"

JJ sat on the floor beside Kid. "I don't like it, but it's what we deserve. We've been trying to get out of this hole we dug ever since we robbed that store in Hunt's Peak. All we did was dig ourselves in deeper. Well, not this time. I'm done. I surrendered myself to God, and He's the only one who gets to decide what happens now even if it does mean prison."

Kid pulled the blankets in tighter. He tied in with the Franklin boys to keep Marshal Cook from arresting them. Now he'd done a lot worse and caused a lot more pain – one man shot to death, two more lynched, families who lost everything because of what he stole.

JJ was right. He deserved a lot worse than prison, but God had still forgiven him. Wasn't that enough?

He bowed his head. "I surrender."

Kid looked out the window and let out a sigh. Drifts still covered the landscape, but he could see patches of grass peeking through in places. Another month or two and it would be time to leave.

It had been the worst winter they'd had since coming to Wind River, with one blizzard after another buffeting the cabin. They'd run out of coffee and meat, and their wood pile was almost gone, but he wouldn't have missed it. They had had time alone with God, time they needed to prepare for what was coming.

He'd made peace about prison. In a way, he looked forward to it. They needed to get on with their lives, and that meant squaring things with the law. It was justice.

Go to Hunt's Peak.

Kid bristled. He knew he'd heard right, but it didn't make sense.

He needed to be sure before he said anything to JJ.

That night, what he heard kept rolling around in his mind. Maybe he was still trying to figure a way out of prison. He didn't think so. Why Hunt's Peak?

When he drifted to sleep, he saw a man. He couldn't make out his face, but the man called to him. "I'm in Hunt's Peak."

Kid woke with a start, his heart beating in his chest.

Yellow warbonnets dotted the land around the river. The mallard ducks returned north, filling the air with the sound of flapping wings and quacking as they rode along the path leading out of the hideout. Kid took one last look. This had been their home for the last five years, and he would never see it again.

They headed toward a nearby ranch where they sold the extra horses. Then they rode to Saint Mary's Station and bought supplies they needed before heading to Hunt's Peak.

Hunt's Peak. He didn't know why they were headed there, but when he told his brother about what he'd heard and about his dream, JJ said he'd had the same dream.

They'd only been Christians for a few months now, but Kid had read lots of places in the Bible where God spoke to people in dreams, so that was where they were headed.

The Wind River Mountains to his right stretched as far as he could see. A stream created by the snowmelt ran down the ridge and emptied into a lake. "It's kind of nice."

"What's kind of nice?" JJ said.

"Oh, being able to ride our horses through here at a pace where we get to see all the beauty God created."

A familiar thunder sounded in the background, and Kid glanced back at the large dust cloud pursuing them. They swatted their horses to full gallop away from the oncoming posse.

Kid yelled over the roar. "How do you think they knew we were here?"

"Maybe someone at the ranch knows us," JJ said. "You think we should stop and wait for them?"

"No, God told us to go to Hunt's Peak, and that's what I aim to do, posse or no posse."

Despite their determination, the posse drove them southwest instead of southeast. When they pushed far enough to be out of sight, they rode through Sandy River to hide their tracks. By nightfall, they were able to lose the lawmen. They stopped to make a cold camp.

"I'll take the first watch," Kid said. "I'll wake you in four hours."

JJ nodded and climbed into his bedroll.

Kid walked around the campsite, making sure everything was secure. Looking at the vast expanse of stars adorning the sky, he felt God's hand in it even though they'd rode in the wrong direction all day.

The only way to avoid the posse now was to ride toward Green River, the town they'd almost destroyed.

The next morning, the posse caught up with them again, and they had to ride hard to evade it. Early the next day, a deluge drenching the ground covered their tracks, and they lost the men chasing them.

They rode a little farther, and the torrent stopped, but clouds still darkened the sky and released enough moisture to drizzle like a leaky pump.

Kid adjusted himself in the saddle but couldn't get comfortable. The oil duster he wore hadn't kept the rain from seeping into his clothes and boots. "God, this isn't funny."

JJ chuckled.

"I have an idea."

"What's that?" JJ dumped the water out of the brim of his hat and put it back on his head.

"Nobody in Green River ever got a good look at us.

"So."

"Once we get there, we could check into the hotel."

JJ glared sideways at Kid. "You crazy? We robbed the Green River Bank twice in one month, and we held up the payroll train going there three times that same summer."

"Yeah, but like I said, they never got a look at us, and that beard you grew over the winter makes you look different."

"Not that different, and you don't have a beard, and that handlebar mustache you grew doesn't cover your face at all. The townsfolk there would like nothing better than to get that reward on our heads to make up for the trouble we caused them. They might even lynch us."

Heat rose up Kid's back. "I don't care." He was in a foul mood, and he knew he shouldn't take it out on his brother, but he couldn't help himself. "I'm tired and saddle-sore, and I'm soaked from this rain God keeps pouring on my head. I'd be more than willing to serve twenty years in the Wyoming Territorial Prison just for a hot meal, a bath, and a soft bed."

"It's bad enough we're even in the area."

"Come on. Don't you want to be dry and warm, let alone get good food in your stomach? It's another week to Hunt's Peak, and I'm done in from running from that posse."

A monarch butterfly flittered around them and landed on a nearby bush.

JJ stroked his beard and looked in the distance.

Kid's foul mood dissolved. When JJ looked like that, he was about to give in. "Just for tonight?"

"Oh, all right."

JJ sounded annoyed, but Kid knew better.

They rode into town and stopped at the Field Hotel.

"Good day, gentlemen," the hotel clerk said. "It looks like you were caught out in the rain."

"You got that right," Kid said.

"We'd like a room and two baths." JJ dipped the pen in ink to sign the registrar. He paused for a moment then signed and handed the pen to Kid.

Kid looked at the book, and his chest tightened. His brother had signed his real name, Joshua Jackson. He felt a check inside. It was lying to sign the wrong name. *Lord, whatever happens is in Your hands.* He signed his real name.

The hotel clerk didn't even look, just handed them the keys. Kid let up a silent prayer that the clerk didn't decide to take a closer look later.

When they entered the room and closed the door, he turned to JJ. "Do you think it's a good idea signing our real names?"

"Nope." JJ pulled off his boots. "But I'm not lying anymore."

Kid let out a sigh. "Maybe we can at least get a good night's sleep before the clerk checks our names and goes for the sheriff."

Chapter Twenty-Seven

The next morning, JJ sat at a corner table in the hotel dining room reading the newspaper and drinking his coffee while his brother devoured his eggs, pancakes, smoked ham, biscuits and gravy, and coffee.

A young waitress poured him some more coffee, and he looked up long enough to nod his appreciation. He turned the page, and his eyes set on the name, Sheriff Drew Porter. "Uh oh!" So, Porter was the sheriff in Green River now. If he saw them, they'd never make it to Hunt's Peak.

Kid glanced to where he was pointing and stood. "Let's go now before Sheriff Porter starts making his rounds."

JJ' shoulders slumped and followed his brother up the stairs to their room to get their things. They rode out of town at full gallop for about two miles before they relaxed and slowed their horses to a trot.

Kid pointed to a group of children playing near an old mine. JJ smiled as he watched the four boys and three girls chasing each other. His good mood slipped when he read the sign in front of the boarded-up mine shaft.

CONDEMNED BY ORDER OF MINING COMMISSION

Dirt and pieces of rock fell from the rotten timber as if to show why.

"That mine looks like it's going to cave in any minute," Kid said, "especially with the rain we've been having."

The children chased each other into the cave opening.

JJ's heart skipped a beat. "We need to get them out of there."

They dismounted and ran to the mine. Kid brushed past JJ and dashed through the opening.

The ground rumbled and shook as dirt and rocks crashed down in front of him. "Kid, look out!" A piece of the mountain plummeted, blocking him from the children and his brother.

He coughed, shook himself, and looked around. In front of him, a barrage of dirt and rocks obstructed the way.

"Kid, can you hear me?" No answer. "Kid!"

He fought back the panic. He had to think clearly if he wanted to get anyone out alive. He found a rock and pounded it on the stone blocking the entrance. He listened, holding his breath.

Pounding came from the other side. JJ took a second for it to sink in and decided what to do next. He beat the rock again, this time using Morse code.

Kid's head hurt, not bad, but it was so dark… no light coming in at all. That couldn't be good. No light meant no air.

He called out. "Everybody all right?"

A voice sounded in the darkness. "Yeah, but I can't see."

Another voice broke through sobs. "Me too."

Three more voices. Then only silence. That left two unaccounted for. Kid reassured them with a calm voice. "Stay where you are. Everything's going to be okay."

A tapping pounded on the rock wall he leaned against. Kid felt around for a rock and hammered out dots and dashes to answer to JJ's question.

Five kids accounted for. Not hurt bad. No opening I can see. Don't know how much air.

JJ blew out a breath and found a piece of wood to use for digging, but the boulder was too big for him to break it up without tools. He needed help quick and supplies – shovels, pickaxes, maybe even dynamite.

The only town close enough to get the aid in time was Green River, and any rescue attempt would involve Sheriff Porter. He beat on the rock saying he would be back soon.

If dynamite was needed, he wanted to be the one to set the charges. He wasn't going to trust his brother's life to anybody else. He would have to come up with a plan to get Sheriff Porter to let him help with the rescue attempt or his brother and those children were as good as dead.

Before Drew could react to the sudden burst through his door, he looked into the barrel of a Remington army revolver in the hands of JJ Jackson. He had a full beard, but Drew would know him anywhere.

"Are you alone, Sheriff?" JJ glanced at the back room.

Drew groaned. "Yeah."

"Sheriff Porter, sit down. I need help, and I don't have much time to explain."

He raised an eyebrow. He couldn't believe he'd be helping JJ anytime soon or ever.

"The mine outside of town collapsed." JJ gouged at the back of his neck. "My brother and seven children are trapped, and I need men and equipment to get them out."

Drew leaned forward and drew a fist to his mouth. "I'll do everything I can, but the only place you're going is in one of those jail cells."

"Sheriff, you let me come along and help in any way I can, and when it's all over, I'll turn myself in."

"What about Kid? If he survives, will he turn himself in too?"

The muscle in JJ's jaw twitched. "Na, but you can't tell me this town wouldn't be happy with at least one of us behind bars. After all, I was the one who planned those bank and train jobs."

"No deal. Once I arrest you, Kid will find a way to break you out. You hurt this town bad. They couldn't take that kind of pain."

"Sheriff Porter." JJ's voice softened a bit. "You may not believe me, but we gave up outlawing about a year ago. We're working hard to mend our ways."

Drew snorted.

"I'll give my word I won't try to escape, and you know I keep my word. How's that?"

"What if I don't agree?"

"Then there's no reason for me being here. You go ahead and do what you can, but you'll need someone on hand who's an expert with explosives. What do you say?"

Drew crossed his arms. It would take a week to get someone who knew what he was doing. In the meantime, with no food or water, those children would die. He had no choice.

JJ followed close behind as Sheriff Porter galloped off in the direction of the mine.

The sheriff raised his voice over the thunder of horses' hooves. "You really are something, saying you've given up outlawing."

"It's the honest truth. We came clean with God after the lynching."

"So, you got religion." Porter slowed his horse. "Well, let me tell you something. You'll never be the man your brother Jed is."

JJ pulled up on his reins and halted his horse. "How did you know about Jedidiah?"

Porter turned his horse and faced him. "He's the preacher in Hunt's Peak."

JJ's heart dropped to his stomach. "It couldn't be the same man. Jedidiah was killed in the war."

"I don't know where you heard that, but he showed up in Hunt's Peak looking for you a few days after you took off with the money you stole. Been praying for you ever since."

This had to be some kind of a trick. "If you know him, what's he look like?"

"Light brown hair, blue eyes like Kid, close to six feet tall, a cleft chin."

All the air left JJ's lungs.

"As far as you changing your ways, I don't believe it," Sheriff Porter said. "If it were true, you'd both turn yourselves in."

"Jedidiah's been alive all this time?"

"Yep." Sheriff Porter turned his horse away and rode toward the mine.

JJ swatted his horse and hurried to catch up.

Kid felt around in the dark until he gathered all the children close to him. One had awakened, but another lay unconscious, still breathing. He wished he could see to know how badly hurt she was. At least all seven were alive.

The darkness disturbed him in a way he didn't expect. He felt like he was falling at times and would set his hand on the ground to steady himself. The dampness caused a musty stale odor, but the hardest part was the closed in feeling like being buried alive.

The children whimpered and sniffled with an occasional sob.

Panic rose from his gut, but he squelched it. "I tell you what we're going to do. We're going to pray. Now all of you join hands."

He heard them fumbling. Two hands grabbed his. "Dear Lord, we know You can see us in this darkness, and we know You're bigger than this mountain. We're asking You to get us out of here safely and to help us not be afraid. Amen"

"I'm still scared," a girl's voice cried out.

"Well then, we'll just have to sing," Kid said. "You can't be afraid when you're praising God 'cause He's right there with you. Do you know *Jesus Loves Me?*"

"Everybody knows that song." A boy's voice pierced the darkness.

"Good. I want you all to sing it with me. 'Jesus loves me, this I know. For the Bible tells me so. Little ones to Him belong. They are weak but He is strong…'"

As he sang and prayed with the children, the presence of God calmed his fears, but the air grew thin, and it became harder to take a deep breath. He told the children to lie down and try to sleep, though he doubted they'd be able to.

He heard pounding on the rock.

Help here. Don't fret.

He pressed his lips together. There was only one place JJ could have gone, Green River and Sheriff Porter. He'd worry about that when they got out of here.

He pounded a message back with the rock. *Air thin. Not much time left.*

JJ inspected the work. A crew of men worked at the mine entrance with pickaxes and shovels, but little progress had been made with the boulder blocking the entrance. Little was the wrong word. They hadn't made a dent in it.

He strode to Sheriff Porter. "They don't have much air. These men aren't going to get through in time. We have to use dynamite."

"Get the charges set," Sheriff Porter said. "I'll tell the men to keep working. Maybe they'll get lucky."

JJ opened the crate and set the charges where the rock would crumble, causing the least impact to the mountain. *Lord, help me do this right.* When he was done, he turned to Sheriff Porter. "Everything's ready."

Porter cleared the men out of the mine.

"Are you sure this is going to work, Mr. Reddinger?" Isaiah Grayson, the father of a couple of the children, addressed JJ by the alias the sheriff had decided to call him.

Mr. Grayson dressed in a black morning suit, like a banker, and had an air of authority about him. "It sounds dangerous. What if the rest of the mine falls in on the children?"

JJ understood why the man was concerned. If he made a

mistake… A chill shot up his spine.

"Don't worry," Sheriff Porter said. "Mr. Reddinger's an expert at blowing things up. You can trust him to do this job as if his own brother were in there."

The irony didn't escape him, but he was too scared to get a chuckle out of it. He finished setting the fuse and tapped a message to Kid. *Get ready.* After lighting the fuse, he ran to the opening of the mine and jumped behind a rock. "Take cover." He didn't bother to look up to see if they listened to him.

First nothing. No sound, no shaking, not even the sound of breathing. Then, the explosion rumbled through the mountain. Smoke and debris flew out of the opening in cascades.

He ran through the dust cloud toward the entrance, his heart beating like a drum. Kid had to be all right. He had to be.

The haze thinned as his brother staggered out holding a little girl in his arms. Six other children clung to him as he led them out of the mine.

Mr. Grayson took the child from Kid's arms and hurried her to the doctor. Sheriff Porter ushered the other children into the arms of their mothers. The rest of the crowd rushed toward JJ and Kid, shook their hands, and slapped them on the back.

Kid fell to the ground and gasped for air.

The doctor and Sheriff Porter huddled together in conversation over the little girl. Porter stepped in front of JJ to face the crowd. "Sarah's going to be fine, just a bump on the head."

A flurry of shouts and hurrahs.

The sheriff held up his hands to silence them. "Let's give these men room to catch their breath. We'll have a chance to give them what they deserve later." He turned and caught JJ's eye.

JJ nodded, fully aware of the double meaning.

The crowd dissipated, leaving in small groups until only JJ, Kid, Mr. Grayson, and Sheriff Porter stood in the clearing.

Mr. Grayson placed his hand on JJ's shoulder. "I'll never forget what you did here." He strode to his wagon where his family was waiting. He turned, tipped his hat, and rode off.

JJ let out a sigh.

"Don't think this lets you off the hook." Porter pointed a finger in his chest. "If these people knew who you were, they wouldn't be thanking you with a pat on the back. You have ten minutes to say your goodbyes, then I want you in my office. Don't make me come looking for you." He tromped off.

JJ turned to his brother, reached out a hand to help him up, and grabbed him in a bear hug. It didn't matter what happened now.

Kid hugged him for a moment then placed his hand on JJ's shoulder. "What kind of deal did you make with him?"

"It was worth it. You're alive. Now you can go to Hunt's Peak."

"What do you mean, I can go to Hunt's Peak? We're going there together."

JJ swallowed the lump in his throat. "I hurt this town a lot."

"In case you forgot, you didn't rob them all by yourself. I was there too."

"Yeah, you were the one who kept telling me we shouldn't rob the same bank twice in a month, but I was too stubborn to listen, felt like I had to prove something."

"Maybe," Kid said. "But what in the Sam Hill does that have to do with the bargain you made with Sheriff Porter?"

He turned his back, not sure he could keep it together if he looked at Kid.

"JJ, tell me." Kid circled until he faced him. "Now!"

"I told him..." He kneaded the back of his neck. "I told him if he'd let me help with the rescue and if he'd let you go, I'd turn myself in. I gave my word."

"You can't." Kid paused for a moment. "Unless you reckon it's time to face up to it. I'm not leaving you to do this alone."

"That's not all." He tried to find the right words. "Jedidiah's alive. He's a preacher in Hunt's Peak, started a church over there. Kid, he's been looking for us."

Kid stared at him with his mouth open. "If he's alive, we both need to go. How are we going to get you out of this?"

"I can't. Sheriff Porter worried you'd try to break me out of jail. I gave my word I wouldn't escape."

Kid's steel-blue eyes narrowed.

"It was the only way Sheriff Porter would agree to let you go free." JJ placed his hand on Kid's shoulder. "I guess this is good-bye."

"You're not doing this."

"What?"

"You have to be with me when we see Jedidiah. I'll flatten you and drag you along if I have to."

JJ furrowed his brow. "You want me to break my word?"

Chapter Twenty-Eight

Drew looked at his pocket watch. JJ should be coming through his office door any time now.

The door opened and JJ walked in.

Drew stood propped against the wall with a peacemaker in hand. "Before we do this, I didn't have anything to do with the Franklin brothers getting lynched."

"Never thought you did." JJ unbuckled his gun belt, handed it to him and stepped inside the nearest cell.

Drew clanged the door shut and locked it. He sat in his desk chair and leaned back. JJ Jackson was now in custody. A satisfaction swept over him. It had been years since he started hunting JJ. He'd sleep well tonight.

Let him go free.

Drew jerked up. He glanced toward the cell. JJ was pacing back and forth. He hadn't said anything. Drew couldn't have heard right. God would never tell him to free a criminal like JJ.

Let him go free.

No. Even if this was God's voice speaking to his spirit, he would never set JJ free, not after all the harm he had caused.

The next morning, Kid watched from a hidden alcove as a crowd gathered at the Green River Community Church.

A woman with a green gingham dress waved a greeting to another woman and stepped over to her. "Martha, I was so worried. How are your young'uns?"

"They're fine. Oh Hattie, I don't reckon I've ever been that scared in all my born days. If it hadn't been for those two young outlaws..." Martha wiped an eye with her handkerchief.

Hattie patted her arm. "I heard Kid Jackson had them all hold hands while he prayed for them."

Martha's voice choked up. "My Sally said he had them sing *Jesus Loves Me*."

"You'd think he was a Christian."

Mr. Grayson stepped into the church. A man dressed in a grey sack suit rushed over to him and shook his hand. "Sir, how are your two young'uns?"

"No worse for wear. Sarah's on the mend, just has a slight headache."

"It surprised me the Jackson brothers risked getting caught for a few kids."

"JJ and Kid saved their lives, all right," Mr. Grayson said. "And I mean to tell the newspapers and my father-in-law what they did. JJ gave his word he would turn himself in if Sheriff Porter let him help with the rescue, and he kept it. He's in the jail as we speak."

"That's amazing, an outlaw keeping his word like that."

Two women chatted as they sat down.

"Claire, did you hear? They have JJ Jackson in jail. He surrendered to Sheriff Porter."

"I know. I hear tell Sheriff Porter wouldn't have even known about the mine accident if JJ hadn't told him."

"I reckon the Jackson brothers have made up for all the crimes they've done in this town."

The church bell rang, and the crowd found their seats. Kid pressed in behind them and stood in the doorway. The preacher brushed by him on the way to the pulpit.

"Excuse me, Preacher," Kid said. "I hate to be interrupting your service, but I wonder if I might have a word with you good folks. My name's Jonathan… Kid Jackson."

A dimple creased the preacher's cheek. "After what you and your brother did for the children in this town, the least we can do is hear you out. Please come forward."

Kid didn't know what to say, but he had to try. He let up a silent prayer for God to give him the words. "I'm here to plead for my brother's life 'cause twenty years in prison's mighty close to being a life sentence."

Mr. Grayson stood up. "I, for one, would be willing to help in any way, but I don't know what we can do."

Kid wiped his hands on his trousers and looked at the congregation. "Last fall, we made our peace with the Lord. We planned to turn ourselves in to the law, but God told us to go to Hunt's Peak down Colorado way first, and that's where we were heading when the cave-in happened. My brother went to get help from Sheriff Porter."

He pulled on his collar. Maybe this was a mistake. Why would they listen to him, an outlaw? "I could try to get JJ out of this if he'd let me, but he won't hear of it 'cause he gave his word he wouldn't escape. But if the town puts pressure on Sheriff Porter to release him from his promise…"

An elderly woman stood up. "Other outlaws got religion, and it didn't take. Those who did really get saved were willing to face up to what they did. It doesn't set right helping JJ Jackson escape."

Kid glanced at the preacher and then to the pulpit where a Bible lay. *Lord, give me the words.* "We gave up outlawing, a year ago, when we bowed our knees to God. Now I'm not denying we deserve prison, but God told us to go to Hunt's Peak first.

"Now, we know why. Sheriff Porter told JJ our brother is there. He's been praying for us. All these years…" He cleared his throat. "We thought he was dead. After we see him, I have little doubt we'll be back here accepting whatever we have coming."

He picked up the Bible. "This book talks about God giving each of us mercy and grace when we turn to Him, and confess our sins, and go about changing things. Isn't that what this here church is all about?"

Mr. Grayson, the banker, the preacher, and half a dozen others burst into the sheriff's office. Drew lifted an eyebrow and set down his coffee cup. Whatever they wanted, he would fight to the death before he let another man get lynched in his town.

"We want to talk to you about JJ Jackson outside," Rev. Barnes said.

The sheriff grabbed his yellow boy Winchester and followed them out onto the street where the entire town gathered around him.

Rev. Barnes cleared his throat. "We hear JJ gave his word to turn himself in so he could help rescue his brother and those children from the mine."

"Yep, and he kept it." Drew delivered a stony glare, hoping it would give them pause. "I have him in a jail cell, right now."

"We want you to release him from his promise not to escape."

Drew's jaw dropped. They couldn't mean it. "If I do that, Kid Jackson's going to break him out of jail." He scanned the crowd and saw Kid in the back. What was he up to? "In case you forgot, he hasn't been arrested. He's standing right back there."

Kid at least had enough shame to lower his eyes.

"That's right," Rev. Barnes said. "We want you to come to

church with us and leave your office unlocked and the keys on the desk."

"Are you crazy? That's JJ Jackson in there. You remember, the outlaw, the one who robbed the town, not once, but twice, not more than two years ago? Remember JJ, who wasn't content with all the money he got from the town bank, so he robbed the payroll train bringing money into the town three times? That JJ Jackson? That's the no-account outlaw you want me to let prance out of here?"

"That's right," Rev. Barnes said. "He's made up for everything he's done to this town when he sacrificed himself for those children trapped in that mine. We want you to release him from his promise and look the other way. Do it for this town you swore to protect."

Drew crossed his arms. "And what if I don't?"

Mr. Grayson stepped forward. "Sheriff Porter, it would be a shame for a career lawman, such as yourself, to lose his job like you did in Bear River."

Heat rose to the back of his neck. He didn't care how important Mr. Grayson was. He was the law, and he wouldn't let anyone intimidate him any more than he allowed the banker and vigilante committee in Bear River off the hook for murder after the lynching. "I could go somewhere else. I have before."

"Be that as it may, you might find it difficult if certain people were to spread word it would not be in a town's best interest to hire you."

"Are you threatening me?"

"Not at all." Mr. Grayson placed a hand on Drew's shoulder. "Look, you're a decent man, and you've been a good sheriff. Forget what I said. I didn't mean to browbeat you, but when the law and doing the right thing aren't the same, you're a good man who'll listen to the Lord."

Amy, his wife, come out from the crowd. His face flushed as she took hold of his hand. She was in on this? "Drew, what is God telling you?"

Everything in him said this was wrong, but he'd only heard God speak to him a couple of times in his life where he knew for sure it was God. This was one of those times, but it didn't make any sense. He didn't want to let JJ go, let alone forgive him.

Now he wished he hadn't told Amy how God had been dealing with him. "Fine."

He stomped back into his office and slammed the door. "JJ, I'm releasing you from your word not to escape. You're free to do whatever you please. I expect you won't be here when I get back." He threw the keys on his desk and left.

JJ stared at the keys, not knowing what to think. Was Sheriff Porter giving the crowd outside a chance at him? He never thought the sheriff was that kind. He paced and waited for something, anything to happen.

The door creaked open, and his chest tightened.

Kid stepped through, took the keys off the desk, and unlocked the cell. "Let's go."

Dazed, JJ grabbed his gun belt and followed Kid out into the street where their horses stood saddled. Nobody stopped them. The streets were deserted as if it had become a ghost town overnight.

They rode out of Green River and past the mine before JJ found his voice. "How'd you do that?"

Kid shrugged. "Do what?"

"How'd you pull off a miracle like that and get the sheriff to release me from my word and then leave so you could help me escape? I know with God all things are possible, but I'm impressed. How'd you manage it?"

Drew trudged into his office. JJ's cell was empty, the door wide open, and the keys on his desk. He picked up his tin coffee cup and threw it across the room. Coffee spattered everywhere.

He had a meeting with the governor next month. How was he going to explain that he let the Jackson Brothers go because God told him to? If he told the truth, which he would, he might be the one in jail.

Chapter Twenty-Nine

JJ and Kid trotted their horses through Hunt's Peak. JJ's face burned as he passed the general store nestled against the livery stable. The last time he'd been there, they'd robbed the place.

They rode further. The bear cage jail cells cast an eerie presence where the sheriff's office once stood, but the building had been torn down. He was just getting used to the idea of prison, but the thought of ending up in one of those small cages caused him to sweat.

The saloon stood deserted in the center of town. It had a few missing shingles and needed a coat of paint, and the roof was caving in. The crowd of men who used to loiter in front was gone.

Eli's Dining Hall had been built across the street. JJ peered through the large window in front. Every table had men and women sitting at it. It looked like Eli did well in his new business. That explained the condition of the saloon.

Some buildings were torn down. A group of children played beside a new, freshly painted, green schoolhouse erected in their place. Purple wildflowers grew in the field beside the school.

The road ended at the other side of town where a church and house, both painted white with a picket fence around them, stood as pillars. The sign in front read *Hunt's Peak Community Church, Rev. Jedidiah Jackson*. A monarch butterfly perched on it and fluttered its wings.

Kid gazed up at the building. "He most likely won't know who we are. The last time he saw us, we were young'uns."

JJ set his hand on Kid's shoulder. "Let's go."

A man with sandy brown hair knelt at the front of the church. He was older and a little heavier than JJ remembered, but it was him. They stepped closer.

"Dear Lord, I know You have them in your hands and that You'll bring them back to You. Keep Joshua and Jonathan safe until then. Let me see them again before –."

"Jedidiah." JJ's voice thickened. "It's us, Joshua and Jonathan."

Voices startled Jed, and he spun around, not sure if he heard right. He gaped at the men standing in front of him. Mid-twenties, that would be about right.

The one man had blue eyes like his own and blond, curly hair like Ma, and a handlebar mustache. He looked like Jonathan might at that age.

The deep brown eyes and strong bearded face of the other man was the image of his pa. He gulped and stood to his feet. "Joshua, Jonathan, it's really you."

They nodded.

He let out a holler and grabbed them in his arms. All three embraced one another.

Jed pulled back, heat rising to the back of his neck. They had a lot to answer for.

They stuck their hands in their pockets and lowered their heads but kept their eyes on him.

"Outlaws! Of all things, you became outlaws? Ma and Pa would turn over in their graves if they knew. How many folks have you robbed out of their life savings? How many have you hurt with your wicked ways? If you were a little younger, I'd take you to the woodshed out back. Outlaws."

A glimmer of light in their eyes fostered hope in Jed. The dark lifeless stare of miscreants he had tried to help in the past wasn't there.

"We've done some powerful backsliding." JJ's voice cracked.

Jed let out a sigh and motioned them to sit. "When I got back from the war, I heard what happened. I spent two years on the trail looking for you. I had just missed you when I rode into Hunt's Peak. A couple of years later, I'd heard you took off from Denver City, rather than face what you'd done."

"We never robbed that store in Denver City," Kid said so quietly Jed almost didn't hear him.

"I know that. So does Mr. Cooper. Marshal Cook found the culprit shortly after you left town."

His brothers stared at him, their mouths gaping open.

"When we robbed that first train," JJ said, "we thought we were going to be arrested for robbing Mr. Cooper's store. If it had only been the Hunt's Peak robbery, we would have gone back and faced up to it."

Jed motioned for them to sit down. "Mr. Freeman dropped the charges the day I married his daughter."

JJ groaned.

Kid put his face in his hands. "We deserve everything we get."

JJ flashed Kid a sideways grin. "Jed, how do you know Mr. Cooper?"

"Mr. and Mrs. Cooper telegraphed me after you took off. My wife and I went to Denver City to meet with them. Mr. Cooper felt bad about not believing you. He still thinks of you as his sons. When Grace's folks died and we were left with the store, Mr. Cooper sold his and moved out here to help us. They've sort of adopted us as well."

Kid groaned. "I feel like I'm ten years old again and about to face Pa after pouring pepper in the punchbowl at the church social."

Jed chuckled. "Why don't we go meet my wife and boys, and you can tell me what brought you back here? You'll love Grace, sweetest lady in the world, spirited too, like Ma."

He entered the parsonage and breathed in the aroma of fresh baked bread. A very pregnant Grace wrapped her arms around him. Her belly nudged him when the baby kicked. Jed kissed her on the cheek. "Grace, I want you to meet the prodigal brothers." He turned and waved his hand toward them.

Grace's mouth dropped open. "Joshua, Jonathan?"

They nodded.

She tried to hug them, but her belly got in the way. "Welcome, I'm so glad you're here, but how… why… what happened?"

"I was praying for them at the church like I always do before supper," Jed said, "and they just showed up. They haven't told me the whys and wherefores yet. I'm sure they'll tell us the whole story while we're eating one of your home-cooked meals."

"How does steaks and baked potatoes sound?" Grace said.

"Like manna from Heaven. Where's the boys? I want my brothers to meet them."

"Mrs. Cooper came for them while you were at the church."

"Oh, that's right." Jed turned to his brothers. "The Coopers keep the boys once a week to give Grace a chance to rest. You can meet them tomorrow."

"Supper will be in an hour." Grace headed to the kitchen. "Then we'll talk." She popped her head back in the room. "The three of you might want to check out the newspaper while you're waiting. There's an interesting article about the two of you on the front page."

JJ's eyes grew wide. "I swear we haven't done any outlawing in almost a year."

Jed lifted an eyebrow and picked up the paper. His brothers twisted their mouths and fidgeted with their hands while he read the article. He sat in his chair and continued reading without looking up, feeling no need to hurry. They'd worried him for nine long years. He would enjoy making them squirm a little.

"I need to hear about this. What have you two been up to lately?" He turned the newspaper over so they could see the front-page headline.

Jackson Brothers Rescue Children Trapped In Mine

Their eyes opened wide as JJ snatched the newspaper and read it. When he was done, he handed it to Kid. "Looks like we're heroes."

Kid read the article.

"Is it true?" Jed said.

JJ shrugged.

"I've got to hear about this," Jed said, "but if I don't wait for Grace, she'll never forgive me."

A few hours later, JJ and Kid finished telling the story of their lives as outlaws, their surrender to God, and their adventures coming to Hunt's Peak.

They didn't tell the glamorous version the dime novels or newspapers reported but the truth as best they could recollect it. They didn't justify their actions or blame anyone else for the decisions they'd made. They said the time in the cabin with God had taught them there were no excuses, only confession and repentance.

Jed was convinced God had done a work in them.

JJ's voice cracked. "We don't blame you if you want to disown us, but we're glad we got to see you again before–"

"First off, nobody's disowning anybody," Grace said with a hint of anger in her tone. "Jed's been praying for you two every day since he came home from the war. He never missed even when I was birthing our sons. Do you know what their names are? Joshua and Jonathan. So, you stop that right now."

"Yes, ma'am." Kid smiled sheepishly.

"My wife's a stubborn woman. Best you listen to her and just nod your head."

Grace threw her napkin and hit him in the face.

"See what I mean?" Jed cleared his throat. "I praise God He's brought you to your senses and that I had a chance to see you again, but after you've visited for a few days… I hate to mention it, but it's the right thing to do."

JJ leaned back and nodded.

"The reason the town was so willing to help in our escape," Kid said, "is because I gave my word we'd be back within a couple of weeks to turn ourselves in to Sheriff Porter."

"It's the right thing to do." JJ's Adam's apple bulged. "I wish there was another way to square things with the law other than spending the next twenty years in prison…" He cleared his throat.

"No way around it," Kid said. "God will give us the strength to do what needs done."

Grace crossed her arms. "Didn't you read the newspaper?"

Jed's brothers looked at her with their brows furrowed. He smiled. He could always tell when she was up to something.

"Yes," JJ said, "but we did too much outlawing to expect they'll lessen our sentences just 'cause we did something right."

"Not the front page." Grace left the room. When she came back, she turned to the third page of the paper and pointed at an article circled in ink. "This."

"No," Jed said. "We didn't get past the part about them being heroes."

JJ grabbed the paper from her and read it out loud. "Frank DeWitt, an outlaw who rode with the Durman gang and robbed trains, banks, and stagecoaches received amnesty from Wyoming Territorial Governor Thayer yesterday.

"Governor Thayer said Mr. DeWitt had not broken any laws in three years and has shown a repentant attitude toward his previous crimes. Governor Thayer said any outlaw who has not committed murder and who has shown a similar attitude will be considered for amnesty if he is willing to surrender himself into a lawman's custody." JJ set the newspaper on the table.

Kid picked it up. "The Durman gang never got away with more than a couple hundred dollars. Don't know if that deal would be offered to us."

"We have to try," JJ said. "It's the only chance we'll ever get."

"So, what do we do," Kid said, "stroll into Sheriff Porter's office and say 'Howdy, we're back, and we want amnesty'?"

Jed looked up. "You mean Drew Porter? He's a good friend of mine. I could talk to him."

"No, it's best we do it ourselves," JJ said. "He needs to see we mean what we say. What do you think, Kid?"

"It's the only way."

"Jedidiah, we don't want you to be harboring fugitives," JJ said, "but would you mind if we stayed a couple of days? I'd like to get to know my family again before we take off. We might never have another chance."

"We need to go to the sheriff and let him know what's going on."

JJ turned pale.

"Don't fret about it. The sheriff's my best friend and one of the first converts at the Hunt's Peak Community Church. Eli Hansen was elected part-time sheriff when Drew Porter left for Bear River."

Chapter Thirty

Jed and his brothers strode to the corner table of the dining hall where Eli sat looking over the week's receipts and drinking his morning coffee. Eli glanced up.

"Mind if we sit down?"

"Preacher," Eli said, "you know you're always welcome and so are your friends."

They took a seat. Eli's brow furrowed as he studied their faces as if he was trying to conjure up the memory. He choked and sprayed his coffee across the table. His voice lowered. "What are you two doing here? I shouldn't even be talking to you two. I should be arresting you."

"Hear us out, Eli," Jed said. "Then do what you think is best."

Eli wiped his face with his napkin. "Go on."

"My prayers have been answered," Jed said. "Joshua and Jonathan have asked God to save them from their sins. The prodigals have come home."

"Praise God." Eli looked around the room as if he expected someone to shout "outlaws," but the hall was empty. "What are you going to do now? You're still wanted by the law, and near as I can figure, you're both looking at twenty years at least."

"We're turning ourselves in to Sheriff Porter in Green River when we leave here," JJ said. "We hope he'll talk to the governor of Wyoming for us about getting amnesty."

"Not likely," Eli said. "It's political suicide to go against the railroads in these parts."

"We know," Kid said. "We're leaving it in God's hands."

"What do you need from me?"

"I know I'm asking a lot," Jed said, "but could you hold off arresting them for a few days to give us a chance to visit? Once they turn themselves in, I may never see them again."

Eli leaned in closer. "You best be gone by the end of the week or I'll have to take you into custody. I am still the sheriff after all."

"You're a good friend," Jed said.

"Just make sure they stay out of sight." Eli wiped the back of his neck with his hand. "If somebody sees JJ and Kid Jackson prancing around town, I might not have a choice."

As they approached Jed's house, JJ saw the Coopers standing on the front porch. He halted his steps.

Mrs. Cooper face lit up like the last time they'd seen her, but the scowl on Mr. Cooper's face reminded him of that last day in Denver City.

Kid stood motionless.

JJ put his hand on his shoulder. "We have to face them sometime."

"Yep."

They trailed Jed to the porch. JJ twisted his tattered cowboy hat in his hands. Mrs. Cooper ran to them and gave them both hugs. They each kissed her on the cheek.

"Why don't you boys take a walk with me?" Mr. Cooper motioned toward the porch stairs. "There's an old woodshed behind the church where we won't be overheard."

JJ shot a look toward Kid. He almost wished he were young again when this could have been settled with a trip to the woodshed.

They followed Mr. Cooper into the shed. Kid, eyes lowered, crossed his arms and leaned against the wall.

JJ faced Mr. Cooper, determined to look him in the eye no matter what he had to say.

"I hear you surrendered your lives to God and are planning on turning yourselves in." Mr. Cooper delivered a scorching glare to each of them then.

JJ started to answer. "Ye..."

"Quiet. I'll have my say first." The vein in his neck throbbed. "I'm having a hard time believing you up and got religion after all this time. Mighty convenient if you ask me. We've spent seven years fretting that you'd get killed, or worse, that you might murder somebody and wind up at the end of a rope."

JJ wanted to defend himself, but he couldn't. It was all true.

"It wasn't just us." Mr. Cooper's voice raised, and he stepped toward them. "Do you know what you put your brother through? He might be able to swallow the line you fed him because he wants to believe it so badly, but I won't be hornswoggled again."

JJ swallowed hard. He didn't expect forgiveness, but he thought Mr. Cooper would know they weren't lying. After all, he knew now they hadn't lied about robbing his store. He didn't blame him for believing this was all a trick after all they'd done.

Mr. Cooper picked up a stick, broke it in two, and tossed it across the room before boring into them with a glare that made JJ's insides quiver. "If you are going after this amnesty, you're probably doing this so you can get away with all the things you've done wrong without having to spend one day in prison." When they didn't say anything, he said, "Answer me."

JJ resisted the urge to look away. "We deserve this going over, but we're not lying about getting right with God." His voice grew thick. "Are you saying we've done so much wrong we shouldn't even try?"

"I don't know." Mr. Cooper's tone softened. "Would you be willing to do that? Would you be willing to give up on a pardon?"

"I don't rightly know," JJ said. "I figured God was helping us with this amnesty thing, but maybe we were trying to make things easier for ourselves. What do you think, Kid?"

Kid uncrossed his arms. "It's not our call to make."

JJ let out a husky sigh. "I never did think we'd get off scot-free. It wouldn't be right after all we've done."

"We should pray about it," Kid said. "We'll do whatever God wants."

Mr. Cooper leaned against the wall with his arms folded.

JJ stuck his hands in his pockets and prepared for the next onslaught.

"I have to admit," Mr. Cooper said, "I'm amazed."

Kid's Adam's apple bulged. "What do you mean, Sir?"

"I figured you'd make excuses," Mr. Cooper said, "that you'd tell me it wasn't right for you to spend the rest of your lives in prison when you've seen the error of your ways. I didn't expect this."

JJ lowered his gaze.

"You really have repented of your crimes?" Mr. Cooper said. "And you are willing to accept any punishment handed out?"

"Mr. Cooper... Sir." JJ's voice cracked. "We spent our whole lives running from God. We're done. I just wish we could make things right with you before we go. I know you can't ever forgive us, but we–"

"Welcome home, boys." Mr. Cooper extended his hand. JJ and Kid grabbed it, and he pulled them into a bear hug.

JJ returned to the porch with Mr. Cooper and Kid, where the others waited.

Mr. Cooper walked up to Mrs. Cooper and put his arm around her. "Mary, God has seen fit to bring our boys home."

Mrs. Cooper cried and wrapped her arms around them.

JJ wiped his face to keep from tearing up. They kept calling him and Kid the prodigal brothers, but that wasn't really true. The prodigal never robbed anyone. The truth was they didn't deserve forgiveness from Mr. Cooper, Jedidiah, or God, but he was grateful for it.

"I think it's about time you met your namesakes," Grace called out. "Josh, Johnny, come here."

Two boys, covered in dirt, ran to the front yard. The older one, around seven years old, looked mostly like Jed. He had his pa's cleft chin and sandy brown hair and his ma's green eyes. The younger was the image of Kid at five years old, a towhead with curls and blue eyes.

"How did you get dirty so fast?" Grace tried to wipe the oldest boy's face with her apron. "Just look at you."

"Ah, Ma," Josh said.

"I'm not dirty, Ma," Johnny said.

Jed snickered.

"You're no help, Jedidiah." Grace put her hands on her hips. "I'm trying to get them to stay a little cleaner, and you laugh."

Jed placed his hands in the air in mock surrender. "Oh, Grace, you're asking the impossible when you ask little boys to stay clean."

"I guess it can't be helped. I wanted them to be presentable when they meet your brothers."

"They don't care," Jed said. "Boys, I want you to meet your uncles." He motioned to them. "Uncle Joshua and Uncle Jonathan. You were named after them."

"Are you really outlaws?" Josh said.

"Joshua Jackson," Grace scolded.

"It's all right, Grace." Heat rose to JJ's face. "It's a fair question. Yes, Josh, I'm ashamed to say we are, at least we used to be."

"Wow," Josh said, "my uncles, real live outlaws. Could you teach me to shoot?"

"Being outlaws is nothing to be proud of," Kid said. "And you best be learning to shoot from your pa when you're a little older."

"But we want to be outlaws like you," Johnnie said.

"Sons." Jed crossed his arms and glared at them. "Your uncles used to steal from people, but now they know it's wrong. They don't want to be outlaws anymore, and neither do you."

"You boys go around to the pump and get washed up for lunch," Grace said. "You'll have a chance to visit with your uncles later."

"Ah, Ma," Josh said, "We're not that dirty."

"Do what your ma said." There was a warning in Jed's tone.

"Yes, Sir." Both boys ran to the back of the house.

"I don't know what to do with those two." Grace wiped her hands on her apron. "Ever since the boys at school told Josh you two robbed banks and trains, they've had a bee in their bonnets."

Jed's jaw clenched. "A trip to the woodshed might give them something else to think about."

"Why don't you let us talk to them?" Kid said. "Maybe we could let them know what outlawing is really all about. Don't think they'll have a hankering for it if they hear the truth."

"Maybe," Jed said, "but I'm not going to let this go on much longer."

Chapter Thirty-One

Kid sat with JJ on the front porch, enjoying the cool breeze when their nephews ran up to them.

"I did it," Josh said smiling from ear to ear.

"I helped," Johnnie said.

Kid raised an eyebrow. "You did what?"

"We became outlaws like you," Josh said.

"What!" JJ's brow furrowed.

Josh pulled coins from his pockets. "We stole money."

Kid's stomach knotted. "Where did you get that from?"

"The store," Johnnie said. "We took them when Pappy was looking the other way. Can we join your gang now?"

"No, you can't join our gang!" JJ stood up. "Our gang is dead. They were lynched because they stole things."

Johnnie's eyes widened.

Kid's stomach quivered. How many young boys looked up to them and aspired to become outlaws after reading about them in the newspapers? More ripples in the pond. "It's sinful to take things that don't belong to you."

"But you were outlaws, and nothing happened to you," Josh said.

JJ leaned against the railing of the porch. "It will. When we leave here, we're going to Wyoming where we'll probably spend a long time in prison. We might never get to see you, or your pa or ma, or Mr. or Mrs. Cooper again."

"That's not all." Kid stooped to eye level with the boys. "We hurt a lot of folks because of what we did. Folks like your ma and pa."

JJ placed his hand on the boys' shoulders. "Is that really what you want?"

Tears ran down Johnnie's face and threatened to fall from Josh's eyes. Josh wiped his face on his sleeve. "What do we do?"

Kid let out a breath. "First off, you're going to return that money to Pappy Cooper and tell him what you did."

"But he'll be mad at us," Johnnie said.

Kid nodded. "Folks are going to be mad at you when you go around taking their stuff."

Josh kicked a pebble on the ground.

"I'll tell your ma we're taking you to the store." JJ walked into the house.

The boys fidgeted on the porch. Kid hoped they'd learned their lesson.

JJ came back a moment later. "Let's go, boys."

Josh and Johnnie followed JJ to the store. Kid walked behind in case they had second thoughts and decided to run the other way.

They didn't have far to tread before they stood in front of the store. Jed's boys gazed up at it. JJ knew how they felt.

"I'm scared," Johnnie said.

"That's another thing about being outlaws," Kid said. "There's always something to be afraid of."

Josh grabbed Johnnie's hand and walked through the door.

Mr. Cooper greeted them with a somber expression.

The boys meandered to the counter and stood there, shuffling their feet. JJ marched up behind them and nudged Josh.

"Pappy Cooper." Josh laid the coins on the counter. "We stole this from your store when you weren't looking. I'm sorry."

"I'm sorry too," Johnnie said.

Mr. Cooper looked down. "I thought you liked me more than that."

"We do, Pappy." Johnnie's eyes watered. "We love you. We just wanted to be outlaws, so we could join Uncle Joshua and Uncle Jonathan's gang."

"And now you've changed your minds?"

Josh tucked his hands in his pockets and looked at his shoes. "They told us how bad it was being outlaws, and how they hurt folks, and how they were always scared, and how they're going to prison because of it."

Mr. Cooper placed his hands on the boys' shoulders. "I saw you take the money. I hoped you would bring it back on your own. I'd planned to have a talk with your pa." He glanced at JJ and Kid. "I'm glad your uncles were there to help you decide to do the right thing."

"Us, too." Johnnie wiped his face on his shirtsleeve.

"I forgive you, boys," Mr. Cooper said. "But don't let me ever catch you stealing again, or we'll go round and round. I can't abide liars and thieves." He winked toward Kid and JJ

"We promise, Pappy," Josh said, "never again."

"Mammy Cooper has cookies baking. I think you boys can mosey over to the house on your own. I want to talk to your uncles."

"Thanks, Pappy." Josh darted out the door.

Johnnie ran after Josh slamming the door behind him.

Kid wiped his hand across his mouth. "They wanted to be like us."

The men remained silent for a moment as shame swept over JJ causing his face to flush. "If we had enough sand to tell you the truth before that day in Denver City…" His voice grew thick. "I reckon you didn't have a choice but think the worst about us."

"I told you I forgive you," Mr. Cooper said. "You did good today. You kept those two boys on the straight and narrow."

"If God allows us to go free," JJ said, "we want to try to help boys get a good start the way you tried to help us. We've been talking about it since we left South Pass City."

"That sounds like a fine thing to do," Mr. Cooper said. "But right now, why don't you get some of those cookies before your nephews eat them all?"

Kid's face lit up, and he rushed out of the store.

JJ laughed and followed him.

After devouring the cookies, they made their way home. JJ let up a silent prayer this would make a lasting impression on the boys.

"Are you going to tell Pa what we did?" Josh said.

"Nope," Kid said, "you are."

"But he'll take us out to the woodshed," Josh said.

"Yep," JJ said, "that's just what he'll do. Our ma and pa died when we were a bit older than you. When we started thieving, we didn't have a pa to clean our plows."

"If we had," Kid said, "we wouldn't be fretting about going to prison."

"It's going to hurt," Johnnie said.

JJ squelched a smile. "Then maybe you'll remember your backsides if you ever figure on doing something like that again." He spotted Jed through the open door of the church. "Looks like your pa's in there. Best to get it over with."

"What do we say?" Josh said.

JJ crossed his arms. "You tell him what you did, and you're ready to take your medicine. A man takes what he has coming with as little fuss as he can manage." Another one of his pa's sayings. He hoped he could follow the advice when his time came.

Kid placed his hands on their shoulders and gave them a slight push through the door.

As they shuffled into the church, Jed glanced up. "What's going on here?"

Josh slumped his shoulders and stared at the ground. "Sir, we stole money from Pappy's store, but we gave it back. We're real sorry."

The muscle in Jed's cheek twitched. "Boys, get to the woodshed now! I'll be there directly."

Josh's eyes widened. "Yes, Sir."

The boys backed up and spun around before running out of the church.

Jed glared at his brothers. "What is going on here?"

JJ lowered his eyes. "They wanted to be like us."

"So, I bring you into my home, and my boys want to follow in your footsteps?"

"Jedidiah," Kid said.

Jed held up his hand. "Don't! I'll talk to my outlaw brothers after I deal with my outlaw sons." He stormed out of the church.

"Maybe it wasn't such a good idea coming here," JJ said.

"God wanted us to come."

JJ's stomach churned. "I don't want them looking up to us. Maybe we should leave now."

"Let's see what Jedidiah has to say when he comes back."

They didn't have to wait long. Jed came back a few minutes later with two teary-eyed boys in tow. The boys strode up to their uncles.

JJ stooped to eye level. "So, are you ever going to do anything like that again?"

"No, Sir," Johnnie said.

Josh rubbed his bottom. "I'll never do that again."

"That's fine, boys," Jed said. "Now go to your room and stay there until I come and get you."

"Yes, Sir." The boys ran out of the church.

JJ swallowed. "We're mighty sorry we caused the boys to look up to us. We'll leave if you want us to."

Jed wiped his hand over his face. "I owe both of you an apology. They told me what happened."

JJ looked at his feet. He appreciated what Jed said, but the boys never would have done such a thing if it hadn't been for him.

A few days later, JJ and Kid saddled their horses. JJ stroked his beard. All those years he thought Jed was dead, years that wouldn't have been lost if they hadn't robbed the store.

"It was good having you," Jed said. "Even if I never see you again here, we'll be together in Heaven."

"It's only twenty years." Kid said. "We can all stay alive that long."

"No matter what happens," JJ said, "we had this time together."

Jed gave them bear hugs and stepped back for the others to say good-bye.

Grace waddled up and hugged them. "I'm glad the boys and I got to know you. I hope you meet this little one who's coming soon too. I'll be praying."

Mrs. Cooper didn't say anything. She just hugged them and cried.

JJ patted her back. "Hey, now, no need to fret."

"I know." Mrs. Cooper wiped her eyes.

Mr. Cooper stepped forward. "I don't know how this amnesty thing is going to turn out. I hope you don't have to spend one day in that prison."

"Sir," Kid said.

"Don't you interrupt me, Son. This may be the last time I get to tell you boys some things."

JJ looked at his feet. When they needed help, the Coopers took them in as if they were their own flesh and blood. Even though Mr. Cooper had forgiven them, that time was over forever.

Mr. Cooper took JJ and Kid in his arms and hugged them, then pulled back. "I'm proud to call you my sons." He cleared his throat. "Well, I guess you best be on your way."

JJ nodded. Even if he went to prison for the rest of his life, this trip was worth it to hear Mr. Cooper say that. He and Kid stepped to the two little boys who were standing by their mother.

"Are you going to prison?" Josh said.

"Probably," Kid said.

"Will you be back?" Johnnie said.

"We don't know." JJ messed Johnnie's hair. "You boys make sure you do what your pa says."

"Yes, Sir," Josh said.

"Be good now," Kid said, "and stay close to God. He'll show you the right path."

"We will." Johnnie wiped a tear rolling down his cheek.

They mounted their horses and rode off in the direction of Green River, Wyoming. When they passed the town limits, JJ looked back, one last time, and prayed he'd see them again.

Chapter Thirty-Two

Drew had finished making his rounds and was heading back to his office when he noticed a light from the oil lamp in the window. He drew his Colt 45 and cracked open the door to find JJ Jackson standing in the middle of the office, smiling at him.

He pointed his revolver in JJ's face. "You got sand. I'll give you that. Did you really think I wouldn't arrest you if I saw–?" A hammer cocked behind him. He groaned and holstered his gun.

"Howdy, Sheriff," Kid said.

"I should've known."

"We want to ask you a favor," JJ said. "Will you hear us out?"

Heat rose to the back of Drew's neck. "Yeah, I'll hear you out since Kid has that gun pointed at my head, but I'm not doing you any more favors."

"Fair enough." JJ nodded to Kid.

Kid twirled his Smith and Wesson and handed it to him.

Drew glanced at JJ's hip. No gun. Realization came over him. "You boys giving yourselves up?"

"Yep," Kid said. "The firearm was to get you to agree to listen."

Drew placed a hand on his desk to steady himself and slid into his chair before drawing his Colt 45 again. He spoke in raspy tones, not sure if he could believe this. "All right, go on."

JJ picked up a newspaper lying on the desk, pointed to a circled article, and handed it to him.

Drew read it with furtive glances toward them. The gist of the article was about some outlaw who got amnesty, but what did that have to do with… No. Maybe they blew up too many safes and scrambled their brains. "You don't mean you two?"

JJ shrugged his shoulders. "We need somebody who'd be willing to talk to the governor for us. Maybe some lawman who knows about the mine accident and that we've changed our ways."

He raised an eyebrow. "And what makes you figure I know that?"

"We're here now," Kid said.

Drew remembered saying once he'd know JJ and Kid really had made things right with God if they ever willingly turned themselves in. Didn't this prove they had? He pointed to the paper. "But this will never work."

"Probably not," Kid said.

"Even if I were to do this, there's not much chance of the governor listening. DeWitt was small time, not like you two. If he says no, what then?"

JJ shrugged. "We go to prison. I told you we surrendered our lives to God. We needed to go to Hunt's Peak to see Jedidiah, but we're here now."

Drew stared them down, trying to make up his mind. They were being straight with him. He knew that. Otherwise they wouldn't be here.

"This is the only chance we'll get," Kid said. "Will you do it?"

Drew holstered his gun. "Yeah, I'll do it."

They ambled to the cells, and JJ opened one of the cell doors. "Which one do you want us in?"

"Doesn't matter." Drew didn't bother to make sure they locked themselves in. He was too stunned. He picked up the newspaper and reread the article. The cell door clanged shut.

JJ paced five steps to the cell door and five steps to the sod wall waiting for the trip to Cheyenne. So small and no window. He never did like small spaces, but he might have to get used to them.

Sheriff Porter unlocked the door. "It's time to go."

They stepped out of the cell.

JJ held out his hands. "Aren't you going to handcuff us?"

Sheriff Porter raised an eyebrow. "Do I need to?"

"No," Kid said. "We're not going anywhere."

"Don't prove me wrong."

JJ almost wished Porter would cuff them. He'd made his decision, but that didn't mean he wasn't tempted. Every urge within him wanted to run, to get away while he still could.

They followed Sheriff Porter to the train depot.

Mr. Grayson marched over to them. "I hope you gentlemen don't mind. I'll be riding with you to Cheyenne. I'm going with Sheriff Porter to see the governor on your behalf."

Warmth went through JJ. It felt good to have someone on their side. After what they'd put Porter through, he doubted the sheriff would be disappointed if they didn't get pardons. "No, not at all, Mr. Grayson. We're beholden to you."

"You saved my Tommy and Sarah's lives. It's the least I can do."

The four men climbed aboard the train and took their seats on two benches facing one another. The train rolled out of the station.

Sheriff Porter leaned in. "I want to warn you what to expect. When we get to Cheyenne, I'll turn you in to Marshal Donner, the lawman in those parts. He's going to lock you up and get a hold of the judge to schedule your trial. We'll go straight to Governor Thayer, but we might not get to see him in time. Sometimes these trials move fast, especially if you're pleading guilty."

A lump caught in JJ's throat. "We are." The idea of being locked away in a small cell terrified him. "We know you'll do your best."

"If you end up in prison, I'll write and let you know what he says. If the governor gives you amnesty, we'll get you out of there as soon as we can, but if he says no, it's over. There's nothing more we can do."

Mr. Grayson leaned toward them. "Even if you do go to trial before we see the governor, Sheriff Porter and I are going to request to say a few words in court. That might help some when the judge sentences you."

JJ appreciated their kindness even if he didn't understand it.

For the rest of the trip, Sheriff Porter didn't treat them like prisoners. He and Mr. Grayson chatted with them like they were friends taking a train ride together. Before they knew it, the trip was over, and they were in the marshal's office in Cheyenne.

JJ's knees grew weak. The thought of twenty years in prison overwhelmed him. He lowered his eyes and waited to be locked up.

Sheriff Porter shook Marshal Donner's hand. "You remember me, sheriff at Green River?"

"I remember," the marshal said.

"Got a couple of prisoners for you, JJ and Kid Jackson."

Marshal Donner raised an eyebrow. "How come you don't have them in handcuffs or at least your gun pointed at them?"

JJ wondered the same thing.

"No need," Porter said. "They traipsed into my office and turned themselves in."

Donner unlocked one of the jail cells. "Get in here."

JJ and Kid walked into the cell. Kid lay on a cot and placed his hat over his eyes as if he didn't have a care in the world.

The cell door clanged shut behind them. JJ tried to get a hold over his fear as he paced the length of the dirt floor.

"Judge Thomas is in town." Marshall Donner locked the cell door. "You won't have to wait long for your trial. I figure he'll want you before him tomorrow."

Porter's brow furrowed. "I'll go see the governor, right now."

JJ grabbed hold of the bars on the door. "Thanks, Sheriff."

Kid tipped his hat and nodded.

Marshal Donner escorted Porter out.

JJ started pacing again. Five steps up. Five steps back. Back and forth. He stepped to the door when Marshal Donner returned.

"Your trial starts tomorrow. Everyone wants to see the infamous outlaws. Be prepared for a circus."

"Great," Kid said under his hat without lifting his head from his bunk. "Always wanted to be in the circus."

The next morning, Sheriff Porter visited them. "The governor is out of town until Friday. I'll see him as soon as I can, but it's not going to be in time to keep you from going to trial or being sentenced."

JJ grabbed hold of the barred door. He couldn't shake the dread resting on his chest. "You did your best."

"It's not over yet."

Kid set a hand on JJ's shoulder. "Thanks, Sheriff."

"Take care of yourselves." Sheriff Porter shook hands with them and left.

JJ stroked his beard. "Do you figure prison's as bad as everyone says it is?"

"I don't know," Kid said. "Looks like we're going to find out."

A few moments later, Marshal Donner stepped in and unlocked the cell door. "It's time."

JJ held out his hands. The marshal handcuffed him and Kid and escorted them outside where he and six deputized men escorted them through the streets. The crowd pressed against the deputies, trying to get to them. Apparently, the guards were more for their protection than to keep them from escaping.

They passed by a vendor who shouted, "Get your popcorn; get your peanuts."

Donner had it pegged. It was a circus, and they were the main attraction.

As they passed the saloon, some soiled doves called out, "We love you, JJ. We love you, Kid."

A couple of years ago, JJ would have sought out their attention. Now all he felt was sorrow and disgust that they would idolize him.

Another group of women in black dresses covering them from their necks down and black bonnets on their heads played tambourines. "We all deserve the wrath of God. Repent before it's too late."

JJ wanted to say he already had, but he kept quiet

Some men mumbled, "Prison's too good for them."

"I'll get a rope," one man said.

He tried to keep his head down, but it almost did no good when one kid threw a tomato at them. He was grateful when one of the deputies chased the boy away before his aim improved.

They reached the courthouse, but the circus moved inside. Every seat was occupied. Those who couldn't find a bench crowded in the back.

Marshal Donner escorted them through the throng to the front where Sheriff Porter and Mr. Grayson sat.

A distinguished looking older man in a grey morning suit with a well-groomed beard and salt and pepper hair sat beside Mr. Grayson. He had to be someone important the way everyone stirred up dust greeting him and shook his hand a little too enthusiastically. Three men asked if they could get him anything.

A man with a notebook and pencil pressed through the mob. "I'm from the *Cheyenne Post*. Kid, is it true you killed eight men in fair gun fights?"

JJ's hands clenched into fists.

The reporter turned to him. "I heard you quit outlawing because your crazy schemes got your gang lynched."

"Ignore him." Marshal Donner stepped between them. "You have bigger problems." He turned to the newspaperman. "Step away from my prisoners now."

The man backed off but stayed nearby.

Donner escorted JJ and Kid to stand behind a railing on the right side of the courtroom. His deputies took positions in various places throughout the building.

"Please stand," the bailiff said. "This court is now in session. The honorable Judge Thomas presiding."

A judge with muttonchops and eyeglasses entered through the side door and sat behind the bench. A low scuffle filled the room as everyone found their seats.

Judge Thomas addressed them. "Joshua Jackson, Jonathan Jackson."

JJ and Kid stood.

Judge Thomas read the paper in front of him and lifted his eyes over his spectacles. "You have been charged with sixteen counts of armed bank and train robbery. How do you plead?"

JJ cleared his throat. "Could we see the list of charges, Your Honor?"

"Bailiff, show them the list."

They looked it over, but JJ noticed a couple of robberies missing. "We have to tell them," he whispered to Kid.

"You're right, but it's not going to change things. It might even make them worse."

JJ looked at the last robbery on the list–Bear River, 1875. He set the list down and squared his shoulders. Maybe what Sheriff Porter and Mr. Grayson had to say would lessen their sentences. Either way, they had to tell the truth. "Guilty on all counts, Your Honor."

"I'm guilty too," Kid said.

"Your Honor, there's three robberies not on that list. We're guilty of them too."

"Let me see if I have this straight," Judge Thomas said. "You're pleading guilty to these charges as well as three not on the list?"

"Yes, Your Honor," JJ said.

"Yes, Sir," Kid said.

"What three robberies?" Judge Thomas said.

"The bank in Laramie in July of seventy-three was us," JJ said, "and the same bank in August, that year."

"Also a payroll train headed for Denver City in seventy-one," Kid said. "That was the first."

"Was that in Wyoming or Colorado?"

"Wyoming," JJ said. "We hadn't reached the state line yet."

"Bailiff," Judge Thomas said, "add those robberies to the list."

The bailiff nodded and wrote something down.

"You realize by pleading guilty, you are placing yourselves at the mercy of this court." Judge Thomas looked overtop his spectacles. "I can sentence you to any prison term I deem appropriate within the confines of the law."

"Yes, Sir," Kid said.

"What about the money you stole?" Judge Thomas said. "Do you plan to make amends by returning any of it?"

JJ swallowed. The judge would never believe them. "We wish we could, but it's gone. We went through all of it."

The judge shook his head. "Convenient. I know some here want to speak for you." He waved his hand in the direction of Sheriff Porter and Mr. Grayson.

JJ glanced at them and nodded.

The judge leaned forward, and a hint of a smirk crossed his mouth. "But I see no need to have them do so. You've already admitted your guilt, but you're still unwilling to make amends by returning what you stole. I've had enough of the newspapers and dime novels making you out to be heroes. You're criminals, and in my court, you'll be treated as such."

JJ's stomach knotted. They would get the whole twenty years. Why not? They hurt a lot of people. It was justice.

Judge Thomas wrote something down before delivering a glare meant to strike fear. It worked. "Joshua Jackson, Jonathan Jackson, I sentence you each to twenty years in the Wyoming Territorial Prison for each of the fourteen counts of train robbery and five counts of bank robbery to be served consecutively. That comes to three hundred and eighty years, sentences to be carried out immediately. Dismissed."

Cheers erupted from the crowd. JJ stood stunned. A deputy came forward and chained their hands and feet.

Sheriff Porter pushed through the crowd. "This isn't over yet."

Two deputies grabbed their arms and pulled them outside. The prison wagon, a black box on wooden wheels with a barred window waited for them in front of the courthouse. The judge must have ordered it before the trial began.

The guard jumped down and swung open the door. The deputies hoisted them into the wagon.

JJ plopped on the floor next to Kid and tried to get comfortable. The chains kept him from stretching out. The door clanged shut, the wagon jerked, and they were on their way to prison.

"I didn't figure it would happen like that." A dull pain rested on JJ's chest. "I expected twenty years, but three hundred and eighty? I don't want to die in prison."

A banging sounded on the side of the wagon. "Quiet back there."

"The judge didn't even let Sheriff Porter or Mr. Grayson talk," Kid whispered. "He treated us like we were criminals."

JJ looked at the chains around his wrists and ankles. "We are criminals."

"God will see us through this."

"How? We have the rest of our lives in prison staring us in the face."

"Don't give up hope yet," Kid said. "Sheriff Porter hasn't talked to the governor yet."

"Yeah, I guess." But he knew at that moment, they would never get out of prison alive.

Chapter Thirty-Three

The wagon rolled through the large prison gate. JJ tried to keep the panic from overwhelming him. "Well, this is it."

"I doubt we'll get cells close to each other."

"Not likely. If we don't see each other again, Kid, take care of yourself."

"You, too."

The door to the wagon sprang open. Guards grabbed hold of JJ's arms and half dragged him and Kid out and through a dark hallway. The gate clanged shut behind them as they were shoved into a small room. The guards removed the chains, and JJ rubbed his wrists.

"Stand there." One of the guards pointed to the wall.

When they did, another man took photographs of them.

"Sit on those stools."

They did what they were told. A man with a large razor blade brushed shaving foam on Kid's head.

"Hold still." The man shaved Kid's head and face.

JJ gaped as blond curls fell to the floor. The barber finished with Kid and shaved JJ. His long dark hair and beard joined Kid's locks at their feet.

"Get undressed," the guard said. "Throw your clothes down here."

JJ removed his clothes and stood naked, shivering before the guards.

One guard gawked at every square inch of Kid's body and barked out comments that the other guard recorded in a ledger. "Blond hair, blue eyes, skinny, around five foot ten, mole on the right side of his neck, scar on upper right leg on the inside, half a dozen marks on his back."

The guard finished with Kid and moved to JJ. "Brown hair and eyes, medium build, around five foot ten, dimple lines on face. Where did you get those lash marks on your back?"

"When I was a kid, the man we were sent to live with liked beating me."

"Marks across his whole back. Too many to count."

JJ never thought of himself as modest, but standing naked in a room with guards looking at him and one of them poking at various parts of his body made heat rise to his face.

The guard finished and stepped back.

The other guard handed them cotton drawers and black and white horizontal striped wool trousers and shirts. "Put these on."

JJ slipped into the prison uniform, grateful for the covering even if it was a little large and itched.

A large man in his thirties with graying temples and a handlebar mustache stepped through a nearby door and stood in front of them. "I'm Warden Kimball. You will address me as Warden or Sir. Joshua Jackson, step forward."

JJ took a step toward him.

"Mr. Jackson, you're now Prisoner One Seventy-nine. Jonathan Jackson, step forward. Mr. Jackson, you're Prisoner One Eighty. From this moment on, you don't have names. You will answer to your numbers. Do you understand me?"

"Yes, Sir," JJ and Kid said in unison.

"Mr. Harris, cell number twenty-seven's empty. Since we're full up, get an extra bunk and put them both in there."

JJ was so relieved he almost smiled. They wouldn't be separated.

The guard who gave them the clothes nodded.

The Warden stepped in front of them. "Can you read?"

"Yes, Sir," JJ said.

"Mr. Harris will give you a list of rules," Warden Kimball said. "Make yourself familiar with them. You'll rise at 5:30 every day but Sunday and work hard for your keep. Follow the rules, and we won't have any problems. First rule. No talking at all."

A chill traveled up JJ's spine. They wouldn't be allowed to talk to each other for the rest of their lives? How could they stay in the same cell and not talk to each other? He didn't hear most of what was read after that.

JJ's face turned ashen. Kid wanted to reach out to him. He had to know there would be opportunities to talk.

Warden Kimball continued. "You'll also be expected to keep your cell clean and your bedding in good repair. That's means every morning, fold your bedding and place it under your pillow."

That was good news. Neither one of them liked to live in filth. He assumed prison would be a place of refuse and disease.

"At certain times, you'll be allowed outside your cell to exercise, but don't step beyond the width of the cell door. If you have any requests, wait there until a guard comes by."

Kid threw a glance toward his brother. It would be hard on him. JJ hated closed in spaces ever since that time with Mr. Greer.

"If you get sick, report to the guard, but you better really be sick. Any deviation from these rules will be met with swift punishment. A record is kept, so good behavior is in your interest. Mr. Harris, give them the rules."

Mr. Harris handed them the list.

Warden Kimball stopped pacing. "Are there any questions?"

JJ tried to break through the fog in his head to form words. "Yes, Sir."

"Prisoner One Seventy-nine, you may speak. What's your question?" Warden Kimball said.

"When are we allowed to talk to the other prisoners?"

"Unless you have to communicate to complete a work project," Warden Kimball said, "you're never allowed to talk to the prisoners."

"But I'm at sea about this." JJ swallowed back the lump in his throat. "Are we allowed to talk to the guards?"

"Only if you have a question or request or if they ask you a question," Warden Kimball said.

JJ darted a glance around the room. Guards at the only door. No way out. Trapped. He took a deep breath and exhaled it to calm himself. "Sir, how are we supposed to interact with each other?"

"You won't," Warden Kimball said. "Use your imprisonment to reflect on your crimes. You're not here to make friends with other prisoners."

Whatever the punishment for talking was, he was sure it'd be worth it. He couldn't not talk. He'd go crazy. "Sir, what happens if we do talk to other prisoners?"

"The first time, no matches for your candles. You'll find this a dismal place with no light in your cell after your workday."

That wasn't so bad.

"The next time, you'll be given a ball and chain to wear for a week. If you persist, you'll find yourself chained to the furnaces in the cellar for five days with only bread and water."

JJ took gasping breaths, trying to get some air. Just like Mr.

Greer's cellar.

"It gets mighty hot during the day and cold at night, and it's damp and dark. You'll be left alone there to decide it's not worth it to defy us."

JJ's lungs felt they were about to explode. He tried to slow his breathing.

"We generally don't have problems with the prisoners after that, but if we do, we have more severe methods."

Mr. Harris and another guard marched them past a row of whitewashed brick cells.

Kid shot a sympathetic look toward JJ. He looked like he'd been hit in the gut with a tree branch. Kid figured since they were in the same cell, they'd have a chance to talk later. They had to. JJ couldn't make it if he couldn't talk for the rest of his life.

The muscle in Kid's jaw twitched. As much as he teased his brother over the years for talking too much, it wouldn't be easy for him either.

The door to each cell was an iron grate that crisscrossed in front of all the cells. They reached cell number twenty-seven on the first floor, and Kid followed JJ into their six-by-six-foot room.

Against the wall were two bunks with straw-filled mattresses stacked together and a small nightstand. The chamber pot hid behind a small grated door near the floor, and the smell of urine assaulted Kid with the knowledge they weren't emptied often.

He brushed past JJ and climbed onto the top bunk. There was barely room for one person to stand, let alone two.

The clang of the steel door locked behind them. Kid squinted to look out of the gated door. There weren't any other prisoners. He hadn't noticed any on the way to his cell either. They had to be on work detail. He doubted they would ever be let out for any other reason.

The guard stayed close by, close enough to hear if they talked. JJ paced, staring at the floor.

Evening approached, and Kid watched through the grated door as the prisoners returned to their cells. White men, black men, Indians, Chinamen, and even a couple of women made up the line. Kid was most surprised about the two boys who couldn't have been more than twelve years old.

They marched in what the guards had called chain step. Each prisoner, his head down and his right hand on the shoulder in front of him, shuffled along. Each time they stopped, one or two prisoners would step out of line and enter their cell, and the guard locked the door.

Except for the footsteps and the sound of the doors clanging shut, silence covered the prison like dirt on a grave. The process took about a half hour before guards locked all thirty prisoners in their cells.

A guard paced the halls in front of the cells. Kid listened to the footsteps clicking against the concrete.

Soon guards delivered food to each cell. When the food arrived, boiled potatoes, a slice of bread, and a cup of water, Kid groaned. He figured he had seen his last good meal for a while. Still his stomach growled with hunger. He hadn't eaten lunch, so he devoured the food.

JJ stared at his feet, not making any effort to eat. Kid knew that look. His brother was brooding. This wasn't the time to risk talking, but he did point to the potatoes and gave him a look meaning he better eat something.

He ate a few bites, then paced four steps to the door, four steps back.

Kid lay down on his cot and counted the footsteps of the guards.

JJ jumped, startled by Kid's voice. He had just drifted to sleep. "Quiet, Kid. We'll get in trouble."

"It's all right. I counted the footsteps of the guards making their rounds. We have a few minutes to talk. As long as we whisper, they shouldn't be able to hear us."

JJ's mouth dropped open. His brother was smart, very smart, but counting guard's footsteps. Even JJ hadn't expected that. "Are you all right?"

"Fine. I'm just fretting about you. You're brooding."

"I'm not. I'm just…" An overwhelming dark cloud gripped his soul.

"You need to stop. Sheriff Porter's going to talk to the governor. It'll be all right."

"Kid, it doesn't matter. The governor's not going against the railroad. We're stuck here for the rest of our lives, never able to talk, never getting out of our cells except to work. Three hundred and eighty years. Twenty was bad enough. Why didn't they just hang us?"

"Quiet, the guard's coming back."

JJ lay on his bunk as the guard's footsteps clicked against the floor. For the first time in his life, he had given up hope.

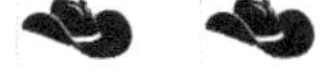

A loud horn blared throughout the prison and woke Kid with a start. He squinted his eyes trying to peer through the darkness to where the noise came from. The image of his cell took form. Wyoming Territorial Prison. It must be five-thirty.

He climbed down from his worn cot, lit a candle, and folded the horsehair blanket, placing it under his straw pillow. He bumped into JJ a couple of times. Guards marched through cellblocks, unlocking doors, and delivering plates of food.

Kid licked his lips, viewing his tin plate of eggs, pancakes, and boiled potatoes. The smell of the eggs made his mouth water, and he devoured his breakfast as if it were his last meal. The eggs were runny and the potatoes only half done, but at least they weren't starving him to death.

He would have liked a cup of coffee instead of water, but this might turn out being a blessing. He didn't have to drink the awful coffee JJ used to make on the trail. He almost felt like himself as he stepped out of the cell and lifted his hands over his head to stretch. He glanced back.

JJ had only eaten a few potatoes before setting aside the plate full of eggs and pancakes. He wasn't even pacing. Instead, he sat on the bed with shoulders slumped, staring at his feet.

Kid glanced around and whispered, "JJ." He knew the guards were probably close enough to hear, but he had to take a chance. JJ didn't even get off his bunk. "You need to eat."

"Quiet. Do you want us to get sent to the cellar?"

A guard strode to them. "Prisoner One Seventy-nine, Prisoner One Eighty, attention."

They stood in front of the guard.

"You're on report for talking. No matches this week. Next time, it'll be the ball and chain. Have I made myself clear?"

JJ flashed an angry scowl toward Kid.

"Answer me. Do you understand what I'm saying?"

"Yes, Sir." Kid cast a glance JJ's way and shrugged his shoulders trying to give an apologetic gesture.

He stared at JJ. "What about you?"

"Yes, Sir." JJ voice was so low it sounded muffled.

When the guard marched away, JJ trudged back into his cell, plopped on the cot, and put his face in his hands.

You've got to snap out of this. I can't do this without you. Kid wished he could tell him that.

The shuffle of the chain step pounded in JJ's ears as they marched closer to his cell. He stared at the line only two cells away. The prisoners stopped and a Shoshone placed his right hand on the prisoner in front of him and pointed his head toward the floor.

One cell away. The guards herded an old black man and a Mexican to the end of the chain step. Like herding sheep.

The sheep and herders reached his cell. JJ joined the line first. Kid placed his right hand on his shoulder and squeezed. That squeeze meant more to him than Kid could ever know.

Chapter Thirty-Four

They had been assigned to work the prison farm and were ordered to milk cows and collect eggs in the barn. JJ collected the eggs, so that left Kid to milk the big smelly cows.

He took his place on the milking stool next to the first of ten cows and stared at the udder. "JJ."

"You're not supposed talk to me."

"This is work-related."

JJ glared at him.

"How do you milk a cow?"

For the first time since the trial, JJ grinned. "We were raised on a farm. How can you not know how to milk a cow?"

"I was the youngest with five older brothers, and you usually did it. I never learned how."

JJ snorted. "First clean the dirt off the udder."

He wiped off the udder and turned toward, JJ waiting for more instructions."

"You have to warm your hands."

He rubbed his hands together.

"Then you want to grab hold of a couple of the teats, squeeze near the top, and pull it gently down. Make sure you point it in the bucket."

"What's going on in here?" the guard said.

JJ bristled. "Just teaching him how to milk a cow, sir."

"Well, get a wiggle on," the guard barked.

JJ showed him how to milk the cow, and Kid struggled to get the milk out of the teats, but JJ's grin was gone. Kid saw something in his brother's eyes he hadn't seen since they lived with Mr. Greer -- terror.

"You have to tell me what's wrong. I've never known you to be afraid like this before."

"Please, Kid, we'll get in trouble. I'll tell you tonight when it's safe."

"Your way for now, but tonight we're going to talk."

They went back to work without saying another word and spent the day working with the animals and spreading manure. When dusk fell, they shuffled back to their cells in chain step. Kid again gave his brother a squeeze on the shoulder, hoping it would help.

Later that evening, he lay on the top bunk in his dark cell and counted the guards' footsteps. "JJ, it's time. The guards won't be back for a few minutes. Now, are you going to tell me what's got you so spooked?"

"I'm not scared of them. It's me."

"What's that supposed to mean?"

"I hate being locked up ever since...."

"I know that, but you never let it eat at you like this before."

"The worst part is not being able to talk to anyone –– to you."

Kid waited, knowing there was more.

"I've always been able to handle things. When I was in charge of the gang, I couldn't ever show fear. If I was scared, I'd talk to you until I got over it."

"You always could wear a body out jabbering all the time."

"Here I can't. If we get caught, they'll make us drag around a ball and chain. And if that's not enough, they'll chain us in the cellar. You heard the warden, a dark, hot room, alone… as if being locked in this cell's not bad enough. Kid, I think I'm going plum crazy. I can't get a handle on it."

"Quiet, they're coming." He lay awake counting the footsteps of the guards. Now he understood. Those old demons had come back to haunt JJ.

He waited for the guards to travel out of hearing range. "JJ."

"Yeah."

"You know I'm still here even if we can't talk much."

"I know."

"You can always talk to God. He'll help you through this."

"Why would He? I deserve this."

"God's not mad at us," Kid said, "He loves us. We're here 'cause we need to get things square with the law. We're already right with God."

His brother said nothing.

"JJ?"

No sound.

He let out a gusty sigh. He couldn't say any more. The guards were coming back.

JJ lay on his cot in the darkness, listening to his own labored breathing, and tried to gain control over the emotions threatening to drown him. It had only been two days. How would he handle the rest of his life?

He thrashed about on his bunk as he traveled back in his dream to when he and Kid had been trapped on Mr. Greer's farm.

It had only been a month since their parents had died. They never had enough food to eat, Jonathan was always hungry, and it was always too hot or too cold. Jonathan still woke up crying at night wanting Ma and Pa.

Joshua promised his brother as soon as they could come up with a plan and get a hold of Mr. Greer's gun, they would run away, but it would be a while. At twelve years old, he couldn't take care of himself, let alone Jonathan. They would have to stay another couple of years.

One night, Jonathan burst into the shed with a wild look in his eyes, holding Mr. Greer's volcanic revolver.

"Kid, what did you do?"

"Mr. Greer was cleaning his gun. He looked the other way, so I took it. Now we can leave."

His chest tightened. "If he was cleaning the gun, there aren't any bullets in it."

Jonathan opened the empty gun chamber, and tears filled his eyes.

Joshua grabbed the gun. "It's all right, don't cry. I'll figure a way to get it back before he sees it's gone." He opened the door of the shed, but it was too late. Mr. Greer stood there, glaring down with his arms crossed.

"So, you're thieving from me now." Mr. Greer grabbed his arm and dragged him to the barn. "I'll learn you good."

Jonathan ran after them. "It was me. I stole the gun."

Mr. Greer stopped, spun around.

Joshua pulled away to step in front of his kid brother. "It wasn't him. You saw the gun in my hand."

"Jonathan, I'm going to give you a whipping you won't forget for lying to me." Mr. Greer snatched up Joshua. "After I deal with this one." He yanked him into the barn and tied him to the posts.

He tensed and prepared himself for the beating. Mr. Greer grabbed the horsewhip. He heard the swish and caught a short breath. Pain covered his back. He tried to focus on anything, but the swish landed again. It hurt too much. He heard screams and realized they were coming from him. He blacked out.

When he half-opened his eyes, the beating had stopped. Mr. Greer cut the ropes around his wrists, and he fell to the ground.

Greer grabbed him by the arm, and he winced and let out a yelp as he was dragged to the trapdoor of the fruit cellar.

"I'll learn you to steal from me." He opened the door to the cellar. "You'll most likely end up in prison, you no good thief. Guess I should show you what it's like in there." He pushed Joshua down the stairs.

He cried out as his body tumbled and banged into each step. He lay at the bottom unable to move. He heard Greer's feet on the steps and glanced up. Greer chained his ankle to the cellar wall and set a bucket of water and a loaf of bread where he could reach them.

"All they get in prison is bread and water, so you best make this last. I'll fetch you in a week."

The trapdoor shut, and footsteps faded as the monster went to beat Jonathan. So dark. he could barely see his hand in front of his face. He dragged himself to the nearest corner and curled up in a ball.

"I'm sorry I let you down, Kid."

JJ woke with a start. His heart pounded, and he wanted more than anything to wake Kid, to talk, to get his mind off the nightmare, but they were in prison, and he couldn't.

He stared wide-eyed at the ceiling, wishing Mr. Greer hadn't been right. *God, I know I deserve this. I'm sorry I'm letting You down again.*

Chapter Thirty-Five

Kid sat on his bunk and stretched, grateful for the extra two hours sleep and because today was Sunday. A church meeting would be all JJ needed to snap him out of the mood he'd been in. The guard delivered eggs, potatoes, pancakes, sausage, a glass of milk, and coffee. He knew right then Sunday would be his favorite day of the week.

After breakfast, he joined the lock step taking them to a large hallway with wooden benches. A podium stood in the front. Guards surrounded every corner.

A young preacher, no older than him, smiled at the prisoners as they found their seats. The preacher led the men in a couple of choruses of *Amazing Grace* before delivering his sermon in a calm tone.

"God loves you. You are here because you've sinned, but God wants to save you from your sins."

Kid prayed at the end of the message. *Lord, I pray others in this prison might come to know You.*

Guards called out numbers. "One Seventy-nine."

JJ jumped up to get his mail. Two letters. The first had no return address, and he gingerly opened it. It was from Mercy. She'd read in the newspapers where they were and wanted to write to encourage him. As if anything could do that. She also included her new address. He read on.

> *I have a decent home in a new town where nobody knows me, thanks to you. I've even started attending church. I can't wait to hear from you. Please write me soon.*

JJ folded the letter, returned it to the envelope, and tucked it in his shirt. He was happy for her, but he wasn't about to write. She needed to find somebody decent, not some outlaw spending the rest of his life in prison.

He gazed at the second envelope. The return address had Sheriff Porter's name on it. He didn't want to expect good news, but hope was starting to well up inside despite his efforts to tamp in down.

His hands trembled as he ripped open the envelope, unfolded the letter, and scanned down to the important part.

> *The governor said he would consider your request, but it doesn't look hopeful. He doubts he will grant the amnesty.*

He dropped the letter on the floor as the dark cloud chasing him for days encompassed him.

"Prisoner One Seventy-nine," a guard said. "Pick up that trash."

He picked up the paper and threw it away, then shuffled to the bench and waited for the guards to take him back to his cell.

Kid traipsed over to the guard. "Sir, can I have a Bible in my cell?"

The guard nodded, and the preacher gave him one.

Let Kid read the Bible if he wanted. JJ wouldn't find any comfort there. The fog thickened until it walled him in on every side. Not even space in his gloom to pace.

Kid waited for the guard to march out of hearing range. He leaned his head over the edge of the cot so he could see his brother. "You have to trust God. He won't let us drown. You have to hold on."

JJ turned away. "I don't want to talk to you anymore. God's not going to rescue us. Didn't you hear that preacher? We're here 'cause we sinned. We deserve everything we get."

Footsteps. The guards would be back soon, but he had to risk it. "You're not figuring right. God loves us."

"Leave me alone." JJ spoke too loudly.

Kid cringed. The guards were too close. They had to have heard. The footsteps came closer.

A guard stepped to the cell door. "You've been warned. It's the ball and chain for a week."

JJ wouldn't speak to him after that even at night. His brother dragged around the ball and chain, but he acted like the weight in his heart was heavier. A week later, when the guards removed the chains from their ankles, JJ shuffled as if it still burdened him down.

Kid could see he'd lost weight. Kid had thinned some too, but JJ didn't eat most of what he was given, and Kid had to keep after him to eat that much. At this rate, he was going to get sick.

He already had dark circles under his eyes and looked pale from the lack of sleep. Kid could hear him thrashing around every night.

After a week, Kid stopped trying to talk to his brother at all since he wouldn't answer anyway. When JJ needed him the most, he didn't know what to do.

JJ glanced up from gathering the eggs in time to see Kid tramping his way. Why couldn't he leave him alone?

Kid's steel blue eyes narrowed. "I tried to be patient with you, but you have to get yourself together. The amnesty will come through any day now."

"Why can't you drop it?" He knew the guards would hear him, but something in him snapped, and he couldn't stop shouting. "There isn't going to be any amnesty. Didn't you read the letter? Sheriff Porter's already talked to the governor. He's not going to do it. You're the most stubborn man I've ever met. We're not getting out of here."

The guard marched in. "Prisoners One Seventy-nine and One Eighty."

JJ stomach's knotted.

The guard tilted his head toward the door. "To the warden's office now."

They marched through the field with the guard following them. The lump residing in his stomach grew until it squeezed the air out of him. His gaze darted across the prison yard, looking for a way of escape. No way out.

They arrived at the office and stood in front of Warden Kimball. Mr. Harris whispered in the warden's ear.

"So, this is the third time you were caught talking," Warden Kimball said. "Do you have anything to say?"

JJ opened his mouth but couldn't utter any sound.

"This was my fault, Sir," Kid said. "I goaded him into talking to me."

Warden Kimball raised his eyebrow. "Is that so?"

"No Sir," he rasped out. As scared as he was, he couldn't let Kid take all the blame. "I was talking too."

"Only after I started it," Kid said.

"One of you is going to the cellar. Prisoner One Eighty, since you're the one who starting talking first..." Warden Kimball looked at the guard, and the guard nodded. "You'll be the one who is punished. Prisoner One Seventy-nine, you can return to your cellblock, but no matches for two weeks."

"No!" He pulled away from the guard. "You can't do this to him. It was my fault, all my fault."

Mr. Harris grabbed hold of his arm, and he tried to swallow back the fear.

"Chain them both to the furnaces."

The guards marched them down to the lower level of the prison. JJ swung wildly. He couldn't stop himself. "NO!"

One of the guards hit him to keep him from fighting as they dragged him into the cellar. When he saw the chain, he flung his arms and hands around, trying to get away. Pain shot through the back of his head, and he fell with a thud and lay on the dirt floor where he landed, barely conscious.

The pitch-black cellar smelled damp and moldy and rivaled the blackness besieging his soul. He rubbed his ankle, trying to keep the chain from digging into it, and pulled on it to see how far it stretched. No more than a foot away. The heat smothered him and sweat poured from his pores. Just like that cellar at Mr. Greer's. He drew his knees up to his chest and rocked.

Lord, please take the guilt and fear away.

He slipped back into his nightmare. Mr. Greer had chained him in the cellar. Someone called. "JJ… JJ, are you all right?"

He woke with a start, his heart pounding, as he tried to slow his rapid breathing. His dream again.

"Are you all right?"

"Kid, is that you?"

"Who else would it be?"

"How come I can hear you?"

"I'm chained to the other furnace no more than three feet away."

"How come the guards can't hear us?"

"They're not here. I guess they figure we're not going anywhere. So now we have time for a little chat. I'm going to talk, and you're going to listen until I hammer some sense into that thick head of yours."

JJ's breathing slowed to a normal rate. He sat trapped in this dungeon, the thing he feared most, but the terror had dispelled and the heavy burden of guilt weighing him down had dissolved. "All right. Say what you need to."

"Did you forget that year we spent in the cabin with God? We may be here 'cause it's justice and because there are consequences for what we did, but God isn't mad at us. Jesus died on the cross for us. He took our punishment because He loves us."

JJ leaned against the wall and allowed Kid's words to rebuke and comfort him. "I guess I forgot that."

"That's why you've been so scared. *'Perfect love casteth out fear.'*"

"You're right."

"I'm not done," Kid said. "When we were in Hunt's Peak praying, all of us came up with the same thing. God told us we could try for that amnesty. You remember that?"

"Yeah."

"Then why don't you trust God to help us through this spell? I don't care if it's been two weeks or two years. I'm not giving up on Him. Even if the amnesty never comes through, remember Bear River? We could have been shot dead in the street like Gus or lynched like Bob and Paul. God has been merciful to us. He's given us so much better than we deserve."

A sense of calm swept over JJ for the first time since the trial. He could see now how wrong he'd been and how much he'd troubled Kid by his lack of faith. God had given him so much. Instead of being thankful, he was wallowing in the guilt and shame from the past. "You done now?"

"Yep."

JJ's voice thickened. "Would you pray with me?"

Chapter Thirty-Six

Sunday came again, and JJ choked up singing the day's hymn. "Jesus paid it all, all to Him I owe, sin had left a crimson stain, He washed it white as snow." The guilt was gone.

After church, they both received letters. JJ opened his first letter and read it.

> *Dear Joshua,*
>
> *You're an uncle again. Grace birthed a fine little girl that's as beautiful as her ma. We named her Rose after Ma.*
>
> *Grace, Mr. and Mrs. Cooper, and the boys all send their love. Mr. Cooper said to tell you he meant everything he said when he last saw you. We miss you both.*
>
> *Jedidiah*

The second letter was from Mercy. After letting him know she'd grown closer to God, he read the real reason she wrote.

> *You may want to feel sorry for yourself and not write to me, but I'm not going to let you. I'm writing you every week whether you answer me or not. You loved and helped me during the worst time of my life, and I'm going to do the same for you.*

It didn't make sense for him to answer the letter. She could never have a future with him. She needed to get on with her new life. Even so, he wanted so much to hear from her again.

When he returned to his cell, he wrote about everything that had happened since they last saw each other. He stopped short of telling her he loved her, even though it was true. Instead, he told her how proud he was that she was putting her trust in God.

A month later, a new warden came to the prison and the rules relaxed. Prisoners were allowed to talk in their cells after the day's work was done.

JJ had been doing better since he repented of his self-pity, and he was so thankful for the change. They settled into the prison routine.

Days turned into weeks, and weeks into months. Another letter from Mercy came every week, and JJ couldn't help looking forward to them. He was pleased she was growing closer to God although she had a difficult time making friends in her new town.

The cells grew colder and the prisoners were issued black wool coats and extra blankets. Instead of working in the garden, they spent the winter cutting ice out of the river and making candles for the prisoners.

Mercy wrote that she told everyone in the church about her past. If she was starting a new life with God, she wasn't going to begin it with a lie. In another letter, she'd written that the pastor and his wife had welcomed her even if the congregation hadn't.

Every time JJ got a letter from her, he would write and share what he'd been learning from Scripture and try to encourage her. He couldn't write much about his life in prison. Every day was like every other day.

The next summer, they went back to work in the garden planting potatoes. Others in the prison received pardons and early releases, but they heard no word.

One evening, after reading another letter from Mercy, JJ approached the subject. "It's been a year now. Looks like we're not getting that amnesty."

"You're all right with that, aren't you?"

He paused for a moment. He wanted to be free from this place, and he wished he could see his family and Mercy again, but he had a peace about it he didn't understand. "God knows best."

The next day, he wrote Mercy a letter telling her they weren't going to get amnesty.

> *Your friendship has meant more to me than you can ever know, but this is the last letter I'm writing to you. There is no future between us. It's time for you to live your life. This is good-bye.*

Joshua addressed the envelope and let out a heavy sigh. As hard as it was saying good-bye to her the first time, this was even harder. Since she had given her life to Christ, a closeness grew between them that wasn't there when he'd asked her to marry him. He loved her too much to allow this to continue. *Lord, help her through this. Help me too.*

A few days later, he was weeding in the garden. A monarch butterfly fluttered by, and when he glanced up to watch it, he saw Mr. Harris march over to him and Kid. "Follow me. The warden wants to see you."

JJ couldn't think of any rules they'd broken, but even knowing he might end up in the cellar didn't disturb the peace of God that was his constant companion now. They followed Mr. Harris across the prison yard into the office and stood in front of the warden.

"Apparently, you have friends," the warden said. "Mr. Harris, have them change into their regular clothes, and take them to the front gate. Sheriff Porter's waiting."

JJ's heart raced. He could barely believe what he was hearing.

After changing into their old clothes, including two tattered cowboy hats, the guard escorted them to the front gate. Sheriff Porter stood on the other side holding reins to three horses.

JJ ran up to him, slapping him on the back. "Wahoo, we got the amnesty?"

"Not yet," Sheriff Porter said. "Governor Thayer's considering it, but he wants to see you first. Don't get your hopes too high because you might be coming back here."

JJ pressed his lips together. Despite himself, his hopes had been stirred once again. He couldn't bear the thought of coming back here now, but he still prayed, "Lord, Your will be done."

When they strode into Governor Thayer's office, JJ felt like a gaggle of geese took residence in his gut. No matter how much the sheriff cautioned him, he knew this was it.

Sheriff Porter motioned to the desk where a stocky man with a bushy mustache stood. "I'd like to introduce you to the honorable governor of the territory of Wyoming, Governor John M. Thayer. Sir, this is Joshua and Jonathan Jackson."

JJ and Kid both held their hands out.

"It's an honor to meet you, Sir," JJ said.

Governor Thayer ignored their outstretched hands and motioned for the three of them to sit. "When Sheriff Porter first came to me, I had no intention of giving you amnesty. You've stolen more money than any other outlaw in this territory."

JJ didn't know what to say to that. It was true.

The governor stood and emptied a bag of mail onto his desk. "Do you know what this is?"

JJ thought about saying mail but knew that couldn't be the right answer, so he shrugged his shoulders.

Kid spoke. "Mail?"

"That's right," Governor Thayer said. "These letters came from every family in Green River. I've been bombarded for a year now, and they all say one thing. They demand I give you pardons. They claim you two are heroes who risked your lives to save a mine full of children. I still have my doubts, but you can't fight the railroad and stay in office."

JJ tilted his head to one side. "I'm out to sea here, Sir. Why would the railroad want us to have pardons?"

Governor Thayer turned to Sheriff Porter. "They really don't know, do they?"

The sheriff had a grin on his face like he was busting to tell them something. "No, Sir."

Governor Thayer rang a bell, and his assistant came to the door. "Mr. Smith, could you please have Mr. Grayson and Mr. Jefferson step into my office?"

The man left and came back a moment later with Mr. Grayson and the important man JJ had seen sitting with him on the day of the trial. They shook hands with Mr. Grayson and the other man.

"Gentlemen," Governor Thayer said, "these men don't know whose grandchildren they saved."

"Joshua, Jonathan, I'd like to introduce my father-in-law, Mr. Benjamin Jefferson," Mr. Grayson said.

"Pleased to meet you, Mr. Jefferson," JJ said.

Kid nodded to them.

"Mr. Benjamin Jefferson," Mr. Grayson said, "is the president of the Union Pacific Railroad, and I'm the division superintendent for all of Central Wyoming. I'm married to his daughter. When you saved my children, you saved his grandchildren."

JJ clasped a hand over his mouth.

"I want to thank you, gentlemen," Mr. Jefferson said, "for risking your lives and freedom to save my grandchildren."

Governor Thayer stood to his feet. "I won't ruin my career for the likes of the two of you, but if you ever break another law in Wyoming Territory again, nothing will save you. Effective tomorrow, I hereby grant you, Joshua Jackson, and you, Jonathan Jackson, a full pardon for all unlawful acts committed on or before July fourth, eighteen-seventy-seven. Congratulations."

JJ couldn't contain himself. He jumped up and let out a holler. Kid just stared with his mouth open.

"Sheriff Porter tells me you have family in Hunt's Peak," Mr. Jefferson said.

"That's right." JJ couldn't stop grinning. "That's where we'll be headed."

"The railroad's moving to Hunt's Peak," Mr. Jefferson said. "If you're interested, I might have some jobs for you working at the station there."

JJ fell in the chair behind him.

Joshua Jackson climbed aboard the train with his brother, Jonathan.

He had butterflies in his stomach not only because he was seeing his family again but because when he'd telegraphed Mercy, she'd agreed to meet him in Hunt's Peak.

"You were right," Joshua said. "God not only gave us better than we deserve, He gave us more than we could even think to ask for."

"Yep," Jonathan said. "We have amnesty, and a family to go home to, a ma and pa in Mr. and Mrs. Cooper, a brother and sister-in-law, two nephews, and a niece."

"Don't forget about Mercy."

"Yes, her too," Jonathan said. "Not only that, imagine us having jobs with the railroad."

Joshua smiled. He was thankful for all of that, but he would have added one thing to that list. Jonathan had been his best friend and only family for all these years. That's what Joshua thanked God for that day.

The End

About the Author

Tamera Lynn Kraft has always loved adventures. She loves to write historical fiction set in the United States because there are so many stories in American history. There are strong elements of faith, romance, suspense and adventure in her stories. She has received 2nd place in the NOCW contest, 3rd place TARA writer's contest, and is a finalist in the Frasier Writing Contest.

Tamera has been married for forty years to the love of her life, Rick, and has two married adult children and three grandchildren. She has been a children's pastor for over twenty years. She is the leader of a ministry called Revival Fire for Kids where she mentors other children's leaders, teaches workshops, and is a children's ministry consultant and children's evangelist and has written children's church curriculum. She is a recipient of the 2007 National Children's Leaders Association Shepherd's Cup for lifetime achievement in children's ministry.

You can contact Tamera online at her website: *http://tameralynnkraft.net*

www.ingramcontent.com/pod-product-compliance
Lightning Source LLC
Chambersburg PA
CBHW071154180726
48291CB00007B/2449